UNSPEAKABLE THINGS

UNSPEAKABLE THINGS

Kathleen Spivack

ALFRED A. KNOPF
NEW YORK
2016

THIS IS A BORZOI BOOK PUBLISHED BY ALFRED A. KNOPF

Copyright © 2016 by Kathleen Spivack

All rights reserved. Published in the United States by Alfred A. Knopf,
a division of Penguin Random House LLC, New York, and distributed in
Canada by Random House of Canada Limited, a division of
Penguin Random House Canada Ltd., Toronto.

www.aaknopf.com

Knopf, Borzoi Books, and the colophon are registered trademarks of
Penguin Random House LLC.

Portions of this book appeared, in slightly different form, as "The Rat" in The
Chattahoochee Review and "The Tolstoi String Quartet" in Carpe Articulum.

Library of Congress Cataloging-in-Publication Data
Names: Spivack, Kathleen, author.
Title: Unspeakable things : a novel / Kathleen Spivack.
Description: First Edition. | New York : Alfred A. Knopf, 2015.
Identifiers: LCCN 2015035393 | ISBN 9780385353960 (hardcover) |
ISBN 9780385353977 (eBook)
Subjects: LCSH: Refugees—Fiction. | BISAC: FICTION / Literary. |
FICTION / Historical. | FICTION / Cultural Heritage.
Classification: LCC PS3569.P56 U96 2015 | DDC 813/.54—dc23 LC record available at
lccn.loc.gov/2015035393.

Jacket images: (violin) © Florilegius/Mary Evans; (envelope) Subjug/E+/Getty Images
Jacket design by Kelly Blair

Manufactured in the United States of America
First Edition

To music, which forgives everything.

CONTENTS

CONTENTS

UNSPEAKABLE THINGS

Chapter 1

THE RAT

In the drafty reading room of the New York Public Library, Herbert opened his latest letter from the little Rat, his old friend Anna Zygorzka. Her letters were slow to arrive, and each one bore the marks of a censor, who dutifully opened and read and then indicated the readership before sending it on to New York. Even David, who worked in the war office somewhat connected with censorship and foreign mail, could not predict the letters that arrived occasionally, tattered and humble, addressed in fine, studied handwriting. Herbert smoothed the paper, which crackled as he spread it out in front of him. He fixed his spectacles more firmly onto his nose and bent down happily. *"J'arrive!"*

Beside him on the bench, his grandchildren sat quietly. Philip studied his toes while he held a green balloon. And Maria, in her ruffled smocked dress and little sweater, bent over her English book as seriously as Herbert now bent over the handwriting of his letter. Maria's lips did not even move as she read; she was concentrating. Although the first signs of spring were coming to New York, the interior of the library was cold and drafty. Herbert wrapped his coat more tightly around his shoulders, looking over to smile at the children. How good they were! So quiet and dear. He went back to the letter.

Herbert and Anna Zygorzka, second cousins, had been writing to each other for years. They corresponded in various languages, including Esperanto and French. Sometimes they alternated. Anna wrote to Herbert in German, and he answered in Russian. Then they corrected each other's letters and started over again. And during that time, they also corresponded in chess.

Herbert smiled as he deciphered the numbers and letters. "Aha, now I have you!" Anna had written in large, distinctive handwriting. "Check to your queen!"

Herbert bent over the letter in delight. "We shall see," he thought. "We shall see." He looked more closely. Undoubtedly, he could find the loophole in this. Then he laughed. She had done it. He had taught her well. But this was not the end of this particular game. Herbert still had a few tricks up his sleeve. The Rat would regret challenging the old chess master. He smiled.

"Well, my dear friend," he read in her large triumphant hand, "are you not proud of me? Guard your queen indeed, my old fox!"

Herbert imagined her nose twitching in triumph. That exquisite ugliness! Her dark, shiny eyes, peering at the chessboard—he had loved to watch her sniffing around the game. He imagined her little snort, a muted shriek of delight when she saw an opportunity for triumph. The Rat!

Underneath, Anna had written, in an equally exuberant scrawl, a few quick words. "The good news, my old dear friend, is that I am coming. I shall arrive soon. I cannot say more. Speak to David." And then, as if to paraphrase her German, she wrote the same message hastily in French. *"J'arrive!"*

Herbert put the letter aside for a moment. As if disbelieving the message written, he bent to it again. *"J'arrive!"* How could that be?

Anna's image rose in his mind. The seaside. Summer holidays with his parents. The arrival of his second cousins from Hungary. The other side of the family. The two mysterious girls, slightly younger, both, than he and his brother. Anna and her younger sister. *The two girls.* The two boys who awaited their arrival; a mystery unfolding.

What a disappointment it had been when he had first seen the Rat. She was small, unprepossessing, with a long nose. And could it be? Whiskers growing out of the mole next to her nose. Well, three long hairs, to be exact. A Rat with severe curvature of the spine, which caused her to move in a painful, crablike way, hunched over, peering upward over spectacles.

Anna and Herbert had looked at each other. Could this be the fabled cousin, so long awaited? Anna's younger sister was normal in every way. Only, she was too young to do anything more than tag after the Rat and Herbert and his brother, whining to be included. So he was stuck, summer after summer, with the Rat for a companion. And a deformed Rat at that. A Rat who had to spend most of every day lying on a sofa, a Rat who could not stand straight when she walked, who moved slowly, painfully, with a little cane. A Rat with the most beautiful eyes, the most seraphic smile. A Rat with the face of an angel, made more beautiful by the imperfections that called attention to her beauty. This Rat had the power to enchant. She trembled inadvertently from time to time, as if this power were far too great for her little body to bear.

One day, the Rat dared to intrude upon Herbert's silent avoidance of her. It was during one of her little slow-paced promenades. Herbert hated to watch her progress down along the sea; it was so slow and cramped. The Rat came right up to him, to the rock on which Herbert sat, thinking drearily of the meaninglessness of his life. He didn't look at her directly, though he had covertly observed her approach.

Anna took a deep breath, gasping as she came to a halt beside him. "Why do you avoid me?" she asked without any preamble. "Is it the way I look?"

"No," Herbert lied. He yawned.

"Come." Anna held out her hand. "We can still be friends." She touched his sleeve. A fine vibration was coming off Anna and it flowed from her hand through his body. Anna was shaking, her breath coming quickly in little gasps. She pressed her knees together and turned her head away.

Herbert took her arm and, still not looking at her, accompanied her back to the house. He was furious with himself.

"You know why they call me the Rat?" Anna said, still trembling, peering at him with deep, beautiful eyes. "Do I not resemble one?" Herbert tried to be polite. "It's true, isn't it?" persisted Anna. Herbert wanted to tear off her shawl, gaze at the nape of her neck, her twisted spine.

Anna shuffled beside him, bent over at a strange angle, leaning on Herbert. "You know," she said forthrightly, "it's lucky Papa has money. For I will probably never marry. And then," she added sadly, "who would want to marry me?" Herbert felt her resignation. He said nothing, walking beside his cousin, a girl already burdened by rejection. Her little pawlike hands pressed his elbow. "It's true."

Herbert searched for something to comfort her. "But, Anna, you are intelligent, educated. Don't give up hope. A young lady like yourself has a long life ahead." He repeated platitudes.

"Do you really think so? Oh, Herbert!" Anna turned her face to his, looking upward. "Do you really think so? Do you think anyone will ever want to marry me?"

"Of course," replied Herbert. "Plenty of gentlemen will want to."

"Oh!" Anna's lovely eyes misted over with joy, and her face crinkled into a smile.

Herbert was delighted with the effect his words had on her, although he noticed that she looked more like a rat than ever— a happy rat. Then inspiration hit him. "Anna, do you know how to play chess?" he asked.

She looked suddenly downcast again. "No, Cousin Herbert," she said.

"Well then, I shall teach you," said Herbert, feeling important. "We must not be idle just because it is summer."

Soon Herbert found himself spending time with the Rat as she lay on her sofa. All summer Herbert and Anna played chess together, and the Rat was happy to follow his lead in other things as well. When Herbert read philosophy, the Rat read every book he recommended. She listened when he read aloud to her— poetry, drama—and Herbert was delighted to have an audience for his developing interests and adolescent self-importance. The Rat had a passionate intelligence and was not afraid to debate with him. A willing pupil, her pleasure in learning was intense. Herbert found he liked to spend time with her, liked to watch her long nose quiver at an idea, sniffing out the exact meaning of each phrase. Her little hands trembled with excitement; her whiskers vibrated with joy.

At the end of the summer, the Rat was disconsolate. Her eyes were magnified with the tears that fell, unwiped, on the chessboard between them. She was more hunched than ever. They took a last walk together, their intensity augmented to the point where neither of them could stand it. "Let me," whispered Herbert softly. "Let me touch you just one time." Anna squeezed his hand. Gently, Herbert pulled back her collar and exposed the top of her spine. "I just want to look at you," he murmured. Anna held his other hand all the while, squeezing tightly as she trembled, her body pressed in upon itself. He let his mouth graze her queerly shaped body. Neither of them said a word; this was to be their secret. When Herbert had finished letting his lips travel the length of her deformity, Anna swooned. She would have permitted him everything, but he caught himself.

He rearranged the shawl about her shoulders, helped her straighten her dress. She was still trembling. "Come," said Herbert. He was overcome with the emotion of the situation; he wanted her, would always want her in a desperate way. "We will write each other during the year. And we will see each other next summer." The Rat lifted her head, her eyes shining. "Yes," said Herbert. "And we will correspond in different languages, we will write our thoughts and feelings and what we are reading, and we will continue our chess. Yes!" he continued, inspired by his own brilliance, and by the happy compliance of this Hungarian girl. "And next summer, we shall pick up again. For this must only be au revoir, not good-bye." He put his hand on her little paw, and her trembling stopped. She brushed a tear from her whiskers.

"Oh, Herbert, what will happen to me?"

During the school year, they continued their separate lives, he in Vienna, she in Budapest. Their friendship grew through correspondence. Anna shared his passion for literature and language. Ever since that first summer, while they had continued to correspond during their absences from each other, Herbert thought about her incessantly: her deformity, her eyes. Yet on the surface he was getting to know other young ladies. It was as if Anna existed in a secret compartment, a delight to be pulled out and played with only during the summers. Their meetings each summer holiday were filled with joy. Always she approached him with shining eyes that drew him toward her secret. He loved to caress her hump. More was forbidden, and when he tried more, she tightened her legs and shook her head. Then the next minute she was welcoming him, and it was Herbert who had to draw the line. He did not know if he hated or loved her; he was fascinated, and yet there was something forbidden in the skirts of her dresses, something that he both sought and shunned. "Let me look at you," he said. "I just want to look."

Herbert, of course, was to make a proper marriage, a proper *Christian* marriage, as was appropriate to his career in the Austrian government. His mother had found him Adeline, and Herbert fell dutifully, romantically in love with the beautiful pianist.

The Rat was unable to attend the wedding. Anna, the emblem of his youth, was far away at that point. Her family had achieved the unimaginable. They had managed to buy for Anna and themselves a Russian count. A penniless Russian count, but a count nevertheless. The terms of this marriage were, among others, that the Rat was to leave immediately for Saint Petersburg, taking her fortune with her.

"And so, dearest cousin," the Rat wrote, "what choice do I have? They do not explain to us the need for such a rush. But I am only a lady Rat after all, and so I go to meet my husband happily."

Now, so many years later, in this suburb of war-torn Europe named New York, the Rat's letters began to reach Herbert again. "Our last game, do you remember?" she wrote. "I was so stupid not to cover my bishop. I lost the whole game on that. Well, now we begin again." Herbert smiled at her resolute handwriting and decisive approach. "I shall go first, my friend. Do not think you can so easily win now. I have been studying, yes, studying chess. And other things as well!" And then, as if there had been no break ever in their correspondence, Anna, choosing the first black pawn, opened the game again.

Of the intervening years, she wrote not one word. And Herbert, hardly knowing where to begin on his and Adeline's life and experiences, also wrote not one personal word in response, except to mention that he was living now in New York with David and Ilse and their dear children. Herbert had decided that it was no use writing anything too personal, especially as he was now writing to a *poste restante* in Leningrad rather than to a real address. Who knew who might be reading, in fact, might even be writing, these letters concerning chess?

"And so, my dear lady, we will write of books. Literature. Yes, the literature we are reading and what is new and what is happening and what we both think about it," Herbert decreed. "I have just discovered a new Italian writer," he appended hastily to one letter to Anna, in which he had successfully avoided a threat to his last remaining knight. "His name is Leopardi. Do you know him?" Herbert then proceeded into a quick discussion of Leopardi. "Perhaps I shall find a copy and send it to you," he suggested at the end of the postscript, knowing it was a futilely generous suggestion.

Anna's response came six months later. "Leopardi, no, I have not heard of him. But then, I do not hear of many writers here. . . ." The words were faint and wistful. "Now, dearest Herbert, watch out for my bishop," she wrote more insistently.

Try as he might through his many connections, Herbert could not locate the actual whereabouts of the Rat. Perhaps she was a spy. Always the letters bore the return address of the central post office. He was careful to write very little of importance in his letters—not even in invisible ink.

At first, it had been a surprise when her notes had started to come to him in New York. He had been waiting in the Public Library for a meeting with a member of a committee for refugees, when a shabby man had jostled him. "I beg your pardon, Herr Doktor," the man had muttered, showing bad teeth. "But I believe this is for you." He had shoved the small envelope into Herbert's hand, and then, just as furtively, disappeared somewhere into the stacks again.

"Who is that man?" Herbert later asked some of his committee members. But no one, of course, knew. "Who are you?" Herbert demanded the second time this happened.

"A friend," replied the man. He looked at Herbert, shook his head once in warning, and disappeared again.

From then on, Herbert never asked. "Thank you, my friend," was all he said, receiving these infrequent letters. Herbert smoothed out the crumpled paper and tried to figure out why, after all these years, Anna had decided to play chess again.

At night, Herbert held Anna's letters up to a candle to decipher if there were an invisible message beneath her spidery inked scrawl of numbers and letters. But there was none, just the chess game, the continuation of their adolescent passion shared.

There was very little else in the Rat's letters. The Rat had always included paragraphs in numerous languages, not forgetting Esperanto. The correspondence between Herbert and Anna had always included at least one passage in Esperanto. It had been Herbert's idea, one summer vacation together, that all the cousins should learn Esperanto. He assured the others that a universal language, in this case Esperanto, would eventually transform mankind's ability to communicate and thereby bring about world peace. Herbert and his brother, as well as the Rat and the Rat's sister, seized upon this idea enthusiastically, and for a while Esperanto became their private communication, especially during mealtimes with the families.

Then, years later, Herbert, for a time, gave lessons in Esperanto, zealous in his efforts to promote this universal language. He lectured and wrote in the newspapers on language and brotherhood; and this continued to be an interest long after he had entered government service. But German, Hungarian, Russian, and French had all proved more useful. Herbert had used his abilities in language to learn a bit of Serbo-Croatian and Bulgarian; his tongue twisted around these savage sounds. Somehow, in the clash of nations, Esperanto was, if not forgotten, at least put aside.

Herbert's wife, Adeline, had not showed the slightest interest in all these language studies. For her, music was the only language she paid attention to. She sat at the piano, in a white dress, at dusk, and played the flowers to sleep in the garden outside. Herbert could not interest Adeline in reading; she felt literature too far removed from the real life of feeling. Adeline had been so beautiful, Herbert remembered. Yet, perhaps slightly . . . silly, Herbert had to admit. But it was her silliness he loved, after all. It was befitting in a woman. Or so he had thought at first. Later he had become a bit impatient with it, but in the beginning of their relationship he had found it charming. Yet, he would perhaps have preferred to spend more time with the little Rat, to pass happy hours in conversation, sharing love of books, of ideas, of chess. But this was not to be.

"J'arrive!" Now, in the library, Herbert reread those last words. "Expect me! I arrive before you know it."

At that moment, both Maria and Philip, Herbert's grandchildren, who had been sitting so patiently beside their grandfather, began to twitch uncontrollably. Maria smoothed her dress again and again as Philip opened his mouth in a wide yawn and began to howl at the top of his voice. Maria roused herself out of her seeming passivity to cry anxiously. "Stop it! Stop it, Philip.

Immediately, do you hear? Stop it!" But Philip did not stop; he was just warming up for an operatic yowl.

Herbert looked anxiously around him. "Ach, little ones, little ones," he said, reproving them gently as he put Anna's letter in his waistcoat pocket.

Most annoying, Maria's grandfather was refusing to pay attention to her. Maria pulled on his sleeve, irritated. "I'm bored," she complained. "Grandfather, I'm bored." Her grandfather appeared not to hear. "I'm tired of waiting here." She let her voice rise to a little whine, just loud enough to disturb the soft whispers about them in the library.

Her grandfather appeared to shake himself out of his reverie for a moment, long enough to look at her and pronounce in an automatic and authoritarian voice, "Show me a bored child, and I'll show you a lazy child."

With slightly more compassion, he patted her, but he still seemed abstracted. He softened, realizing it must be hard for the children always to wait here. Still, there was no place else for them to be.

"A bored child is a lazy child," he repeated more kindly. "Is that not true, *Liebchen*? Now surely you must have something to do. Where is that book you were reading?"

"I'm tired of reading."

In the half-light of the library, far down the corridors and in the reading room, elderly anxious faces turned away from books and newspapers toward the commotion and clamor of Herbert's grandchildren.

Maria, in a frenzy of anger, reached over and yanked Philip's hair. "Shut up!" she hissed at him. This had the effect of making Philip yell even louder.

"Children," Herbert clucked helplessly, reaching into a pocket for two shriveled candied violets with which to pacify the children. But the proffered candies did no good: both children were squirming uncontrollably. The waiting gray heads looked toward Herbert and the children pityingly. Herbert was intensely embarrassed. In response, he closed his eyes, letting himself lapse into a delicious torpor, almost sleep. He pushed the noise of children far away, time for his nap.

But somewhere behind him, Herbert sensed a commotion, a reverberation of confusion that shattered his dream state. The light in the library fractured into shards, as if the noise of fingernails on a blackboard had cracked it. There was the sound of scuffling somewhere, perhaps in the stacks, and then protesting, muffled shrieks.

In answer to that, Maria leaped to her feet. "Grandfather," she commanded, "stand up. Something is happening." She reached over and raised little Philip to his feet beside her. Philip, surprised, stopped crying, stuck in mid-yowl.

Near them, the sounds of more scuffling. Herbert still tried to feign sleep. He tried to block out the sounds of a struggle and then, almost beside him, the faint sounds of terrified squeaks. "Grandfather!" Maria pulled at his coat. Herbert reluctantly opened his eyes.

At his feet, as if hastily deposited there, lay a small dusty bundle. But this bundle was shaking; this bundle was alive. Herbert looked more closely. The bundle opened its small dark eyes, eyes that suddenly welled with tears and, as suddenly, with laughter. Could it be? "Anna?" he asked falteringly.

"Yes, my dear Herbert. You see, *J'arrive.*' I have arrived! I am here." The creature closed its eyes again, but the long, pointy nose quivered as tears of joy rolled down her cheeks. The whiskers swayed, catching the tears; three long whiskers, now gone completely white.

"Anna?" Herbert bent down and raised the bundle to its feet. "Oh, my little Rat, but what have they done to you?"

"*J'arrive. Je suis ici.* I have arrived," whispered Anna, clinging to his arm.

"My little Rat." Herbert cradled her, surprised. The pointy little face looked up at him.

"Oh, Herbert, do not worry. I am here now; that is what matters."

"My dear friend." Herbert wondered how he would cope with this surprise.

Anna's face took in his wonderingly. She passed a tiny hand over his cheek, as if in disbelief. Then she peered at the children, who, suddenly silenced, stood watching. "And these?" she asked.

"Yes," replied Herbert. "These are David's children. My grandchildren."

"Children?" Anna breathed.

"Yes. This is Maria, and this is Philip." Herbert put his arm around the two children, who stood stock-still, staring at the creature beside their grandfather.

"Dear, dear children," Anna said. The children stared.

The Rat was tiny, no doubt the smallest woman Maria had ever seen; smaller than Maria herself. Anna, now completely bent over at right angles to the ground, twisted in a grimace of shoulder and torso as she took in the presence of the grandchildren.

Maria looked back into the face of the creature, the curved, eager mouth fringed by three long white whiskers. The huge dark eyes peered damply, red-rimmed, through spectacles. Anna's eager face strained to penetrate the heart of the onlooker. Maria was fascinated, and immediately she fell in love, although she did not know what that felt like. She could not look away from the Rat's face and little body.

"They call me the Rat," Anna said, presenting her hand, unsteady and shaking, to each child in turn. Philip did not utter a word. Maria took the Rat's hand, and curtsied, as she had been taught, quickly and respectfully. "Yes," Anna continued. "Do you not think I look a little bit like a little Rat?"

Maria did not dare answer in the affirmative, for fear of offending the creature. Grown-ups sometimes joked, but they did not expect you to joke back.

The little Rat was by now so deformed that her spine resembled that of a shrimp, curved and curled onto itself, more than it did that of a rat. Maria stared at the long whiskers curving out of the mole near the Rat's nose. The dark red-rimmed eyes smiled kindly. These eyes were ringed with deep circles, the small face grooved with these dark bruised lines. "Yes, these circles are new," Anna said with a sigh, as if divining the child's perceptions.

"My dear little Anna," said Herbert, finally finding his voice.

"It does not matter," the Rat replied, smiling through tears and patting his arm.

"And your hair?" Herbert marveled. "It has gone completely white."

"Yes," said Anna simply. "It turned white overnight. Suddenly. From shock." She looked at Herbert sadly. "But we will not speak of that now," she said. "Now we speak only of our happiness in being together, my dear friend."

"Come, children," Herbert said suddenly, commanding them. In one quick motion, he bent down and picked up the little Rat in his arms. She wrapped her ragged blanket around her shrunken body as Herbert swooped her up. How small she was. Her little body lay in his arms without weight. He felt the sharp curve of her spine, and gently, almost absently, he ran his fingers over it. His fingers remembered the shape of her body, and his own echoed with memories of desire.

"My dear Herbert, where are you taking me?" she asked. A cloud of dust motes rose around her clothes and hung in the air of the library, turning golden in the late-afternoon sun that slanted into the reading room.

"I am taking you back home with me," replied Herbert firmly as he walked slowly, carrying the little Rat in his arms, toward the large entrance doors. "Come, children." He did not turn around to see if they were following, for, as usual, he expected and usually got total obedience from them. Maria took Philip's hand, and the two children, fascinated, followed Herbert and Anna toward the door. "David's wife is a good woman," Herbert said to Anna. "You will stay with us."

"But, Herbert, are you sure?" Anna asked. Herbert didn't answer; he was not sure of anything.

"How did you find me?" Herbert was asking the little Rat as he carried her, weightless, shrunk into a third of herself, in his arms through the streets. He bore her ceremonially, draped across his own body. The children followed, trying to catch the words of the older couple.

"It was not a problem, finally," said Anna. "You have friends. Perhaps I have the same friends. It does not do to look too closely at such matters."

Herbert nodded yes. He was becoming resigned to yet another burden.

"What matters is that they brought me to you." Anna sighed, giving herself up to the luxury of being cradled, carried like a child, to some unknown destination. She closed her eyes and seemed to fall into a soft trance, assuaged at the end of a long journey.

"Sleep, sleep, my dear little Rat," Herbert whispered. His heart swelled.

Maria caressed Philip's hand. "My dear little brother," she thought. She had rarely felt so tender toward him.

When they reached the apartment building, they walked past the inquisitive eyes of Shirley, the elevator operator, who closed the iron grating once they had entered. "Evening, Professor," did not require an answer.

They walked into the little room on the top floor. Maria's mother looked up as they entered the small room that was home. She straightened, wiping her hands on her apron. She had been peeling potatoes, and the brown rinds lay next to the glowing globes, white knobs of potato bones in the half-light. Herbert set Anna down; she tottered feebly, then straightened herself as best she could to her bent-shrimp position. The Rat looked upward, a tremulous, unsure half smile on her face. The children's mother looked back intently. Then she extended her hands to the older woman, drew her close, and, putting her arms around her shoulders, led her to a chair.

"So it is decided, then?" asked Herbert, looking at his daughter-in-law.

"Yes, Papa. It is decided. It is fine." Ilse looked into the face of the Rat.

"Good." Herbert said. *"Danke schön,"* he added quietly, so that only the air around him heard.

"You will share the daughter's bed," said Ilse. Maria looked up sharply, her lips parted. But something in her mother's eyes stopped her.

"Thank you," whispered the Rat. She turned her head painfully, so her eyes met those of the girl. "Thank you, child." So it was decided, and Maria stifled her hot protest.

Chapter 2

NEW YORK, NEW YORK

New York, New York. City of Dreams. New York, like a brace of trumpets, welcomed them. Received all of them, the immigrants. They poured into her huge maw just as the steam poured out of the smokestacks of the large ships that had brought them there. New York, City of Welcome. The trumpets screamed in unison, held to the large smiling mouths of sweating musicians. The sailors sweated in the engine rooms of the large ungainly steamships. New York, City of Refuge. New York, City of Hope. The strident avenues streaked across the city, silver: fiery arrows like long, bright sounds, almost too much for the ear to bear. And still the band played. Louder. More volume. New York, and the gleaming saxophones entered in chorus. New York. And now the trumpets rose to a wail, a cry of pain, and the saxophones sang of darker things. Sadness. Nostalgia. New York, City of Dreams Left Behind. *New York.*

The great ships drew into the harbor, parting a dark veil of raindrops to reveal Miss Liberty, a pigeon on her head. A strange language, sounding to the ears of the strangers like the guttural barking of dogs. Across the water, uptown and downtown, in the gleaming cathedral city, Manhattan, the jarring music lured. New York. Like a faraway walled city of many oblique castles. As in medieval times, there were the lords of the manor, whisked away silently in great soft cars. And there were the serfs, toiling in the streets, to be seen behind the quick, frightened, averted eyes, behind the racks of clothing wheeled through the open air, or, if lucky, behind the wheels of taxis, cunning, swift, opinionated, serfs nevertheless.

The winds swept, merciless, about this city. Like the knife-sharp notes of a clarinet, rising with authority above the insistent throbbing bass notes of everyday street life. The wind pierced the thin bodies of the immigrants. But here, unlike in their native Europe, the skies were blue and clear. The sun shone, jabbing at them through the cold. Snow fell on the city, and for a brief time the snow sparkled in clean light. The sky was blue as a cantata. There was some rain, of course, but never the low skies of Germany or Austria or Russia or Poland.

The immigrants sighed for the gray deceiving light of their native lands. They longed for the cloak of darkness. They had gotten into the habit of scheming. Underground life, in a certain way, suited them. They were not fit for such direct light. New York fixed its pitiless gaze on their struggles and laughed.

But they were to retain their habits of secrecy. Clutching their worn coats about them, those coats of what had once been "good tweed," they huddled, heads averted, through the city's arrowed streets, hiding their eyes from this cold, this wind, this all-seeing sky and sun. How could it be so cold and yet so blue? "Blue, blue, blue," sang the black musicians up in Harlem. But blue was different there: a smoky, aching, shadow sort of blue.

Each week, the ships came into the harbor, disgorging the crippled remains of Europe, already charred, or at least forever marked. "Bring me your huddled masses," Miss Liberty had cried. And so they came. But for many of them, it was too late. Too late to join the concert of trumpets, too late for joy. They feared these bright Americans, with their "Can do" and "Will do" and easy self-assurance and "How do you do" and their too-open gaze. They crept, half-broken, onto the terrain that was New York and wanted only to rest.

But New York moved quickly. How could one rest? And where? The immigrants shuffled along as best they could behind the city's optimistic rhythms, searching the darkest corners, that stubborn, dear, familiar darkness, in which to hide.

The immigrants pulled their coats more tightly about their protesting bodies. The coats were worn, but the wool was strong as steel. What once had been soft was now a rigid woven fabric of determination. Though the teasing New York wind found its way into the garments, the immigrants held on to their European values. Their belief in the triumph of humanitarianism, all those examinations of ethics came into play as they attempted to find meaning in suffering. All that education, all that philosophy and music and history and culture: this was what would hold them upright now.

"Baby, I been missing you," moaned the cheerful musicians uptown. "Oh baby, I's so blue." The instruments wheedled and chorused, while the smoke of nightclubs wreathed around their heads. A shaft of early-morning sunlight illuminated the smoke for a moment. "Baby, I been missing you."

The trains ran through New York, crisscrossing with a wet, nostalgic sound. The traffic poured endlessly through the streets. Impatient, the dark horns of taxis hooted next to the horns of the great ships, swinging into and out of the harbor. And the horns of Harlem played; the music was picking up. Europe seemed far away.

But even while buses rushed through the streets, there was a war going on. America was in it, too. Too late. The immigrants bent their baffled heads and tried to find their way. They had much to tell, no one to tell it to. But for now, that didn't matter. They tried to get on with their lives.

New York, New York, City of Light. The Great White Way, the waste of light. All that light. The immigrants sought a cool refreshment, shadow, which they knew and loved. The museums. The Public Library. The dark recesses of the smallest, poorest cafeterias. The darkened rooms, unheated, of the tenements. If they were lucky, they found work. Somewhere, in a room without light. Anywhere.

So Herbert, too, king mole of all the moles, had found his shadow space in which to operate. The Automat. The New York Public Library, a hushed, dark place where one could conduct one's business in whispers.

Wherever he was, Herbert conducted his business. It was like an inflexible dance, which he must dance until he dropped from exhaustion. And even beyond that.

"May I have this dance?" Herbert waited and received his partners. Heads bent, their walk not a dance but a maimed shuffle, the refugees petitioned for favors. They fell at his feet; they slumped to their knees; they kissed his ring. Herbert tried to avoid, in a self-deprecating way, these attentions. The refugees looked directly into his eyes, and he saw in theirs a will that he do what they wished. He could only submit. "I am your servant," he said, comforting them. "I am at your service." A long, slow dance, with no lack of partners cutting in and out. "I will do what I can," he promised again, and he did.

Herbert kept no records, no written files on his work. He relied on his memory, his good word, and the promises of others. Nothing was ever to be found in writing on anything he undertook. When he died, it would be to leave behind only a few notes on Esperanto, a few old books on chess moves, and a small heap of shiny dust, glittering like gold powder: like flakes of himself, shavings of dandruff or halo dust about his shoulders. Just a small shiny heap on the bed where he had floated, scheming.

Herbert's partners clutched him desperately, dictating the pace and turning in one direction only, inexorably counterclockwise—that is to say, against the clock. He could not persuade them otherwise. He did not know any other steps.

But uptown, elsewhere in New York, the city throbbed with its own beat. The Two-Step, the Chicken, the Turkey, the Herky-Jerky, the Fox-Trot, the Charleston. Disjointed syncopation: new steps invented every day. The dancers, their faces like the masks of grinning animals, bobbed and pouted in their atavistic rituals. Forgetfulness was the name of the dance in New York, waiting to celebrate itself in all its brash optimism. The Yanks were here; the Yanks would do the job. Watch out, Hitler! Watch out, world!

The trumpets blared in their loud promise. Nothing was subtle about New York, nothing.

The sailors, the soldiers, the girls, the coupling, the smoky blues, all cried of entitlement, an arrogance and happiness and optimism untouched by the kinds of losses the immigrants had lived with for centuries. On the stoops of tenements, old men sat uselessly, watching this strange new American race. Old women, and young ones, too, sad and dark-eyed, graven into headstones of themselves, watched with weariness, put down or picked up sewing, then put it down again, wondering. How would they survive such a harsh, bright light?

Dusk was the hardest time. When the diamond lights went on in the big jagged city, when the bluish haze of smoke and evening came down from its perch somewhere up in the sky and curled itself around the avenues, New York began to come alive. A city of night, of jazz, of sound, both comforting and inexpressibly lonely, all at the same time. Hope and despair—loss of a girl, perhaps, or of love. This was jazz.

The immigrants thought of their other losses, all of them—everything lost. For them, dusk was a time of grief, no mocking gaiety to underscore, no irony. Maria, with her grandfather and little brother, after a day at the Public Library, saw the spirit of the city about her. People were moving happily, hopefully, going somewhere. But they were going to the makeshift little room where other people's pasts would always seem more real than any present moment she might ever choose to live.

Always the past, with its stately progression of dances. The formal waltz, partners held in a pattern of arms and posture that might have contained them all their lives had not history happened. Passions so carefully contained that the merest flicker of a shadow was seen in its most significant perspective. The sun slanting toward autumn in the garden, a glance exchanged, a pressure of hands. A knock on the door. A few discreet words—"Herr Hofrat . . ."—whispered. There were warnings everywhere, if one could but hear them carefully. Herbert had gotten the family out of Europe just in time. All but Michael.

He had not properly understood the whispered warnings. Never imagined they could be for him. It was David who had understood them finally, poor shabby David, made for the real world in ways the rest of the family was not. "Herr Hofrat, if you know what is good for you, you will . . ." Eventually, Herbert accepted.

Now he had gotten them into a dance that would never end. A strange dance in a strange city, too fast for them all. The dancers shuffled slowly, pausing to lean and gasp for breath. They would be lucky if Herbert could find jobs for them all, a place to live, papers, false if necessary. Their dance was more of a dirgelike shuffle.

Still, as long as there is life, there is the dance. Though the immigrants kept to their stately formal waltzes, their grandchildren might one day dance to the new rhythms in what would be a revival of jazz. But the first two generations had to live out their lives still in desperate partnership, not quite believing they were in a new place.

In their minds, they would be always young, turning and spinning slowly under the flicker of candles, holding one another at arm's length, the women's white shoulders, the gleam of flowers and eyes and hair, the crackle and gossip of a delightfully scandalized city, Vienna, bourgeois, staid, stuffy, and malicious. The Viennese Waltz—Vienna had even given its name to the form of the dance. The music gathered, the string players hummed along with their instruments, and the city rustled with the sounds of the dance. Only David, Herbert's son, who worked as a decoder in Washington, D.C., sat outside its skirted circle, still bent over the chessboard in the garden, still trying miserably to figure it all out, decode, decipher, live up to his father's expectations.

So it was that he had heard the warning voices, figured out what was going to happen to them all much before it did. But no one would listen to him. Not for the longest time. They were all too busy dancing.

And what had Herbert had to pay to get them all out of Europe, a Europe in flames? Herbert had given: his house in Vienna, his garden, his wife's jewels, the summerhouse by the seaside. He had given his bank accounts, all of them. His furniture, his large office on the top floor of the building that housed the Ministry, his library. He gave up his language; he gave up his wife's sanity; he gave up his profession, and that of his older son, David, and his son's wife, Ilse. Ilse, who could have safely stayed behind.

And finally, when there was nothing else left to give, he gave up his younger son, paying for their escape with sacrificial blood.

The boy was laid on the altar of escape. (Bless me, *bless me,* oh Lord.) With one resolute motion, Herbert slit his second son's throat. Michael thrashed against the doors of his own death, the boxcar carrying him away forever. Why, why? Adeline stared into Herbert's eyes, the last look of comprehension flaring and then, horrified, dying forever. "Forgive me," Herbert pleaded silently. The rest of the family was permitted to leave.

"Father, I forgive you!" But it was too late. Herbert paid.

Chapter 3

IN VIENNA

In Vienna, the Tolstoi Quartet was becoming a nuisance. The Quartet had existed through generations since 1869, the date of the publication of Tolstoi's great novel *War and Peace,* and it claimed a distant relationship to the Russian writer. Its musicians lived on money from the Tolstoi trust and from individual subscribers and patrons, and all this contributed to the growing suspicion on the part of the Austrian government, which had no financial control over them.

But they were Viennese to the core. They were as much a part of the tradition as four pillowed Sacher-Tortes set out on dainty plates with silver forks and doilies at the even more traditional Sacher Hotel. They were as innocent as mountains of whipped cream piled high on Viennese coffee. And inoffensive as *Die Fledermaus,* they still believed in happy endings.

Among their patrons was Herr Hofrat, the undersecretary at the Ministry of Trade. The Quartet performed often at the Hofrats' house. And at the end of each performance, they always included a piano quintet so that their hostess, Frau Hofrat, Adeline, a former concert pianist and Herbert's wife, could perform the final piece with them.

Already there was a mounting whiff of scandal around the

undersecretary; it was said that he was perhaps embezzling funds from the exchequer, and the new government was secretly beginning an investigation that would trace the money to purchases of houses under false names. But the Quartet made it a point never to read a newspaper, never to go to a coffeehouse; they had never even heard the name Sigmund Freud. Music was their life.

Four single-minded men, they were swaddled in protective ignorance. With the help of their wives, they remained like little children who could do only one thing: play chamber music. In their spare time, they looked at musical scores and sang madrigals together. Every minute of the day was spent with one another. They practiced together in the same room with their instruments. They slept with their instruments. But since this group had also managed to marry, eventually this was to be the cause of their downfall.

Politics came and went in Austria, a geographical hub with shape-shifting borders that seemed to specialize in uprisings, assassinations, and operatic drama, but the Tolstoi Quartet stayed as it had always been. The Anschluss happened. The Quartet still gave their concerts. Musically, their repertoire was set; the quartets of Mozart and Haydn were their staples. Over the years, the Quartet had reluctantly added Schubert and then Brahms, and, most daringly, they had now moved on even to the late quartets of Beethoven.

They had always refused to play the newer composers, Mahler, Bruckner, and others. That refusal served to increase their popularity, for the times had caught up with them. The music of Mahler and others was now banned in the German-speaking countries and considered inflammatory and degenerate. The Tolstoi Quartet was praised for its unstinting support of what was truly pure-blood Germanic: its music. And for this reason, until now the Austrian officials had more or less left them alone.

All through Gustav Mahler's tenure, from 1898 to 1907, when he was director of the Vienna Philharmonic Orchestra, and when his music was played everywhere, the ancestors of the present Quartet had remained faithful to the period when it had first begun, and in this way they felt they were not compromising the family money that had been set aside for them in a trust established by the Tolstoi family. Mahler's music would never be stopped, however, not by new German borders: stateless, it wandered everywhere and took life from the sorrows of others, fastened itself like a vampire onto the mouths of grieving parents and the cries of little children.

In 1938, just before the Anschluss, Bruno Walter, né Schlesinger, traveled one last time to Vienna to conduct the orchestra. Then he left for good immediately after. Among the works Walter chose for this final program was the music of his former mentor. The orchestra played Gustav Mahler's Ninth Symphony. This would not be heard again for a long time after. The Quartet did not attend that last concert. They continued to practice and perform their good old Mozart, the lighthearted thump-de-thump of Haydn and all the rest of their old chestnut repertoire.

By 1942, sixty members of the Vienna Orchestra had joined the Nazi Party, and two of these were members of the SS as well. That put the average membership in the Nazi Party among the orchestra at 48 percent, in comparison with the 10 percent Party membership among the Austrian population as a whole. Meanwhile, thirteen or more Jewish players from the orchestra had already been deported, some were murdered in Vienna, and a good number of them died in concentration camps. Half-Jews and those players who were married to Jews were winnowed out later.

Wilhelm Furtwängler was now appointed by Hitler as director of the Berlin Philharmonic during the Third Reich. He was based in Berlin but was responsible for all concerts throughout the new German territories. Furtwängler was highly ambivalent about this appointment, and he never joined the Nazi Party. But he was close to the leaders who set policy. He would be seen by history not only as a gifted and controversial conductor but as the Nazi darling, a traitor, or at least a double agent. He managed to save some of the doomed Jewish musicians, arranging for their escape. But equally randomly, he culled among their ranks, and under his directorship many more were sent to their deaths.

Furtwängler, who had been charged with resurrecting "true Germanic music," was not in the habit of killing off his musicians directly. He covered his tracks. The notorious SS first trumpet player of the orchestra did the dirty work of denouncing the Jewish musicians in their midst, and those who were married to Jews. But Furtwängler kept a soft spot for the old classical players.

The members of the Tolstoi Quartet seemed not to notice anything going on outside of their practice rooms; they persisted as they had always done, keeping to themselves, playing their select concerts, going to the orchestra concerts, and they refused to comment. Timid and shortsighted, they closed their ears to many things.

The Quartet's concerts were always sold out, and there were always long waiting lines to get in. Violent fights erupted outside the hall as last-minute concertgoers and students vied to get tickets. The police were getting a bit fed up with the fracas that went on whenever the Quartet gave a concert, but the men backstage inside the hall, preparing to perform, were not aware of the violence outside, violence that was becoming more and more overt.

When the doors opened, those who had managed to get tickets ahead of time filed in, still seething with hatred. There was the annoyance of chairs clapping open, an epidemic of coughing and throat clearing, and crutches thrown down, clanking on the people in the seats in front. Young people wound wool scarves more securely around their necks, just waiting for the next provocation. As they hefted themselves into the front rows of seats at the last minute, there was the annoying swish of fur coats and silk stockings.

Finally, the first violinist sounded the open A string, which started a round of intense tuning and a last desperate spate of coughing. Then, chins firmly pressed, they drew their bows.

The Tolstoi Quartet played so exquisitely, so at one with each other and with their instruments, that to hear them was to be instantly transformed. The audience breathed in time to the musicians, who breathed in time to their musical instruments. Sore throats were instantly healed, and lung diseases, to which Austrians and Germans seemed particularly susceptible, went into partial remission. Coughing stopped, and the effect lasted for several days. Crutches were forgotten. Arthritics found they could unfold themselves and walk freely out of the concert hall. All discomfort vanished at the soft sounds of bows caressing strings. To listen to them was to be blessed with a sharper vision, to walk out into a world of bright colors and tenderness and an inner softening that took all hurt, all discord away. Even the angry throng outside the theater was calmed by the strains of the music that floated out.

Individually, the men were remarkable musicians, but since they always played together, they breathed as a single unit, not one instrument standing out, no one pushing to be heard. The instruments swooned in their arms and the harmonics vibrated through the hall. The musicians adjusted their breathing, and healing entered their lungs. They were filled by the music: music they knew, music large enough to blot out everything else that was happening in Vienna.

Meanwhile, many of their private subscribers and patrons, including the Hofrats, were disappearing from Vienna. Most of Herbert's relatives were shipped to the camps, including his sister and brother and their entire families. This was never spoken of.

Now Furtwängler, who was himself in danger of being sent to a concentration camp, and who had a very ambivalent relationship with the Third Reich, was sent to Vienna to oversee all musical lack of discipline. He realized that the members of the Tolstoi Quartet, stupid or not, needed some indoctrination, as well as protection, if they were to remain a staple of the Viennese musical appetite. They were to join the Party, as all remaining state musicians were required to do. He summoned them to state offices in the company of the newly appointed Nazi Minister of Propaganda.

The players blinked their eyes, as they rarely went out in daytime. They shuffled their feet, caressing their instruments. "Heil Hitler." The players held up their bows in their right hands and waved them, a feeble protest.

"You are obliged," Furtwängler said, "to rename your quartet in a more acceptable way. A more German way. For instance, we suggest the Goebbels Quartet, after our noble minister."

"Never!" the musicians cried with one voice, and their stringed instruments protested so loudly and discordantly that Goebbels, the new Nazi Minister of Propaganda, had to block his ears and run out into the hall. "Think about it." Furtwängler said, fixing them with a menacing glare. "We are warning you."

The Minister of Propaganda wanted the Quartet deported at once, but Furtwängler intervened. Already European music was being depleted. These feeble men were one of the last links to Vienna's glorious past. "Wait," he counseled Goebbels. "Let's give them one more year and see if they come around. If not, they will disappear. I will guarantee it." They saluted each other smartly.

By the end of the year, the disgraced Tolstoi Quartet was forced to leave Austria. It was too late in the war for Furtwängler to consider a steamboat such as the SS *Koenigstein,* one of the last passenger boats to leave Germany. Ports in South America were now closed. Under Furtwängler's intervention—and money— the Tolstoi Quartet was sent to Bremerhaven, where they were smuggled onto a submarine. There they were flattened and pressed, fitted neatly behind one of the smaller turbines. With its dubious freight, the U-boat *Eva* serpentined toward the Americas, its long black snout snacking and feeding on the fire, chaos, and wreckage it created along its way.

The German submarines plied the waters off the Atlantic coast of the Americas, which allowed them to torpedo at will. They still owned the Caribbean waters and especially the sympathetic shores of South America, where they could refuel and restock. They were bottom-feeders, and on their way they fed off the tankers carrying crude oil from Venezuela to Aruba to New York, as well as off the ships ferrying sugar from Cuba, guns, supplies. The convoys of liberty ships were fair game. The ships carried men and weapons to Europe to fuel the Allied war effort, and the returning convoys carried caskets, corpses, and war brides, the remains of war. Anything could be had for a price, and the waters off the Americas seethed with the ever-hungry torpedoes.

Coming up for air along the coast of Venezuela, the U-boat *Eva* suddenly surfaced. Its menacing turret poked out, took in the blue sky and bright air, inhaled a breath, and vomited just once before it sank again, leaving a half-mile sheen of its own ambergris. Among the assorted debris were Zwieback crusts and pigs' carcasses, potato peels, a corpse or two, and human waste. The Tolstoi musicians were also swept along on a child's rubber raft provided for the purpose.

Released onto the ocean, all blinding brightness, all sudden sunshine, the members of Tolstoi Quartet clung to their instrument cases and whimpered. Along with all other war wreckage, they were swept in to shore on the incoming tide near La Guaira, the Venezuelan port that served Caracas, there to await a ship that would smuggle them somewhere else.

In port, as prearranged, the tramp steamer *Calypso* awaited them. The *Calypso* was slowly getting ready to load. Captain Joe Riley buttoned his trousers as he sauntered out of the doorway, whistling. It was late morning, and he had just left Carmelita, his favorite girl, the one-legged whore of La Guaira. It had been a totally satisfying session; she had given him the best part of the night, and strong coffee and pastry just before he left. He planned to go back to her again that afternoon before his ship left port. Behind him, in line waiting for Carmelita, who was sleeping it off now and would be in no hurry to accommodate them, were his officers, as well as assorted officers and crew members of other merchant ships in port. Joe passed them by, his voracious parrot, Sugar, cackling and fretting on his shoulder as always. A huge but rather cowardly bird, she plumped her feathers up and made a fierce face at the waiting men.

Carmelita was the most popular and, to Joe, the prettiest of the girls in all of South America, or so it was rumored. She was known all over the ports and throughout the ships. Men were fascinated by that one-legged whore and her stump. They just couldn't stop themselves from caressing it. Carmelita was also a talented contortionist. She could put more love into a man than any other girl on the coast. She found places to arouse that they never even knew they had. One night spent with her, and she got into men's minds: they could never stop dreaming or talking about her afterward. They groaned and muttered her name in their sleep. She was the most depraved woman most of the men had ever known, wild and legendary in her endless inventiveness and pleasuring. She left them wanting more, always more.

But Joe always got special treatment, she told him, and she was his girl each time he came to port. The lovely Carmelita was nineteen, and Joe was young for a captain, age twenty-three. Neither could understand a word of what the other said, but they were in love. It also helped that Joe was good-looking, virile, and always paid her several times more than what she asked. This time, he would have a lot to give, the "whole wad," as he said to himself. Arrangements had already been made.

Joe's ship, the *Calypso,* was a rust bucket loosely affiliated with the Allied effort, and she was charged with ferrying goods up and down the coast of the Americas, legally or not. The main purpose of the *Calypso* was to dodge, by any means she could, the German submarines lurking about, and get supplies to American troops. The little tramp steamer was so beat-up-looking that no one took it too seriously. So she operated in relative calm. The *Calypso* carried munitions, sugar from Aruba and Cuba, and general cargo. On this last trip from New York to Venezuela, the *Calypso* had carried a holdful of boxes of cornflakes, toilet paper, fashion magazines in Spanish that had been printed in New York, and a few heavy, ornate coffins, corpses being returned home to Caracas. This all had to be unloaded before the *Calypso* could make the return trip. It was all the same to Joe Riley and his men; as long as they and the owners lined their pockets, everyone was happy.

"A kiss. Give us a kiss," Sugar jabbered. Joe hiked the parrot farther up his arm and fished in his pocket for a piece of banana. He stuck a morsel between his lips, puckered up, and the parrot sidled up his shoulder to peck the morsel from Joe's mouth. Sugar immediately started shrieking for more, but Joe ignored her.

They were loading the *Calypso* now, and Joe walked down to the loading dock to see how it was going. He squinted as a large crate was being jerked onto the deck of the *Calypso*. It hung in the air and swayed. He watched with a critical eye as the crate settled onto the deck of the ship and was lashed down. "Easy. Take it easy there," he called to his men. He fingered the large wad of hundred-dollar bills in his pocket and fed the parrot one more ripe banana morsel.

Then he walked over to the port office, filled out the necessary papers, and pushed the parrot's beak away from his lips. "A kiss! A kiss!" the bird shrieked angrily. But Joe was busy now, and the parrot, waddling sideways, anchored herself anew on his shoulder, chucking and muttering as Joe signed the exit papers.

Next, he had to go find the rest of his crew, make sure that the papers of the scruffy new sailors who had signed on in La Guaira were properly falsified, and then go rouse the last of his men who were in the local jail, sleeping off what had been a bad, or good, night, depending on one's point of view. More money changed hands, the customary bribe to the local port authorities. By this time, Joe was almost ready for his afternoon siesta, so he strolled back to find Carmelita one last time.

As the *Calypso,* reeking of liquor fumes brought along with the crew coming back on board, steamed out of port late in the afternoon, the men working on deck could hear faint groans and clawing from inside the crate on deck. They reported this to their captain, who told them to ignore it. Joe ordered one of his able seamen to make sure the crate was firmly lashed down, and the groans soon became drowned by the winds that howled around the little *Calypso* as she steamed north. At night, during the graveyard watch, the cook's boy would put a pot of rice and leftovers out on deck, and by morning it would be gone. But the sailors knew better than to ask questions.

As the northern shore of Venezuela receded, Captain Joe Riley, pacing the bridge, thought fondly of Carmelita and of their last wild afternoon "siesta" together. She had actually cried when it was time for him to leave, real tears that streamed down along with her mascara. She'd wound her leg two times around his neck and, with her big prehensile toe, scratched him delicately behind his ears, a trick she knew he loved.

"I'll be back soon," Joe said, kissing her stump one last time. He tried to comfort her as well as himself. To make sure she knew he meant it, he took out a wad of bills, counted out two thousand dollars, and put them into her hand. That very same two thousand had been stuffed into his pocket just the day before in a transaction that had been so unpleasant and secretive, he didn't want to think about it. Dear Carmelita, could anyone need the money more? And oh, what wonderful times they had together. He sighed. For sure, he'd never find a girl back home as sweet as that little whore.

Although Joe had agreed to transport his cargo to New York, he knew he could not get past the authorities there. The run was already dangerous enough. He decided to put the crate ashore before the *Calypso* reached New York, somewhere along the New Jersey coast, near Cape May. He went in as close as he could by night, watchful of the submarines. Then he stalled the engines, launched a lifeboat, got the wretched musicians in it, and rowed the Quartet as close in as he dared. He beached them in the shallows, near the barrens, the mosquito-ridden swamplands of New

Jersey. From there, the musicians and their instruments would make their way slowly to New York City by bus. They had some money sewn into the red silk linings of the instrument cases, not much, but they would find a bus somewhere that would get them to New York. Although they had always wanted to enter the gleaming city in triumph, this was not to be. Once on the bus, they cringed, slid down in their seats, and drained the last dregs from their bottles of schnapps. Somewhere, they had heard, there was perhaps a last living relative of the Tolstoi family who would allow them to survive for a time in her coal cellar, or at least until they came up with another, more practical solution.

Chapter 4

ADELINE

Herbert arrived at the psychiatric hospital, where he opened and closed doors. "How is my wife?" he asked quickly, anxiously, of the nurse in the hallway. He was panting, worried that he might be late. "Has she been asking for me?"

"She's fine," replied the nurse, barely looking up. "She's in there. She's been a bit difficult today. Perhaps it is the weather."

"Gracious lady," he said softly. Charm was a reflex for him.

"She'll be all right, I am sure, sir. It's just the shock of it all. Really." The nurse hesitated. "Perhaps you would like a cup of tea?"

"Ah, dear lady, you are too kind." Herbert's face betrayed his weariness.

"In there," said the nurse, gesturing. "I'll bring it in to you. Go now. She's been waiting for you all day. She keeps forgetting where she is."

Herbert looked stricken. "Yes," he said, half to himself. He stood before the double doors of the ladies' ward and squared his shoulders. The steam pipes hissed throughout the old brown building—steam pipes as big as the bus that had burrowed its way through the streets, tunneling him here to visit his mad wife. He was becoming a man of dark places: the library where he received his supplicants; the tenement where he lived with his elder son's wife and children; the cafeterias of New York where he planned and waited and wrote letters; and now this dim, high-ceilinged room where ladies lay, muttering to themselves. He gathered his forces.

"Adeline!" he cried, bounding in what he hoped was an optimistic manner into the shadowed room. Once again, an aureole of light seemed to lift him by his meager hair, catch his large flapping ears and hook-winged shoulders, and propel him forward with energy. He sank in a subservient heap beside the bedside of his wife and took her hands in his. He kissed first one inert hand and then the other. She gave no answering pressure to his clasp. "Adeline, my darling!" he cried, and bent and kissed her lips.

Adeline lay in the feverish dark, plucking the same edge of the sheet between her gnarled hands. "Adeline," Herbert whispered. The invalid did not look up. "Adeline, listen to me," he whispered again, more urgently. She did not stop her relentless quivering and searching, as if her crabbed hands were trying to read the faces of her children in the grayed surface of bedsheets.

"Listen." Herbert pressed his face against the unresisting chest of his wife. "The Rat is with us now," said Herbert. "The Rat." Adeline did not answer, but it seemed as if she had heard.

But still his wife seemed not to notice him. She stared straight ahead. "Speak to me, my darling. I implore you," he begged, touching his large ring, the one that signified his membership in the Freemasons, to her cheek. That ring had saved so many lives. Could it save theirs?

"Herbert, they are trying to kill me," said Adeline. "I saw them. I saw them yesterday." She caught his gaze finally. "I can hear it. The sounds."

"Where, my darling? Tell me." Herbert looked at her tenderly.

"Here. Everywhere. Can't you tell?"

"No, my darling," replied Herbert. He stroked her hair.

He could hear steam hissing faintly through the walls, burping and snarling as it tried to fill the space assigned to it. And if he listened more closely, he, too, could hear the muffled cries of humans, clawing their way into their long death sleep. "No," he lied. "It is only the heat. You are imagining things."

Adeline did not answer; it was not worth it. She turned her head away from him and gazed at the wall. "My Michael." She did not actually say this aloud. But in chorus, the steam pipes began to thrash loudly. Thick clouds rose among their own writhing. The pipes clattered, and patients throughout the building started to beat tin implements together. Plates clanged in the cafeteria somewhere in the dark basement reaches of the hospital. Steam bonged through the passageways and plates were flung onto floors. "Michael," the lunatics cried. Adeline lay inert, still as a grave but, unfortunately, still living. A thin skeleton of a boy tried to wrap his bones around those of others. He moaned once; then the hissing of death stopped. Satisfied, death ate him.

Herbert heard. "I know." He was sweating, pale, but dared not think further. It was too dangerous. Beside him, Adeline lay in her trance state.

Their thin, beautiful boy cried out to him. "Father! Father!" Just those two words. He raised his head from the pile of the dead for an instant; his eye sockets bored into Herbert's own. The muttering of the steam subsided into a faint complaint around the edges of the room.

"Michael!" Herbert cried inside himself, but he dared not speak. "Adeline," he pleaded. He caressed her closed eyes, her cheeks, closing his own eyes around the memory.

"Herbert, wake up! What are you doing?" Adeline shouted, suddenly opening her eyes and sitting upright. "The woman over there is spying on me. I know it. She stole my brooch."

"Shh," whispered Herbert, looking furtively across the room. In the adjacent beds, other women lay inert, muttering to themselves.

"I saw her." Adeline's voice rose to a shriek as she clutched her pink silk bed jacket around her throat. Her bony fingers moved convulsively. "Pig!" she hissed at the woman next to her.

"My darling." Herbert tried to calm her, smoothing back her hair, which sprang up like a thicket of flames around her head.

"Thief! I spit on you. I spit on you! Do you know what they do to thieves where I come from?" she demanded. "Ppfft!" Adeline spit furiously toward the bed next to her, and the spittle ran down the corner of her mouth. Her face was convulsed, engorged with fury.

"My darling," Herbert said mournfully, trying to hold her down and looking wildly around the room. He hoped no one would notice them. But such was the bedlam around each patient that Adeline's privacy was ensured. "Thief!"

"Now, dear. Settle down." The nurse appeared beside Herbert, holding two cups of tea. Adeline thrashed, trying to knock them out of the nurse's hand. "Calm down. There's a good girl." It seemed to Herbert there was menace in the nurse's soft voice. Adeline shrieked once more and then fell back against the pillow. "There," said the nurse. "That's better. Perhaps you would like some tea also?" Herbert gratefully assented, and Adeline, calmer now, took the cup in her hands.

"And what have you been doing?" Adeline demanded of Herbert when the nurse had left. Herbert tried to resume a normal, calm tone. "Professor Zatzki came to see me today," he ventured conversationally.

"And do you remember also Frau Elkin? Helmut's wife?" He sighed.

Adeline brightened at their names. "Ah, yes. Are they here? They, too? It is amazing to think they, too, are here."

"Yes," whispered Herbert. He did not tell Adeline of the losses among their compatriots, those old colleagues who had also found their way, stumbling, into the cavernous library in New York.

"Was it hard for them?" asked Adeline tenderly.

"Yes, my dear. I am afraid so." Herbert did not tell her of the long wait, the papers, the false documents, the money, the connections, the letters, the final seal of the great ring upon papers that said death or life to a Europe gone mad. Europe was eating them all in its gaseous fury. Herbert operated in secret, but he was not alone. There were others—others, whose names he did not know—who carried out his bidding. He looked at his ring and put his hands in his pockets.

"You are a shabby little man," Adeline said suddenly. "You know, I always liked your brother better. I should have married him instead."

"Oh, Adeline." Herbert sighed, pressing her hand to his lips once again. "You are so beautiful." He sighed again, dropping her hand. She would never love him now, he knew. "I am not half the man my brother was," he said. "But I love you with all my heart." "Could you not love me a little bit?" he wanted to say. His heart was breaking. No, he corrected himself, it had broken already. Irrevocably.

"Look at me," cried Adeline. "Can't you see I am no longer beautiful? I, who was always the greatest beauty? Yes!"

Adeline sat up again, throwing her cup and saucer onto the floor with a large satisfied crash. "I was so beautiful," she shouted to the woman in the bed next to her, "that you, you pig, cannot imagine what it was like. Papa loved me the most. I was his favorite. I was a great beauty once. Herbert, tell them how beautiful I was," demanded Adeline imperiously.

"Shh." said Herbert meekly. "You still are, my darling. My beauty. My sweet girl."

Adeline's lips curved in a satisfied sneer. "You see," she hissed at the woman next to her, then fell back onto the pillows once again. Tears came to her eyes, and she started to sob. "Oh, Herbert"— she gazed at him—"I was beautiful once, wasn't I?"

"Shh," said Herbert gently, sorrowfully. "Of course. Calm yourself."

"No," said Adeline, despairing. The tears ran down her face. "Look at me, Herbert. Be truthful for once in your life. Even he wouldn't want me now. Not even your handsome brother." Sobs shook her thin shoulders.

Herbert cleared his throat. "Adeline," he said, as if to change the subject, "you haven't asked after the children."

Adeline seemed to return to herself. She looked at him. "Tell me." She regarded him searchingly, as if to really see him. "The little ones. How are they?"

Herbert smiled at her. "Today I took them with me to the library. They are so good, David's children. Philip sat there like a good boy. And Maria, a little princess. I was so proud." He thought of the children, patiently waiting with him day after day.

"And Ilse? Is she working now?" asked Adeline.

"Yes," said Herbert. "She has a good job now."

"She was never good enough for our family," Adeline hissed, rearing back. "She was never good enough for David. And what's more, the girl isn't even Jewish."

"No," said Herbert. "But she is a good girl. She works hard."

"And common," sneered Adeline. "David could have done much better." Both thought of their elder son, the good one.

"Michael," the steam pipes started to whisper again.

Herbert's head hurt; his eardrums whirled in a blackness of pain. He thought they would burst. "Stop it immediately!" he shouted aloud. Somehow, he was standing on his feet, a small scrunched figure beside his wife's iron bed. "Stop it!"

Adeline shrank back, her dark eyes regarding him with surprise. "But my darling," she began in a coaxing voice, "I did not mean . . . I only meant . . ." The room receded back into its rightful form. "I am sure Ilse does a good job," she said grudgingly. Her voice became conciliatory. "Sit down, my darling Herbert."

Herbert's head cleared and he saw his family united as they once had been: David and Michael played together in a large walled garden under the linden trees. And Adeline, beautiful and proud, gathered the little boys to her and kissed them tenderly. She played the piano; she sang. The boys ran off again, grew up. David in Berlin, Michael at home in Vienna. Then something happened, but he had forgotten what.

The music swelled. The sounds of the children playing drifted up from the garden. The fragrance of linden trees in June was like white sleep. In their bedroom, the shutters were open. The scent of the flowering trees entered the windows of the large house and fell like petals on the bed.

"My darling," Adeline sighed to him from her pillow.

Herbert kissed her beautiful mouth; he stroked her hair. Lowering his body onto hers, he wondered at so much tenderness. Then he remembered something again. His brother. The one she had wanted to marry after all. Only, something had happened there, too. His brother had married somebody else, a nice, common girl. Leni liked to collect mushrooms, Herbert remembered. She was a good cook. A nice, dull girl.

"Die Linden, die Linden," sang Adeline in a white dress. There

were flowers in the room, flowers in her hair. Two little boys played in a pool of sunlight next to her skirts.

Herbert parted the body of his wife and slowly entered her velvet. She opened, receiving him. He pressed his lips to her mouth as she struggled to tell him something. Something about the children perhaps. "Not now," he wanted to tell her. Everything could wait.

But the room reorganized itself with a sudden white clapping sound. "Herbert!" screamed Adeline. "You haven't been listening! Did you hear what I said?" She stared at him, panting, with large terrified eyes. "What are you doing? Don't you see they are killing me here?"

Probing evening fingers of cold were clawing their way into the room, and Herbert shifted slightly in the scratchy overcoat. He was sweating even though it was cold—a chill sweat, as if he were becoming ill. Heavily, he got up from his sitting position next to her. He uncramped himself slowly in the isolate dark. "I must go now," he said to her. "It is getting late and I must go."

"Herbert, I am so frightened," burst out Adeline.

"You are right," he said to her sadly. "You would have been happier with my brother."

"Don't leave me," Adeline pleaded.

"But my darling, I'll be back tomorrow. You know that," he said in a soft, coaxing voice, as if to a child: the child she had become.

"I am nothing," he thought, and a great weight fell onto his heart.

Chapter 5

THE GOOD DOKTOR

A drum roll, a tympani, a clanging together of garbage can lids heralded the start of a new day. Dr. Felix sat in his office on New York's Upper East Side. He surveyed the loving photographs inscribed to him that beamed down from the walls. Beside him, his little dachshund, Schatzie, sat soberly, her jowls grizzling and quivering as she waited for her master to feed her just one more lump of sugar before the day actually began. "Hush, *mein Liebchen*," said Felix, reproving the dog, and at the same time stroking the folds of her flesh, so silky, furred with a fringe of black and white hairs. Schatzie licked his hand.

Felix surveyed the crumpled papers he held, papers taken from under Herbert's mattress, reading and rereading them. "Knight to a2," he read. "Pawn 3 to d5." He threw the papers down in frustration. "Aach!" Chess moves! That was all they were! Herbert planning out chess moves, playing against himself, as always. And for that, Felix had risked discovery. He was fed up. And yet, what if this was code? "Hmmm, Schatzie. What do you think?" The dog nuzzled Felix's hand with a spongy, plush nose.

Every day for the past week, Felix had sat in his office, waiting for the children. And each day, in mounting frustration, he read and reread the papers he had salvaged from Herbert's cot, trying to find the secrets that lay within the careful handwriting. But it was to no avail. Felix sighed to himself and put the papers back in the little upper drawer of the desk, locking it firmly and putting the key in his pocket again. He offered the dog another sugar lump, and Schatzie, groaning slightly, struggled to her feet and wagged her stump of a tail.

In the examining room and in the entryway that led to it, photographs of children looked down at Felix and his current patients. Their sweet little faces and unblinking dark eyes stared out at the world. "For my beloved Uncle Felix." "To Felix with all my love," "Dear Felix, how will I ever forget you?" The words were written again and again over the bottom of the photographs, usually in elegant upward loops, sometimes with a trailing line beneath the sentiments. The handwriting on the pictures was like flowers, decorating the elaborate costumes of the children, the white dresses, the silken curls, the little boys in suits, sailor or otherwise, the girls in white lace dresses with intricate sleeves and wide sashes. All stared soulfully out of the silver frames that guarded them, watching Felix at work every day as he cared for children, the children of America. "The children of America," thought Felix. But they were in truth very like the children of Europe, for they were, most of them, the same children. Only less elegant, less graceful, less courteous. For these were the children of Europeans in America, those who had managed to survive. And a sorry lot they were.

Felix scratched his bushy head, where the gray hairs sprouted like Struwwelpeter's. He consulted his watch yet again, taking it out of the pocket where it lay and screwing his monocle to his eye in order to regard it better. He had the impression time stopped here in New York. The apartment was silent, the floors creaked on their own, and pipes hissed. But Felix was lonely. If it were not for Schatzie, he realized, he would have given up long ago. He tried not to think of Marthe, and of what had befallen her. It was his own fault. His father had warned him not to marry a Jew.

Marthe's father had been a doctor, Felix's teacher. And Marthe had been beautiful and rich. "Rich," thought Felix sadly. So he had married the daughter and gotten the father's practice as well. Until the war: Hitler, and everything had changed. Felix tried not to think about Marthe, but the more he tried not to think of her, the more she came into his mind. Finally, he saw himself pushing her away and leaving Vienna, where he had spent so many happy and lucrative years. Felix, leaving the day after Marthe had been taken, had packed hastily. From the medical practice, he took only the photographs, but there was a special trunk of research equipment, microscope and slides and jars, which he packed and took with him as well.

Scooping up Schatzie, Felix had stood beside the train that was to carry them both away from Europe. Mentally, he made a photograph of himself at that moment. In the foreground, he placed the large trunk. Next to it in the station, Felix himself, a small man, with Schatzie squeezed, unprotesting, under his arm. In his eye, the monocle glared, a manic disk. Felix bit down fiercely on his cigar, and with his free hand, he fingered the gold watch, the one Marthe's father had given him when he had entered practice with the older physician. Then the train came; the doors opened, and Felix and Schatzie had to be helped in. It was only then that emotion overcame him, misting the monocle, which he removed, putting it into his vest pocket, where it rested beside his stethoscope for the rest of the long journey.

Now in Manhattan, a new life, an empty life. But the doorbell rang, signaling the arrival of the first of the children. It was tonsils; Felix already knew that. "Come, Schatzie." He sighed, putting the dog down. He went down the long hall to the large carved door, opening it slowly. Schatzie lumbered behind him. *"Guten Morgen,"* Felix said, opening his door to the small patient, who stood solemnly beside its mother.

"Oh, Herr Doktor, we are so grateful!" The mother, upon seeing Felix, immediately began to gush with relief.

"Not at all, dear lady, not at all." Felix forestalled her with a warning gesture. He moved closer to the little boy, who was just his height. "Well," demanded Felix suddenly, lifting one bushy eyebrow, "have you been a bad boy, hmm?"

The little boy shrank back, clutching his mother's hand tightly. "Noooo," he ventured tentatively.

"No, Uncle Felix," said Felix, immediately correcting the child. The boy complied. "Good," said Felix, leading the way into the examining room. *"Komm,* Schatzie," Schatzie trotted behind obediently. The child and his mother followed.

Felix staggered suddenly. "Ach," he cried. "Bad child, bad child! What have you done to Uncle Felix?" The boy cringed, but the mother smiled down at him indulgently. "Don't be afraid, Hans," her smile seemed to say.

"You see, you are breaking my leg!" cried Felix to the child in a fierce voice. "Now it is I who am sick! Are you going to fix my leg, hmm?" Hans pressed back against his mother, all of his own physical suffering forgotten as he contemplated the figure of this contorted man, sagging to the ground, clutching Hans's body and gibbering, tongue lolling, as he staggered against him.

"Now you must help Uncle Felix, bad boy," Felix said. "Ach, ach, how it hurts!" Felix fell on the floor of his examining room, his leg cramped against him. Schatzie nuzzled her master's prone body, bewildered. She licked him a couple of times. Hans watched this, his round eyes even rounder. "It hurts!" Felix cried. "Now,

Hans," he commanded the boy, "you must help your poor old Uncle Felix." He stretched out a hand to Hans, who, terrified, refused to take it. "Come, you bad boy," Felix cried. "It is you who broke my leg. Now you must fix it." The boy, pushed forward by his mother, tentatively touched Felix's arm. "Ach!" Felix sprang to his feet, and before the surprised eyes of the child and his mother, he bounded about the room, although still managing to drag one leg behind.

Suddenly, he swooped down upon the boy. "Now open your mouth!" he commanded. "Say 'Ahh.'" Felix set the child upon the examining table, screwed his monocle to his eye, reached for the stethoscope, took out a tongue depressor, and peered down the child's throat, all in one motion. He appeared to thrust his bushy head all the way into the boy's gullet.

"'Ahhh,'" said the boy, as if his life depended on it. "'Aaah.'"

Felix snapped the tongue depressor in two and went for the child's ears. All this happened so quickly that Hans never thought to utter a sound. Felix threw Schatzie a sugar cube and reached for the stethoscope that dangled around his neck. He took out his gold pocket watch and counted to himself, breathing in a stentorian fashion. "Bad boy, bad boy!" Felix said to himself. Schatzie licked his pant leg.

"Now, Hans," Felix said briskly when he had finished, "you will be a good boy from now on, hmm?" He bent down and pressed his nose against Hans's, fixing the child in his gaze. "No more troubles for Mutter, hmm?" Hans, terrified, nodded.

"That's better," said Felix, straightening up. "First you will take my medicine. You will be good, and then you will give me a nice picture. *Ja?* A nice picture for my walls."

Hans looked around him and above, as far as he could see, to the grave and smiling photos of children looking down at him.

"Of course," Hans's mother said encouragingly. "Of course you shall have a picture."

"And you, you must get dressed," said Felix to the child. "And then you shall sit in my nice room outside with Schatzie and wait for Mutter, hmm?" Felix looked significantly at the far corner of his office, far from the examining table, where a large screen cut off the final third of the room. The ceilings were high, with decorated moldings at the top. Paint was peeling, and the radiators muttered. But the room was nice and warm. Hans wondered vaguely what was behind the screen. Felix snapped his fingers and Schatzie emerged from the corner, wagging her entire fat body. Deftly, Felix pulled a dog candy from out of a sleeve, and with the other, he plucked a lollipop from Hans's ear. He held the lollipop in the air. "You see, this has been the problem all along!" he declared. "Bad boy, why do you not tell Uncle Felix you hide candy in your ear!"

Hans's mother clapped her hands with delight, as if to encourage the jollity, and Hans managed a wan, unwilling smile. "Bad boy, bad boy," chanted Felix, and he gave the child the lollipop.

"Schatzie, come!" he commanded, snapping his fingers once more, and the dog waddled heavily toward the waiting room. "Hans!" The child walked obediently behind the dog, casting reluctant backward glances at his mother as he went. "Mutti will only be a little while," said Felix. He looked significantly at Hans's mother, at the screen that hid the couch with the silken cover, and motioned the child out. "Sit, Schatzie! Sit, Hans!"

Hans's mother was already unbuttoning her coat, fumbling with the too-small buttonholes. "Now, Hans," warned Felix, "if you are a bad boy, Uncle Felix will know." He raised his voice suddenly, sharply. "Sit," he commanded. Both Hans and Schatzie sat on the little sofa outside of the examining room, next to the umbrella stand, their round eyes looking up at Felix as he wagged a reproving finger at them both. Hans put the lollipop in his mouth and tasted it carefully. He put his other arm around the dog.

"The child will be fine, dear woman," Felix said to Hans's mother, carefully shutting the large oak door to his office. Hans's mother made an imploring gesture toward her son, but Felix raised one gnarled hand as if to forestall her words. "Come with me, dear lady, now," he commanded, leading her behind the screen. "It is only a question of medicine," he said. "The child will be fine, I assure you."

After Hans and his mother had left, Felix sat down once again at his big desk to make a few notes for himself. He scribbled hastily, blotted the paper quickly, and unlocked his desk drawer, placing the note inside. Once again he pulled out the papers he had stolen from Herbert's cot, then held them up to the green-shaded light, as if light would reveal what understanding could not. But he could make no sense of the notes. "P5, k3," he read. Felix snarled, flinging the notes back into the drawer. He shoved them into the back and locked the desk again.

When the doorbell rang this time, he was quickly remaking the couch at the end of the room. He smoothed the silk cover, plumped up the pillows, and readjusted the Chinese screen that separated his sleeping quarters from his office. He moved Schatzie's pillow farther away under the window and plumped that as well. "Come!" he said to the dog, patting the pillow. And Schatzie obediently waddled over to her bed, where she settled herself with a grateful groan. But not for long. The old dog struggled to her feet, jowls jiggling as she watched Felix's departing figure, and followed him, smiling to herself, as he went to answer the door. It was his next patient.

Outside the front door, Maria stood, bundled to her ears, next to her mother. "Aaah!" cried Felix, as if in complete surprise. "And what do we have here, hmm?" He bent down toward the girl and scowled. "Why do you bother Uncle Felix, hmm? Have you been a bad girl again?"

Maria, who had been feeling alternately hot and cold, weak with fever, drew back. Felix looked up at Maria's mother. "So?" he said.

"She is sick," Maria's mother replied. She clutched her neck, drawing her scarf more tightly around herself. "So we must come. I take the morning from my job. Herr Doktor, I implore you!" As Felix ushered them into the front hall, toward the little sofa and the coat stand, Maria's mother fought back tears. "Aach, I am worried!" Maria, in a swirl of light and sound, hardly noticed this exchange.

"My dear lady," said Felix skillfully. Maria's mother pulled herself together. "And your husband?" demanded Felix, changing tone.

Maria's mother shook her head. "David . . . ," she began, but did not finish. Both looked quickly toward Maria. But the child stood stiffly in her little coat and shawl about her head, pale and slightly swaying.

"It is secret, hmm?" Felix barked.

Maria's mother nodded, her own pale face closed. "And now, of course, we have no money," she added in a low voice.

"Calm yourself, my dearest Ilse," Felix said in a low, commanding voice. He snapped his fingers, and Schatzie waddled forward. Almost absently, he gave her another sugar lump. "These are difficult times. We must be calm." He bent down to unwrap the shawl from Maria's head. "And with me"—he looked up at Maria's mother—"you know it is never a question of money. How much do you need?" he asked in a low voice. Maria's mother made a demurring gesture. "We shall see," murmured Felix, "We shall see." He straightened himself halfway. "And from David, there is nothing?" Maria's mother shook her head. "*Ja.* Secret," muttered Felix, half to himself. "Secret, this David. Nothing." Maria's mother stiffened. "Now, now, dear lady," Felix said authoritatively, "We must be calm. These are difficult times."

He bent once again to Maria. "You see, bad girl, how you upset your mother!" he shouted into her ear. "You are a bad girl! And now Mutti is crying. Bad girl!"

"Calm yourself, Ilse," he whispered again to Maria's mother. He motioned to the couch outside his office door. "We must have self-control. Sit here with Schatzie. I take the child now." Maria's mother sank onto the sofa, exhaustion rimming her eyes.

Maria cast behind her a look of despair as Felix took her by the hand and led her into the office. Was she again to be alone with him? A terror seized her heart. "Mama!" she tried to whisper, but no words came out. Looking at her mother on the sofa, Maria realized that there was no help to be had there. Docilely, she allowed herself to be led. Felix closed the big oak door.

"Now," he said, "you bad girl! First we look at your ears, hmm! And then we shall look at Mutter. And then, if you are good, I give you a candy."

Maria looked at the photographs of the children that covered the walls from floor to ceiling. "Would you like to be in a photograph?" asked Felix. "Perhaps today we take a photograph. But only if you are good. *Ja?*"

Felix suddenly fell to the ground in front of Maria, doubled into a fetal position. "Ow ow ow!" he yowled. "You see, bad girl, how you hurt Uncle Felix! My leg!"

Felix grimaced as he thrashed on the floor. Maria stood there, gravely watching him. She swayed with dizziness. "What have you done?" cried Felix. "You broke my leg!" Seeing that Maria did not respond, Felix sprang again as briskly to his feet.

"Come," he said, "now we fix Uncle Felix's leg." Hobbling, he led the child to the examining table and lifted her on. "Bad girl, undress for Felix," he demanded, pressing his bushy brows against her face. Maria was hot with fever, but she felt his still-hotter breath against her. She forgot entirely that her head hurt. Her head, her ears, both seemed bands of ice. Felix took off her clothes and surveyed her small, undernourished body. Maria felt the draft across her chest, but, alternately, warm air rose from the radiator in Felix's room.

"Now," breathed Felix. Once again, he raised the stethoscope to his ears and fastened its huge unwinking eye to Maria's chest. He listened, concentrating, and Maria forced herself to leave her body and float up to the molded ceiling, where, she noticed, a huge stain like a map had emblazoned itself.

"Breathe," commanded Felix sharply. Maria surveyed the happy children, all in white, like angels, who regarded her from Felix's wall. "To my dear Uncle Felix," she read in large grace-ful writing across the bottom corners. The other children looked out at her seriously, as if to give her courage. Maria listened for sounds of her mother outside, but the room was entirely silent.

Affixing a large beak to his head, Felix thrust this beak into Maria's ears. She heard only the sound of his heavy breathing, and the sharp, cold metal hurt. Felix said nothing. After a while he withdrew the cold beak. "Say 'Ahh,'" he commanded, thrust-ing a tongue depressor into her mouth. Maria gagged. "Bad girl. Say 'Ahh,'" said Felix again. She smelled his shaving lotion.

"'Aaah,'" she managed, terrified.

Felix held her wrist and seemed to count to himself. "Lie down," he commanded. Maria lay down, her small, thin body shivering. She felt ashamed of her illness, ashamed of giving so much trouble. Felix said nothing. He pressed his large bushy head to her chest. He listened. Maria listened, too, but for what, she did not know. She smelled his oily hair. His hair tickled her. Once again, she left her body, floated on the ceiling near the water stain, the map. Felix held his breath.

"Now," he said, almost to himself. "What have you done, bad girl?" He took Maria's limp little hand and placed it near his own leg. "You see what you have done?" Maria felt a lump, a huge swelling on the front of Uncle Felix. "You see how it hurts?" he hissed. Maria felt such pity for him. Rocking back and forth, Felix pressed Maria's hand against his lump. "Be still." With his other hand, he held her so she couldn't move, fixing her with a stare. She tried not to look at him.

Maria pictured her mother sitting in a shaft of white light outside the examining room, the dachshund at her feet. Maria hated her mother. She knew there would never be help for her there. She broke out into a sweat. Suddenly, tenderly, Felix was next to her. He held her hand, stroking her forehead. Maria felt obscurely grateful to him.

Felix moved away, and then as quickly he came toward her again, holding something fine between his fingers. Pinching her flesh, he injected something into her, withdrew the needle, and wiped her skin.

"Get dressed," he said. "Mutti is waiting." He adjusted her clothes, tenderness in his hands as he buttoned her sweater.

He led Maria, who was in a sort of swoon, out of the office. As he opened the door, Maria's mother stood up. "The child will be fine," said Felix. "She will be good. Won't you?" he said sharply, addressing the almost fainting girl. Wordlessly, Maria nodded.

"The child needs vitamins. You bring her to me each week. After that, we shall see."

Maria shrank back onto the sofa. "I give her the injections, you know," said Felix, standing above both mother and child. "It could be quite serious, this difficulty with the ears. We must take care." Maria's mother nodded, holding her daughter's hand. "We do not want to operate," Felix said more softly, as a warning.

"Is that not so?" he suddenly cried, stooping down once more to Maria's level. He pinched her cheek. "Abracadabra," he recited, beetling his brows at her. Deftly, he plucked a sugar cube out of thin air and tossed it to Schatzie, who snapped it up immediately with a satisfied smacking sound. "Ah, what have we here?" cried Felix now, And he held one immaculately cuffed wrist near Maria's ear. Suddenly, there was a lollipop. "Bad girl, you hide this from Uncle Felix!" he exclaimed. Maria's mother smiled, the first smile since they had entered.

"Now," said Felix to Maria, "I want you to sit here with Schatzie and rest while I talk to your mama. Don't move," he warned her, fixing her with what Maria knew was a special glance.

"Just wait, my darling," said Maria's mother gently. "I won't be long." As she got up to follow Uncle Felix, she was already unbuttoning her coat.

"Come, my dearest little girl," said Felix, extending his hand to her. "You shall see, all will be well. You must not worry about the money when I am here to help. And the child will be all right, you shall see."

"Wait for me, darling," Ilse said. "Just sit there. There's a good girl. I must have a little talk alone with Uncle Felix now." Maria leaned her head against the back of the couch, and with one hand she began to stroke the sags and folds in Schatzie's neck. She held the lollipop in her other hand. Maria decided never to talk to her mother again.

Before Felix could close the heavy door between the waiting alcove and his examining table, Maria caught one more glimpse of the cold white table upon which she had lain, and the big yellowed screen that guarded the far corner of the room. She could no longer see her mother. But she saw her mother's scarf, and then the good black wool coat as it was flung over the upper part of the screen. Maria closed her eyes. Felix shut the door with a heavy, muffled sound.

Maria wondered if her mother and Uncle Felix were talking about her in there. If so, what were they saying? Was she going to die? Terror gripped her heart. She felt sick and light-headed. Perhaps she was already dead. She looked around her, still feeling the dog's warm, jowly skin, and then she saw the many faces of children. They all seemed to love Uncle Felix so. Maria knew she hated him. Perhaps she had died and gone to heaven with the other children. Maria thought that heaven was a place of love and forgiveness. Had these children forgiven Uncle Felix? Maria knew, from her dispassionate, detached position now, that these children, all of them, were also dead. Otherwise, how could they express such love and gratitude? Maria watched herself be dead. Her hands and feet felt cold, but she did not move. She sat there, waiting, waiting, until the big oak door opened once again. Her mother emerged, laughing, talking to Felix as she adjusted her coat and scarf.

"Ah, dear lady, it is I who am grateful," said Felix as he ushered her out. He put something into her hand. Maria's mother put her hand quickly into the coat pocket. Maria's mother took the little, cold, dead hand of the dead Maria and the dead child floated whitely out of the office. Before too long, they were on the street, and the cold air burned against Maria's face. She was dead; she did not want to feel the air. She did not want to smell the cold, sooty, greasy smell of it as it entered her nostrils. Dead people were cold, Maria knew, and so it was all right to be cold. But not to smell things.

Felix shut the heavy decorated door after they had left. He was ready once again to make his notes. His next little patient would be coming soon, after Felix had his nice lunch of thick bread and butter and sausage, and after Schatzie had her bowl of dog food.

"Come, my darling," said Maria's mother, walking more quickly, happily. There was a spring in her step, a careless hopefulness. "Now we go home. And I make you a nice lunch. Philip will be waiting for us," she went on cheerfully, babbling into the unlistening ears of Maria, who tried to shut out her mother's hateful voice. "Won't that be lovely, a little soup? And then I must go to work. But soon you will be in your nice bed with your nice books. And you will feel much better."

Maria's body burned, but she shut herself off from herself and floated up into the sooty sky. There, assembled with all the little children in white dresses, she looked down at her mother with pity, as if from a great height. From now on, she would be dead. But she would still sit in judgment on her mother and others. And when God came on Judgment Day to ask her opinion, she would tell God what had really happened. In her mind, however, God and the SS were confused. Maria knew she must never tell anything—ever—to anyone. Or else they would all—her whole family, including even little Philip—be put into the camps. And then they would die in the ovens and become smoke. Black smoke, streaming out of chimneys. She thought of little Philip burning, his small body twisting, shrieking. She could never bear that, not even if she herself were tortured. Maria knew that life was a test, a test of courage and silence. She had always understood that, although her parents had tried to shelter her, perhaps, from this understanding. But she knew something from the whispers around her, the mutterings of the walls, the imprecations of the elevator girl, and the absences of her father. She knew from the furtive fear of her mother, from the huddled penury of their lives, and from the sense of being always in hiding, even here in New York.

Maria thought only her grandfather could match—in fact, surpass—her in cunning secrecy. She was brave; she would save her family one day by her silence. They were all in her power, Maria knew, her power and God's. For if she said only one word of what she knew, the Nazis—or God—would find them all instantly, smoke them out like a helpless nest of mice.

No, Maria would never tell anyone anything, not even God, whatever happened to her. Not even her father. Where was he? It was a secret. Maria resolved to be dead at least until her father came back. Then she would hold his hand ever so tightly. But still, she would never tell. She would practice being dead as long as she could.

Chapter 6

AND THEN HE DID

Feverish, Maria tried to adapt her body to fit around that of the Rat's in her cot. Anna took up so little room that after the first night, Maria did not notice the lack of space; she fitted her small bones around the curved ones of the Rat. Maria was to find comfort in the frilled nightgown of the Rat, the sweet, faint smell of the Rat's cologne, and, of course, the Rat's low, thrilling voice. No longer did Maria have terrible dreams; no longer did she feel herself alone. Terror abated when the Rat came into her bed. They lay together through the long nights, when, with no heat and no dawn in sight, the Rat warmed them both with her stories. The Rat talked throughout Maria's childhood. She talked while the others slept, while the thin snores rose in the silence of the room. Anna whispered to Maria in bed, her words inevitable and continuous as the flakes of first snow, falling upon the Rat's adopted Russia.

"I was only sixteen, just a little older than you are now," the Rat began, fondly stroking Maria's hair back from her forehead. "But I was already married. My father had sold me, or perhaps I should say he had bought me a husband. A fine husband, handsome, well connected. But a poor husband. Oh, I did not know it at the time. But he was poor. And weak, too." The Rat paused, her voice trailing off into the shadows.

"And I went away with him—oh, I did not want to go. But I went nevertheless.

"They sent me away, to Russia. To Saint Petersburg, where I lived with my husband. And his mother. And, of course, the whole household. And I had to learn their ways."

From the first, the Count did not touch the Rat. He liked her dowry. Anna was a meal ticket for this impoverished branch of the noble family. But he found women ugly, and the marriage had been only an agreed-upon front for his other, darker desires. Her intelligence repelled him further. He did not care about her deformity, since he never intended to have anything to do with her other than to mollify his mother. "We had no wedding night," the Rat told Maria. Night after night, Anna lay alone in her room while the Count amused himself elsewhere. Anna accepted this, and did not expect otherwise. "Perhaps he had a mistress. Perhaps he was at cards. . . ."

Maria knew better than to interrupt. She lay beside the Rat, staring into the dark. "He went to the theater; sometimes I went with him." Anna was silent then at the memory of it. "He was repelled by me. And so," she continued, "I lived with his family. It was wild and savage; I enjoyed it. And then finally I had the children. His mother had spoken to him, you see."

"You must try to do something with the girl," his mother had protested as the debts mounted. "We want the family name to continue."

The Count went out and got drunk, came home, and mounted the Rat from behind. A few gestures, a stifled cry, a booted leg hastily thrown over her hyphenated body. Two or three plunges in the dark; there, it was finished. This much he would do for his mother. And when it was finished, tears—his. "Forgive me, my little Anna," the Count sobbed. "Can you forgive me?" But it was his fellow officers from whom he was asking forgiveness. One in particular—his immediate subordinate, who had instructed him how to do it in the first place. He bit his lip. He would do this for three nights, approaching her in the dark, thinking of Vanek, and then, when he had thought enough, mounting her in a violent fury until he had spent his seed. Anna knew enough to cooperate, never to cry out, never to feel anything. To respond in any way would have seemed to her the ultimate treachery. Each time, when it was over, her husband collapsed and sobbed on her hunchbacked body in disgust. He pulled out of her without a word and left immediately, going to the barracks at once to drink himself further into a stupor. Was this how men behaved with their wives? Anna was disgusted, but she stroked his hair as he bent and kissed her hand before going. "Of course. Yes. Shh. Go; don't worry."

This happened exactly three times. Three children. Anna, embarrassed by her pain, stifled her cries. It was humiliating, the whole procedure. But the children were beautiful, each one emerging from her torn body. She clutched them to her, precious things. After that, she didn't mind that her husband was never there. She watched with pride as her three children grew.

"And then, one day, my husband was sent to the front." Like other younger wastrel sons, the Count had a career—or rather, that which passed for a career—in the military. He was an officer for the Tsar, and his manners were brutish enough to command any number of wretches having the misfortune to serve under him.

"I was not sorry to see him go," the Rat told Maria. "We had the usual farewell scene. But we both knew it was a farce." Upon saying good-bye to his three children, all under the age of five, the Count allowed his real emotions to show for a moment. His mustache quivered. When he embraced his old mother, he burst into tears. He had done all she had asked of him. Anna observed all this, dry-eyed.

"Life at home went on as usual. Mama was aging, becoming more impossible. I tried to please her. I couldn't. The children grew, did the usual things. I was happy, peaceful. We didn't hear from him for a long time, this husband of mine. After a while, I began to forget him. I was happy, alone with the children, and I realized I was never made for marriage after all."

After a year, still no word came back from the Count. But one day, Anna opened the door to a man whom she recognized as one of the Count's servants. He handed her an envelope with the Count's seal upon it. "The bearer of this message can be trusted. I rely upon your generosity," she read. "Your husband is in danger. He must have money immediately," the servant told her.

The Rat stepped back. "Money?"

"He has lost everything," the servant replied.

"My dear little wife," the Count had written. "All is lost. By the time you read this, your unhappy husband will be . . ."

Anna scanned what appeared to be a deathbed farewell. The Count had thrown away everything in gambling. Anna's money, their house and lands, even the house in the country had been lost in the endless gaming to which at last the addicted Count confessed. "It is a debt to the Tsar," he wrote. "If I don't pay it, I shall be shot. I beg of you, my dear Anna, to send me money immediately. I promise you I shall never gamble again."

"And so," continued the Rat, stroking Maria's hair absently, "I sold everything I had. My furs and jewels, everything. But it was not enough."

A month later, the Tsar's bailiffs came to the door. "Give me a week," Anna pleaded. "I shall go to the Tsar himself and throw myself at his feet. I shall beg for mercy."

The next day, while the children were asleep and the Count's mother was still in bed, the Rat made her way by coach to the palace. Attendants led her upstairs and through a series of rooms and magnificent hallways. Enormous doors shut behind her and finally she was taken into a large study. At the window stood a hooded figure, pondering the sadness of Russia as he looked pensively outward. Anna stood before him and waited, her head bent.

The figure turned. "So, my dear Countess," the man said. "You have come for mercy."

The Rat shuddered. She had never seen eyes like that. Anna sank to her knees. "Holy Father," she murmured.

The man came forward and lifted her to her feet. "Countess," he said, "you come on your knees to me?" His voice had a sarcastic timbre that echoed through the cramped bones of her body. It spread out like ripples in the room. "You come on your knees? And you would like something from me?" The voice was insidious, hypnotizing. "Good," he said. "Now, my child, look at me." The command caused Anna to raise her head until her eyes met those of the apparition.

"And then I knew." Anna shuddered, burrowing her head in Maria's hair. "I was in the presence not of the Tsar, but of Rasputin."

The Monk reached out one finger and touched the Rat's cheek. "Tell me, my child," he commanded. "What is it you want?"

"Save us, Holiness." The Rat burst into tears. "Save us."

The gaunt figure listened, immobile. He looked into the eyes of the Rat. "My dear lady, I already know everything," he replied slowly in his thrilling voice. "Trouble yourself no longer. I will pay your husband's gambling debts. All of them. You and your children do not have to cry any longer."

The Rat gasped.

"But I shall ask of you only one little thing in return."

"And what was that?" Maria asked urgently.

The Rat did not answer. And when finally she did, it was in a low, reluctant voice.

"I ask of you only this, dear madame," Rasputin said. "That for the next two weeks, you shall be my companion."

Rasputin looked into Anna's eyes with a piercing yellow glare. The Rat felt herself go weak. "If not . . ." The Monk did not need to say more.

"And did you do it?" Maria asked.

The Rat was silent for a long time. A shiver crossed her little body.

"Yes," she finally said. "I agreed. And so I went every day to Rasputin's apartments. And there, I did with him . . ." She paused. "Unspeakable things."

In the darkness, both she and Maria were silent. Maria stared into the room, wondering what "unspeakable things" could cover. She thrilled to the dark inclination of the phrase. "Unspeakable things." The words repeated themselves.

From behind the blanket that separated the room, Maria's grandfather's snores rose like wisps of smoke into the thin air. The room was starting to take on the outlines of early morning. Maria's mother slept as if flung down onto the couch. Only Maria and the Rat lay awake in the half-light. And finally the Rat, too, fell asleep, with small, slack, shallow breaths, as Maria lay half-awake, listening.

Ilse was to speak to her daughter later. The next morning, as Maria's mother was combing her daughter's hair, she pulled the child toward her and hugged her. In one corner of the room, the Rat sat hunched contemplatively over her cup of tea. Maria's mother cast a quick look at the older woman. "Maria," her mother said softly, "there are things we should be silent about."

She stroked her daughter's long, shining hair, then deftly plaited it. "We must be silent, do you understand?" Her hands moved efficiently.

Maria could hardly wait to get home that afternoon to see if the Rat was still there. And indeed, there she was, bent over as when they had left her, but this time with a large book propped open and a lorgnette in front of her. Upon seeing the children, the Rat sighed, put down the lorgnette, and held out her arms to them.

Each night, Maria huddled around the Rat's small body and waited for the next installment, spellbound. "My husband," the Rat whispered into the dark, "you know, I never saw him again after that. He was sent to Manchuria. And so . . ."

And so? Maria's heart was pounding with excitement. "And so." The Rat turned over and went to sleep.

The next morning, before everyone else was awake, the Rat picked up the story of Rasputin. "And afterward, he, too, disappeared. That was terrible. But I was not sorry." She was silent for a long time. "And of course the Holy Tsar and his family. It all happened so quickly.

"I stayed with my husband's mother until she died. It was my duty." After her death, the Rat yearned to return to Hungary. "To see my family and friends and your grandfather, who was then still living in Vienna. Yes, all this I wanted. But," the Rat continued sadly, "I had my duty to my husband also. And so I waited and waited to hear news of him. But no news came."

The Rat decided to try to find her husband. "I only knew that I must see him one more time to say good-bye." Taking two servants with her to accompany her three children, she set out toward Manchuria. "I did not know if we would ever return, and so of course I took the children. We traveled all through Russia. Mother Russia." The Rat whispered into the dark, staring outward at the memory. "But I never found my husband again."

"And so, she never saw her husband again," Maria's mother was to tell Maria, many years later. "Nor her two sons. Except for one daughter, who went to England, all were lost."

"What happened?" Maria had wanted to know this ever since the Rat had started once again to tell the story of her travels throughout Russia. Maria knew a bit about Anna's children—mostly of their mischief and misbehavior. But once the Rat embarked on the story of their travels through Russia—herself, the two servants, and these children—there always came the point of absolute silence, when the Rat turned her face to the wall and refused to say another word.

"She never saw any of them again. We don't know what happened. Your grandfather tried to find out. But . . . We can only imagine," Ilse told her daughter quickly, sensitively. Maria's mother immediately continued on another topic in order to forestall Maria's possible questions. But Maria had no intention of not asking questions.

"And then," she asked, "what happened to the daughter?"

"She went to England. Aunt Anna managed to smuggle her out."

Maria thought this over. "And how did Aunt Anna come to us?"

"We don't ask this question," admonished Maria's mother impatiently, pursing her lips.

Maria couldn't wait for night to happen again, to hear the beautiful hunchback's story, whispered obsessively in the dark, into the whorled echoing shell of the child's ear. Unspeakable things.

Hadn't Maria known all this already? The Rat, curled in upon herself, dreaming of Rasputin, her spine a bent half circle, floated in Maria's mind as in their small bed. And Maria's grandfather, his white hair an aureole about his head, dreamed in a cloud of quiet snores behind the army blanket draped over a clothes-line, so close to them both. In the room, Ilse turned over on the couch, where she lay wrapped in a quilt. Next to her, little Philip pressed his nose against her body.

In a dank basement far away, secreted in another place, another city, with the long name—Washington, D.C.—David, Maria's father, husband of Ilse and only remaining son of Herbert and Adeline, peered at a page and tried to type what he saw there. He rubbed his eyes. He was so weary. There was always more news to translate. Always more to decode and try to understand. He tried not to read what he saw beneath the mild reports that came to him from abroad. For he was an alien, and a translator whose usefulness was controlled. David translated the advertisements from foreign newspapers—ads for goods, which were limited, ads for people who sought spouses, even in the midst of catastrophe. The Allies felt that perhaps, in these ads, great schemes might, in code, contain military secrets. David wondered. But he translated into English the desperate hopes for marriage and family that, even in the midst of devastation, reflected the ordinary yearnings for a more ordinary happiness on the part of the German-speaking people. David translated these pathetic ads, then passed the translations on to his superiors. Maybe they could decode them? What did it matter? David dreamed of his family sometimes. But when he thought of his mother, Adeline, he stopped thinking and bent again to his work.

The Rat twitched in her little space, and Maria moved her body accommodatingly to make room for her. Everyone stirred in the little room, as if a wind had touched them, and then every-one, in unison, turned over and slept more deeply.

Chapter 7

THE LABORATORY

After the last little patient of the day had left, Felix took a moment to enjoy a cigar, a glass of wine in hand. Schatzie lay at his feet, adoring. But Felix did not linger too long. For he was a disciplined man with a careful schedule laid out for himself.

He moved rapidly toward his laboratory, as he called it: a small dark closet that he had cleverly converted into a small working lab, complete with a microscope, smuggled in from Germany during those last days, and shelves of slides. He screwed his monocle more tightly to his eye and bent toward the eyepiece of the microscope.

There, a small number of cells lay beneath his eye in their petri dish. It appeared, though he could not be too sure, that there had been some activity. Briskly, Felix tried to focus the eyepiece further. He could not be sure; no, he could not. He moved to the counter beside the instrument and carefully noted the date and time, as well as his hesitant observations.

Felix opened the small refrigerator beneath the counter. His jars lay in their opaque darkness, small bits and pieces swimming in fluid. Felix regarded them gravely, then shut the refrigerator again. Schatzie sighed and shifted position, waiting outside the laboratory door. The laboratory was the one place she was not allowed to go, although Felix was carefully cultivating, in a small dish, some specks of Schatzie's dander.

In another dish, a small section of Schatzie's tail, a very small, scrupulously clean bit of tail tissue, lay in its formaldehyde, ready for regeneration. Felix had taken this bit from Schatzie under local anesthetic; the dog had not even felt it. It was only when Felix had shaved the dog's tail preparatory to the incision that Schatzie, feeling slightly shorn and humiliated, had turned and regarded Felix with reproachful eyes. Felix, before he anesthetized the shaved tail, had washed that part of Schatzie so tenderly that the dog had finally sighed with pleasure. Felix was skillful; the anesthetic had worn off quickly, and Schatzie was her old happy self again, wagging the bare thing with its little Band-Aid on it. Now the hair had grown back. But the piece of Schatzie lay in Felix's cell bank, ready to be immortal. A superdog. With a supertail.

Felix believed in regeneration, the creation of the whole organism from its smallest part. For this reason, he had collected body parts, which he was storing until he could finally discover the secret of growing whole ones again.

His jars were full of mysterious things. The closet smelled strangely: formaldehyde, vinegar, and a kind of protein broth that Felix made himself over a hot plate and fed to the body parts. It was part oatmeal, part liverwurst. The tissues thrived in their milky jars, and seemed to thrash and swim when he dropped the mixture in.

Felix surveyed his collection happily. All seemed healthy, in good condition. "Rest, my little ones," he said, preparing his mixture carefully and filling an eyedropper. The gruel had to be fresh each evening, he had discovered. He had killed an ear by feeding it old gruel. Now he was more careful, and the results, he thought, were good.

Felix's main goal was the study and propagation of genius. What was genius? How could one ensure its survival? How could one produce it? What happened to the bodies of dead geniuses? Did their genes die with them, or could the cells, the genetic code, somehow be preserved? Felix devoted many hours to the study of these questions.

Felix had managed to preserve a piece of skin from Marthe's neck. "One never knows," he had thought in his practical way. "There might come a time when I will need it again." There she lay in her jar. But Felix was not sure he would want Marthe again, even though he wept for her occasionally. Felix liked to weep; he liked the slow, soft letting go of tears: so warm. He liked to weep for Marthe; it made him feel tender, almost sexual. Thinking of her sadly aroused him.

But Marthe was not, had never been, a genius. Her regeneration would have to wait. Felix had more important things to do.

Felix coveted a piece of Herbert, that wily rascal, to round out his collection. He respected Herbert a great deal. It was too bad Herbert was misguided, but perhaps with some genetic engineering that could be changed. Felix had not yet figured out how to get Herbert's consent to donate his tissue. He meant to talk to him, but somehow Felix quailed before the prospect. Best, he thought, would be a section from Herbert's scalp. It was liver-spotted already. Felix might be able to convince him he had skin cancer, offer to remove it. He smiled to himself. That might do. After all, the family trusted him.

He had been present at the birth of Ilse, as a medical student assisting Marthe's father. Marthe's father had been called away, and it had been Felix who had, in fact, delivered the baby. Not only that, he had also delivered Ilse of Maria, a very strange little girl indeed. But an interesting one. They had every right to be grateful to him, grateful even for their lives, which he, Felix, had breathed into them. How strange that they had found themselves in New York after all these years.

Herbert had much to thank Felix for, if only he were to think about it, but Herbert was stubborn and strong; in his own way a great, a very great man indeed. There was something magic about the man, powerful; a great negotiator, a man of principle. Even in Felix's youth, Herbert, "Herr Hofrat," was legendary. Felix was not fit to touch the hem of his greatcoat. Yes. The man should be preserved, thought Felix. He belonged in the collection.

Felix squirted a little red dye onto the slide before him, adjusting the cover slip with a delicate hand, and bent once more to the microscope. He thought he saw the cells wiggle. He had learned to be patient. Regeneration might take a bit of time.

Each month, Felix received a shipment from Europe, jars carefully packed in dry ice, and delivered (emergency, Red Cross) by airplane and then by ambulance to his door. Carefully, lovingly, Felix opened these packages, cradling the jars in his hand. Someone had written on them, identifying the parts. So far, he had managed to collect a bit of the brain of Rolfe Kahn, the physicist whom the Nazis had managed to collect for him. That was his best specimen so far.

Also among his choicest prospects was the left eye of Oswald Herten, the painter. (Felix would have preferred the right eye, which had the better vision, but that had somehow been lost in transit.) He had a scrap of bone from Lenhard Weisen, the famous German Jewish runner who had appeared briefly, during the Olympic Games, but who then had somehow mysteriously disappeared. He had a fragment of thigh from another half-Jewish high jumper; the tip of the earlobe of Heinz Werner, a composer; a few cells from the nose of a famous—now dead—literary critic; and various scraps of body parts of assorted European playwrights, artists, and writers, all of dubious origin, all disappeared now. His network had been good.

His source of supply was his dear old childhood friend who had remained in Austria throughout the unfortunate war. Felix remembered their discussions during medical school. Helmut had always believed in the concept of the "master race," perhaps even more than had Felix himself. Helmut had even tried to dissuade Felix, sometimes strenuously, from marrying Marthe. Perhaps he had been right. Marthe had proved nervous, neurasthenic. Helmut himself had never married.

"Ours is a fine and manly friendship," Felix told himself, thinking of Helmut, his earnest face and keen eyes. It was an intellectual meeting of the minds that endured far beyond any feeling for women.

Helmut was the last person he had seen at the station. Helmut had gripped Felix's hand in his own and looked deeply into his eyes in a firm, manly way when Felix left. "God be with you!" Helmut had shouted after the departing train. Now the two doctors maintained a clandestine correspondence, a brief scientific notation smuggled in with the jars. Felix recognized Helmut's writing on the labels.

"My friend, my dear friend," he thought sentimentally. And tears welled up in his eyes. He wondered when he would see his friend again. Perhaps after all these troubles were over. Felix waited for a sign that he could return to Europe once again. Meanwhile, he rejoiced in Helmut's important position in the Party. Together, they were participating in a great new experiment, the thing they had always dreamed of: the creation of a better, purer society. This, this new society created from the old, would be their true progeny, the child they would create together finally. Felix knew Helmut, in his laboratory in Austria, felt exactly the same. He pictured his friend also bending over a microscope, carrying out his experiments, making his notations on reproduction.

Of course, all human life could not be so serious. Felix respected beauty, too. In various jars reposed various scraps of what had once been famous Jewish beauties. Felix had worried that the SS would not preserve for him these vital parts of these women; he worried, as is the way of soldiers, that they would simply use and abandon the women once they took them in. But he needn't have worried. The police were under strict orders to exercise self-control in these matters. And so the fragments were shipped to Felix in New York, each one carefully classified: Frau Kohner, Frau Schwartz, and so on. Felix remembered with nostalgia the beauty and gaiety of these women.

"Someday you will live again, my darlings," he promised them. He sighed with pleasure. But no, he must go slowly. He must study a great deal before attempting anything so daring. Felix turned to his collection of large and secret books on alchemy, cell biology, and necromancy. There was something to be found in them all. He was not ready yet to synthesize his knowledge. He must study more.

Felix knew he also was a genius, perhaps the most important one of all. He had taken the precaution of preserving a bit from his scrotum, just in case. There it lay, in its own jar, winking at him merrily. Felix remembered the courage it had taken to operate on himself. It had been minor in the end—injecting himself with the novocaine and then, with a surprisingly steady hand, slicing off just the surface layer, a little patch. It had hurt afterward, he remembered. Nevertheless, Felix knew that if his experiments in regeneration were a success, his tissue would be of foremost interest, especially to future generations. After all, he had no child of his own to carry his amazing genetic makeup. But he knew he could produce, once he had discovered the secret, a man-child of his own makeup, springing forth, as it were, from his own loins. Felix was proud of his practical foresight.

He touched the jar containing his own tissue with reverence and love. Felix believed in talking to his specimens. He approached each bit of tissue with love and respect. Reverence for life—he believed in that.

Before leaving his laboratory, after having fed all his jars, Felix caressed his newest acquisition, a larger, round-bellied mason jar, wherein swam the four little fingers of the musicians of the Vienna Tolstoi Quartet. Felix thought of the wonderful music they would make together once he had done his work with them. He remembered the music the Quartet had made in the past. How he loved their Brahms and Beethoven and Schubert. He would make sure the fingers played together once again; not that horrible modern stuff, but the dear old music he and Marthe had enjoyed so much. "Hello, fellows," Felix whispered to the jar's cold, rounded side. He could hardly believe his good fortune.

Felix closed the door. Schatzie, patient as ever, wagged her tail, rising to her feet. "Good girl," said Felix, bending down and scratching her silken ears. Schatzie followed him down the long hall toward the bed behind the screen.

Felix undressed and, reaching into the large wardrobe, drew out a picture of his beloved Führer and set it on the mantel. Then he pulled a corset and some stockings out of the closet and quickly put these on over his short legs. Carefully he applied the lipstick, and then a brassiere followed upon his squeezed chest. "Lie down, girl," he exhorted Schatzie, who obediently bowed her head. Felix fell to his knees before the picture. "*Mein* beloved Führer," he whispered. It seemed to him that the image of the

Führer looked down at him, only him, poor humble servant that he was, with tenderness and approval in his eyes. "My faithful servant," the picture seemed to say back.

Felix writhed in his constricting woman's clothes, the black lace lingerie straining over his crotch, pinching him cruelly, the whalebone brassiere digging into his body. His "broken leg" throbbed.

He took out "Little Hänschen" from between the garter belt and the top of his stockings. He began to stroke it tenderly, crooning, *"Ja."* It was small and velvety; then, as he caressed it, it grew in his hands. Little Hänschen liked to be free; he grew big and strong with pride.

"My Führer, my beloved." Felix sobbed, giving himself to the overarching ecstasy. To whom was he crooning? The hot come began to spurt into his hand, and suddenly he felt ashamed. Delicious shame, the most delectable emotion of all. He stroked more quickly now.

"Forgive me, my father, for I have sinned," he gasped. The familiar litany of his childhood prayers soothed him. Before he knew it, he was crying. The warm tears coursed down his cheeks, and he felt the relief of confessing to his Führer all his sins. The picture forgave him. "I know you are doing your best," the picture seemed to say. "My son, you are indeed my true son."

Felix wept in a luxury of self-abnegation. "Pray for me, Father," he sobbed.

"You are my faithful servant," the glass-covered picture said. Felix straightened his stockings, his makeup smeared. He bent over tenderly and kissed the Führer's lips. He buried his head against the warm side of his faithful dog. "Oh, Schatzie, my dearest," he sobbed, overcome with the emotion. The dachshund licked Felix's hand. Felix thought he could sleep now.

Chapter 8

NIGHT

Snores punctuated the drab air of the room above the city where Maria lay in a half sleep. Beyond the blanket partition, Herbert coughed once, lying on his narrow cot in his own little area of the room. Maria's mother, sleeping on the couch, did not move at all, lying as if she had suddenly fallen, startled, amid a heap of sheets.

In the first circle of the orchestra at the Vienna State Opera, Herbert regarded his wife's sleek shoulders beside him, her smooth hair as she bent her head to the program in her lap. The lights shone about them like beacons, shedding amber on the red velvet interior. All was muted and golden. Onstage, the musicians were tuning up behind their curtain: the crisp sounds of the A from the concertmaster, a spark in the thin air, and then the answering calls of the other instruments as they responded to the tuning note of A taken up from the first violin section. The instruments mooed and lowed in their preparations.

Herbert put his hand on his wife's, and she looked up at him and smiled. "Are you happy, my dear?" he asked her.

"Yes, my darling," she replied, squeezing his hand in return. She leaned her head briefly against his shoulder.

Herbert had heard that Adeline was in love with Herr Mahler, who would be conducting tonight. But he discarded that rumor. Mahler was, of course, a genius. Who wouldn't be attracted to his eccentric power? Herbert himself was one of Mahler's benefactors, even though he found that actually listening to Mahler's music was an ordeal. There was too much pain in that strange music, too much the outraged groan of the outsider. Yes, thought Herbert, too much pain.

He looked at Adeline fondly.

"The children, they were wonderful tonight, weren't they?" she said to him, smiling.

"Yes, but, my dear, you really favor Michael too much," Herbert replied, thinking of the little imp. "You let him stay up too long. He got much too excited."

"But he wants so much to be like his brother. Anyway, what's the harm in letting him stay up with us?"

Herbert sighed. The evening meal had ended with Michael's protesting shrieks as their nursemaid ushered the two boys upstairs.

"No, Mama!" Michael howled, flinging himself against Adeline's knees and holding on. Herbert and David regarded the scene with quiet eyes, though they exchanged a hidden smile. David was prim and full of virtue next to his younger brother.

"Hush," said Adeline, patting the younger boy. "I'll come up and say good night before we go out."

"I want you to stay with me," protested the child, clinging to his mother even more forcefully.

"Come, Michael," exhorted David. "We'll play with the soldiers." At the thought of being allowed to touch David's precious toy soldier collection, Michael disengaged himself in a hurry.

"I'll come soon, my darling," Adeline said regally to Michael as David scurried upstairs behind his brother. She dismissed them, though David continued to follow his mother's beauty with a pleading glance.

"Good night, boys." Herbert watched them approvingly. Adeline smoothed her skirt. From the rooms upstairs Herbert could hear the treble exclamations of the younger boy, and, from time to time, the lower notes of David's voice, calming him. Herbert turned his attention away from them. He was waiting for something else.

"Papageno, Papageno, Papageno!" sang the figure onstage. A waiting body leaped forward onto the apron of the stage and danced to the edge. A glance passed between the figure onstage and Herbert, who watched from the second row of the orchestra seats of the Opera. How had the setting changed so fast? The music was satisfying, harmonious. The figure shook its headdress of tatters and bells and danced away. Herbert could no longer see him in the crowd of figures that swirled onto the stage now, singing as they danced. They carried trees aloft, peeping through the leaves at the conductor. The dancing figure of Papageno reappeared, casting one backward glance at Herbert as he was once more lost in the swirl of the opera production.

With a start, Herbert recalled himself and reached for Adeline's hand. But all he grasped was the rough wool of the blanket that covered him where he lay on a narrow cot in his son's cold-water flat in New York. "Adeline!" Painfully, Herbert remembered where he had left her. He coughed. His lungs hurt, his body, too. Carefully, so as not to wake the children, the Rat, and Ilse, David's overworked wife, he shifted position on the cot. The gray light of dawn was coming in beyond his clothesline partition. It was bleak, and the chill in the room was a dirty one.

Herbert closed his eyes once more and tried to remember Herr Mahler. And Adeline's wild passion for him—a passion that had made her sob each afternoon alone in her dressing room, her hair in disarray, eyes glittering. A passion he, Herbert, had pretended not to notice, even when, at the end of each day, he entered the silenced house, a house shuttered against the mourning animal upstairs. Herbert had pretended he did not see Mahler's rejection of his lovely wife, even while he comforted her through it. "Shh, my darling." And while he held her, her hot face against his waistcoat and asked, "Why are you crying so?" He made a sign behind her back to Papageno. "Leave us for the moment." Papageno obeyed, and with a small answering gesture of the hand, almost imperceptible, he disappeared.

Herbert dressed quickly in the half-light, trying not to cough as he pulled on the garments, stiff with cold.

"My dearest Herr Professor," Mahler had written long ago. "It is only you who can help us now. My wife and I implore you on this most urgent matter. The situation can only get worse, as you, of course, do not need to be told. If you could only be so kind? I realize, of course, that a man in your position . . . I would be so grateful. . . ."

Chapter 9

WHAT HAVE YOU DONE, BAD GIRL?

Maria's head was pierced by a knife so intense, it felt like white heat. A noise, a sound like a sizzle, then a violet explosion. Her eardrum burst; she fell downward into cool absence of everything. "Stop that!" cried her mother.

Maria turned in the bed, cried out, her hand to her ear. Anna froze as she tried to move over and lie still, to make room for the girl. But her lower body had a mind of its own. It flung itself about and, arching, shuddered uncontrollably, flailing upward to meet the demon passion. "Oh." Anna bit her lip. She was hot, open, wanting to be filled. She tried not to make a sound. She tried to push the images away. But the wave started again, a dark pulsation. Obsessive memory and her reaction. And once again she gave herself up to it; she had no choice.

When inner feelings, long buried, start to surface, what can a woman do? She can go quietly crazy, or she can dance. Anna could not sleep; she danced inside instead. She lay twitching while the little girl slept fitfully beside her. "Unspeakable things." Anna gazed at the ceiling. The memories burned into her. Subterranean. Darkly moving, they cried within her for a way out.

There were only two choices. A woman could go deeper into self-paralysis, reclining, mute for years beside the kindly, bearded, prurient Doktor Freud. More and more aroused, squeezing their legs tightly against each other, Viennese women caged their wild desires, forcing them so far inside that not even speech was possible. This was, of course, the best way. Freud preferred his women masochistic, paralyzed, and mute. That way, he could "help." Explicit sexual implications rose from their supine bodies, wreathed both doctor and patient in delicious undertones of what was hidden: that bud between their legs, the will to control its throbbing, to squeeze down even harder; the involuntary, soundless cry. Helpless, lovely, trapped-in-headlights women lay on couches, pretending to maintain stillness as a secret perfumed shudder moved along their bodies. Only their *Doktor* knew.

For the Rat, stillness was not possible. Her only choice was to dance, to dance horribly in a caricature of music as something stirred within her, itched and crazed. She had traveled too far along the path of depravity. Now temporarily in safety, she stared at the ceiling and the memories took over. She twitched and juddered. Her limbs would not be still. Her God would not forgive her. Her memories of violation overtook her every time. Each night she talked and talked, as if to stave them off. She was exhausted by an orgasm of endless talking. And each time when finally she tried to stop talking, the thrill of repetitive climax and the unstoppable fascination overtook her. She was exhausted, but her racked body would not let her rest. One seism after another. The hunchback stared at the darkness, running her hands along her misshapen body, trembling with the force of her memories. She willed herself to lie quietly. She could not. The memories enveloped her. Her body vibrated and quivered around them, contorting her small body while her closed eyes rolled back in her head. The demon stroked and squeezed and forced her open again and again, thick-fingered, relentless.

And when this had exhausted her, it began again. She shook with the force of it, craved it, cried for it, wanted it and wanted it to stop, but still she wanted more. She put her hands on her body carefully to quiet her wild desires. But they sprang up, consuming as wildfire.

As she whimpered with suppression, Maria whimpered also. The child was hot, writhing, as if sensing the torment of the woman next to her. Anna carefully felt Maria's forehead. "A fever," she thought, worried. "Sleep, my child," she whispered to the restless girl as she caressed her cheek. With great effort, she pulled her twisted nightgown down around her legs and slid out of bed. It was nearly morning.

"Penance," thought Anna. There was no other way. She crossed the room. The doors to the large, looming wardrobe were ajar. Carefully, Anna pried one open and slipped inside. She eased herself into the cavernous closet. The stale air enveloped her, a cocoon, muffling everything else. The wardrobe was dark, enfolding, heavy with the thick smell of Herbert's tweed jackets and the extra army blankets and mothballs and winter woolens for the family. Anna took a hot breath and eased herself onto the lower shelf, closing the door behind her. She would sit there, out of the way. She would neither eat nor drink. She would pray a whole day and a night, longer if necessary, starving the demon out of her. Only then could she take her place again in the household. A hair shirt, she thought. I will suffer and pray and drive the demons out.

As she put her hands down, she felt a thick, large envelope. The smell of mothballs overwhelmed her. Instinctively, she snatched the folder and put it inside her nightgown, against her thin breasts. You never know when you might need some papers. Hidden ones. "Thief," she thought, and the word thrilled her.

Finally in the airless cupboard, a clammy, dreamless sleep overtook her.

Outside, the wind screeched and hollered. It was dark in the mouth of the building. The cold whistled through the grates. Somewhere far away, the children's grandfather was floating through the city, doing important things that had nothing to do with them. Somewhere, that snap-jawed thing called "work" would hold Maria's mother forever in its prison. The hours passed.

The cold winter morning moved into Maria's clothing like snakes, wriggling into all the secret places. Her ears ached with a hopeless numbness that filled her head with throbbing sounds. Philip stirred, opened his little round mouth, and began to wail loudly. Her head hurt awfully. "Wake up!" cried her mother. "Do you want to eat something?" Ilse was anxious; she had rushed home on her lunch break and would have to leave again. Light came and went on the walls.

Delirious. The word echoed in Maria's head. *Mastoiditis,* she heard also. That was a less pretty word.

Philip cried, but his sounds seemed far away. He laughed, gurgled, and let Maria know he loved her. But she could scarcely hear him, lying focused in the white hollow that held her. She needed to think very hard about it, curve the space around her so that her ears wouldn't hurt so much, her head. She didn't know that two adults, her mother and grandfather, were preparing for two others to join them. Soon there would be seven, then eventually nine refugees in one small, cold room high over the city. Even now, things were happening around her: people moving; Philip growing into the true companion he would always be for her; her mother receding; her grandfather shrinking also each day, so that only his ears would be left large as ever, sticking out of a tiny, dear little head that was even now shrinking downward on its stem of a neck. His hunched shoulders puffed out under their burden like angel wings under a too-large shabby coat. But for now, her ears ached and she ached with a fever so bright, it purified all else from her mind and body. She floated out of herself darkly, onto the top of the cedar chest in the corner.

"Maria, can you hear me?" Ah, that was perhaps Grandfather speaking. Maria's hand clenched. She heard "No heat" and "the children waiting." And "No heat" again. "I'll talk to the landlord," her grandfather promised. "Don't worry, Ilse." He touched Maria's mother's arm. "I'll talk to him."

Philip smiled and waved a friendly fist in Maria's direction. Maria vomited. She felt prickly all over. The door of the small room where she lay opened and shut, opened and shut again. A doctor came with his black bag, then left. She heard once more that word *mastoiditis.* The word *eardrum. Thrum thrum,* sang Maria's head. *Eardrum. Thrum thrum.* She wanted her mother to stay with her. But her mother had to go to work. She had to work or there would be no food for any of them, her mother explained. "Be a good girl." The door opened and closed again. The clouds and the sun made radiant swooshing sounds through the window, and then Maria was alone.

Alone except for Anna, who, slowly suffocating in the wardrobe, slept like a stone, in a trance. Anna's breathing was slower, more labored. For once, her mind was silent, her body, too. Her large luminescent eyes fogged with sleep; her limbs were languorous and heavy. She pillowed her head against a tweed sleeve; the day was nearing its end.

Maria woke up for a moment, sensing the door opening and shutting again. She fell back into her hot swirl of sleep as well: a sleep that was not really sleep, but, rather, the crawling of many insects toward morning. She felt rather than saw her grandfather come in and leave again with her mother and little woolly Philip. Once more, she was alone, sweating in the chill of the empty room. The door opened; opened and shut again. Maria sensed the change in the light: a shaft of afternoon sun as the day crossed the building. Then the door opened and shut again, this time behind someone else. Someone small. Someone dangerous.

"Well, my child? What is the matter? Have you been a bad girl again?" the figure muttered menacingly, almost as if to himself. He took a step or two toward the girl. "Well?" he demanded more loudly. "Have you? Speak up!" Maria felt her mother silent behind the figure. "A bad girl!" exclaimed the little man. He turned back toward Maria's mother, addressing her directly. "If she doesn't speak, we will make her, *nein?*" he said in a sharp voice. "Speak up, girl. If you will not, we have ways. You know," he continued, "I have my ways." Maria opened her eyes. "You see," exclaimed the figure triumphantly, "she understands. The bad girl understands." At this, he walked into the room.

Maria heard the thump of a gimpy leg being dragged. "Maria," said her mother redundantly, "wake up. Uncle Felix is here to make you better." Maria closed her eyes again. She recognized her mother now for the traitor she was. And she knew only too well the family doctor.

Felix limped to Maria's bedside and stood looking down at her. Maria tried to stay still, although she knew it was futile to pretend sleep. She watched the little stump of a man through half-closed eyes, and he, penetrating, regarded her. "He's so wonderful with the children," the European refugee population told one another. "Children love him."

"Bad girl! Now what have you done?" Uncle Felix muttered between clenched teeth. Suddenly, he gave a loud cry. "Ach!

Schrecklich! Bad girl. What have you done to Uncle Felix's leg?" He clutched his hip dramatically and staggered, half falling onto the little girl's bed. "Ach! My leg!" He paused, regarding the girl directly. "Now, see what you've done to Uncle Felix!" He straightened again. "Would you like to see it? My broken leg?"

Maria tried to worm her way farther under the covers, while at the same time still appearing to be passively asleep. Felix staggered, clutching his thigh. From the region of his hip came a relentless clicking sound. *Click-click.* He raised his dark eyebrows, watching the little girl intently. "You hear that noise? That is my broken leg, bad girl. My leg!" He turned to Maria's mother behind him. She was standing in the doorway, smiling. "Did you see what that bad girl did?" he demanded, watching her for effect. "She broke my leg." Maria's mother laughed. Maria hated her shadow in the doorway, but she feared more being left alone with the pediatrician.

Felix tottered around Maria's bed once more, reeling and moaning. *Click-click,* went the noise of the leg. He reeled to a stop, planted his cane in front of him, and lowered himself onto Maria's bed, sitting down next to the girl. Maria wanted to shriek with revulsion and fear, but if she did, it would give her away. She willed herself to open her eyes, as if pretending to see the man for the first time.

"Now," began Dr. Felix briskly in what was another voice altogether. "Mother says you are not feeling well. What is wrong here?"

Maria did not answer, and the watching shadows in the doorway grew closer, blocking the light with their concern.

"Open your mouth. Say 'Ah,' " commanded Felix, moving closer toward Maria's face. He peered inside. "Hmm. Have you been a bad girl?" he muttered as he peered down her throat.

Maria's ears were cracking with pain. Felix brought his large, menacing face closer to hers. "Do you know what this is?" he commanded, switching on a piercing headlight, which now seemed appended to the front of his face like a second snout. "Hmm? Well, bad girl, answer me!" Maria said nothing, shrinking back as much as she could.

"You see this light?" Felix switched the light off again, on, off. "It's to find out all your secrets." He lowered the snout light toward her again. "All of your secrets, child." Felix let his voice rise from a hiss to a hoarser one. "All of them!" He turned the light on again and bent his head toward Maria's mouth. "Do I make myself completely clear?" he warned, his face close to hers. He held her frightened eyes in his dark pinpointed ones. "Good," he said, as if satisfied by something. "Now, open wide," he commanded in a more hypnotic croon. "Now, my good girl, now turn your head."

Maria could hear his large breath as he regarded the inside of her ear. He smelled of perfume, and there was something shivery at his touch. A cold instrument entered her ear; then the headlight receded again. Felix straightened away from her again, turning to the watching adults. Maria did not hear him say anything, but there seemed a wave of laughter at the door, nervous laughter.

Felix stood up. The shadows of Maria's mother and Philip vanished. Maria could hear them slipping out of the room, far away from her, and light shone through the doorway once again. She was terrified, for she realized that she was alone with Uncle Felix.

"I am just going to give you a little medicine," said Felix. There was a cold draft on her body as the bedclothes were suddenly pulled away. "Turn over for Uncle Felix." The crooning voice came and she was forced to obey. He pulled up her nightgown, and a colder patch of air lifted a chill wind against Maria's body. "Lie still. Don't move," commanded Uncle Felix as he stabbed her flesh. There was a moment of silvery pain, followed by a dull ache. Maria was so surprised, she could hardly register the moment. She let herself float in a flaking cloud of snowflakes. Felix's face broke into a jigsaw puzzle and re-formed. Had anything happened? Maria floated in fever, far away from any other sensation.

Felix pulled the blankets around her neck, tucking them in tightly. He straightened and did something to the front of his trousers. "It's finished now," he said loudly, in a matter-of-fact tone of voice.

Ilse entered the room again, coming closer to the bed and looking down at her daughter with concern on her face. But Maria shut her eyes, refusing even to acknowledge her mother's presence, that large, false, untrustworthy person who had betrayed, and would continue to betray, the girl.

Uncle Felix glowered toward Maria, who lay shrinking in her bed. "Penicillin!" he said. "A wonder drug. Remarkable, my dear lady, remarkable." Creaking, he raised himself from the side of the cot, his body hunched like question mark as he dragged himself onto his lame leg. *Click-click.* The leg straightened.

Maria could see Felix's hand in his hip pocket. She loathed him for trying to fool her, for thinking she could be fooled by such deceptions. "My leg!" cried Felix, hobbling once more around the narrow room and shrieking for effect. Maria refused to smile. "Look," Felix commanded. Slowly, he withdrew his hand from his pocket and opened it in front of the girl's nose. She looked; she could not help it. In his gnarled palm lay a shiny green frog. Felix pressed his fingers together and the frog gave off a metallic croak. *Click-click.* Maria's mother smiled indulgently. "Here, child, this is for you," Uncle Felix said. "Now that you've broken my leg, you might as well have this. My poor leg is completely useless even without my little frog to help me. Here." He put the toy frog down on Maria's blanket, clicking it twice more for effect. "Now I must go."

"Felix, will you stay for some coffee?" Ilse offered as the doctor limped toward the door.

"Ah, dear lady, you are indeed too kind," said Felix in a normal voice.

Within the wardrobe, Anna woke with a start. Suddenly, she felt she would die if she stayed in the wardrobe a moment longer. The mothball odor and the smothering pressure of the stale smell of old wool pressed down on her little misshapen body. Her delicate nostrils quivered and her compressed lungs tried desperately to suck in air. She had slept for the first time in perhaps years, and now, waking, she had forgotten why she had ever entered the wardrobe. She must have climbed in. A ridiculous impulse. Why was she here? How foolish to suffocate like that, a desiccated carcass to be found perhaps days later when the family needed an extra blanket. She must get out, and immediately. She turned on the small shelf and hesitantly put one foot down toward the floor, timidly opening the door to the wardrobe just a crack. But wait, there was someone else in the room. Someone small as Anna herself almost, small and quick and unfamiliar. Looking through the crack, Anna could see Maria still in bed, and the disarray of bedclothes. It was dark again, night at the window. Had she slept away the entire day? A bit of fresh air blew in through the crack in the wardrobe door, fresh to Anna's lips anyhow, and she sucked it in gratefully. But something told her to stay still, hidden and concealed, until the coast was clear. Peering through the crack, she observed the room and the shrieking little man who now inhabited it.

Anna saw him dart back toward the girl. He looked at her, and one eyebrow started working furiously. Up and down. "My face!" he shouted at her. "What have you done to my eyebrow, hmm? Bad girl, have you been bothering Uncle Felix once again?" The eyebrow, as if with a life of its own, waggled furiously on Uncle Felix's face. Maria shrank back, seeing in that eyebrow hordes of black ants. Felix held in one hand the end of a long black thread that seemed somehow to be attached to the frenetic eyebrow. Maria could see the thread protruding out of Felix's coat sleeve.

"They all love this trick," Felix confided to Ilse. He turned back to Maria. "Bad girl, bad girl." Maria slipped softly into the coolness, finally, of sleep. But Anna was wide awake now, watching, startled and fascinated.

Felix turned back just before following Maria's mother into the hallway, toward a hot plate and coffee deliciously steaming. "I'll stay with her just a minute more," he said as Ilse left to prepare the coffee for him. Satisfied that Maria's eyes were closed, he darted, now totally silently, back into the little room from the doorway. But this time, he did not pause at Maria's bed. He moved silently, lightly on his feet toward the army blanket that divided Herbert's space from that of the mother and children. Quickly, he lifted one end of the blanket where it hung on a clothesline. Anna, watching from the wardrobe, cringed back against the blankets, hoping she would not be seen. But Felix had other things on his mind. Even more silently, giving one furtive look behind, he ducked through the blanket partition. He bent down, ran his hands quickly along the top of Herbert's bed, and then slipped his hands under the narrow mattress that lay upon it. Silently, Felix withdrew both hands. He put both hands in his pockets now, hands that no longer grasped a black thread, but something larger perhaps, something more bulky. Felix once again made as if to leave.

Maria, lying, eyes shut, entering sleep, felt the cold rustle of folded wings. Then, dimly receding as she sank gratefully into a possible relief from fever, she heard the heavy limp of Uncle Felix. The door shut behind him, and the thump of his "broken" leg punctuated the loud announcement of his presence, exiting toward coffee, her mother, and a discussion of their mutual pasts.

Carefully, Anna exited the wardrobe. The stiff envelope crackled against her breast. She stood hunched, as if in thought. But for once her mind was clear. She walked over to the child and kissed her. "My darling child, sleep now," she said.

Someone, Maria knew, had entered Grandfather's part of the room. And someone had left it. But no longer on guard, Maria slept. Next to her, on the blanket, a small green frog, luminous eyes bugged open, and neck sac bulging, slept, too. Its striped back caught the light and winked back. *Click-click,* it might have said. But in the afternoon, it, too, was silent.

Chapter 10

THE TOLSTOI QUARTET'S STORY

As Herbert opened the door and stepped out into the early New York morning again, the air came up and bit him with cold. It had a keen animal sharpness, the wind. Herbert pulled his ragged coat about him and hunched directly into it, heading toward the Automat and his appointments there.

Although it was early in the morning, the windows of the Automat were already rimmed in steam. Herbert hurried through the almost deserted streets of New York, barely registering the dim gloom of dawn that uncurled itself around his body, until the animal itself startled awake with bright eyes and a glittering edge of sun topped the buildings that rimmed the East River. The shaft of sun reached down and coaxed him to look up and even to feel cheerful.

"I must do something for the children," he reminded himself. But he had errands to do that did not concern his grandchildren.

As the shaft of sun reached down through the tall, oppressive buildings, the glittering towers of New York began to sing in chorus, a metallic shimmer of sound that reached into Herbert's ears, even though his ears were muffled by a long, grimy scarf and a squashed hat. New York sang in a whine of strained sound that merged with the increasing humming of cars, taxicabs, and even, far away, the sighs of trains and great boats shunting themselves along the river. Herbert hurried and the gloomy streets lightened in front of him. He was a man going quickly toward the vanishing point, that point where perspective meets horizon.

Eighth Avenue was punctuated by small bent figures, hunched against the wind, hurrying somewhere. Herbert stopped at the door of the Automat and then entered its warm odor.

"Morning, sir," the waitress greeted him. As Herbert paused in the steam of the cafeteria, she went back to cleaning. The Automat had opened two hours ago, and already there were puddles of water and mud on the floor, the grime melting from early-morning customers. With a shrug, Helen indicated a back table. "They've been waiting for you," she said.

"Thank you, my good woman," replied Herbert, pulling off his gloves and removing his hat. He struggled to untangle the large scarf from his neck.

"Back there," she said. "I suppose you want your coffee?" Not for him to stand in line. Or lift a tray.

"That would be so kind," answered Herbert somewhat absently in his accent, automatically charming. He took a moment to overlook the situation—the dim restaurant with its few dark tables, and the already-gleaming cases of self-service items: Danish pastries, red Jell-O, whipped-cream hats.

The four men who formed the world-famous Tolstoi Quartet were waiting for him in the back of the restaurant. Two tables had been pushed together in readiness. Herbert quickly took in the dark bulk of musical instrument cases that sat expectantly next to each man. Two violins, a viola, a violoncello; the cases were dark and covered with stickers from travel—travel all over the world.

The Tolstoi String Quartet had a certain European reputation. Named for the writer they considered the most universal, the Tolstoi Quartet sought in its music to overcome barriers of nationalism. But Herbert had never quite forgiven the Quartet for not calling itself the Arthur Schnitzler Quartet instead.

Herbert had often heard them—in the concert hall in Vienna and, even more pleasantly, in his own home. Adeline had delighted in these soirees. Adeline! He saw her at the piano, for in private rehearsal she had played the piano for the Schubert Quintet with these courteous, sonorous men. Herbert did not need to close his eyes to see again the Tolstoi Quartet in his home, the elegance of the men and women, the beauty of their playing, the tears that rose to his eyes even then as he watched his dark-haired wife.

Now, as Herbert walked toward the seated Quartet, a tremor crossed the dank air of the restaurant, metallic with the stale odors of wet wool and ashen coffee. Herbert coughed, clearing his throat discreetly. Four chairs scraped and four heads turned to look. "Ah," cried one. And at that, all four men sprang to their feet and looked sharply in Herbert's direction. Herbert advanced toward them. "Please be seated," he said. "Be seated, my dear gentlemen."

The four men looked quickly at one another. In a rush, their faces contorted with fear and longing, they swooned to the ground. They fell on Herbert as he stood, his threadbare overcoat too large around his body. "Herr Professor, Herr Doktor," they murmured. Each man attempted to clutch the hem of Herbert's coat, and they prostrated themselves further, embracing his ankles and his overshoes.

"Please, gentlemen," Herbert crooned, trying to take a step backward.

"Beloved Herr Professor," the men murmured.

"Please, gentlemen, I implore you," admonished Herbert.

Gently, he reached down and placed his hands on the shoulders of the two men who encircled his feet. "Please."

The men seized his hands and began kissing them fervently. "Our beloved Herr Doktor. We thought we would never see you alive," they said, kissing his ring. "The ring. Your promise."

Tears rimmed the eyes of all four men, and Herbert, too, felt his own tears rise, welcome balm to the wandering soul. He grasped their hands. "My friends, it is I who should embrace you." Herbert's voice was like warm honey.

The Quartet started to sob aloud, and Herbert let the sadness pour out of him, too. "Please, gentlemen, please," he crooned, trying to encircle them all with his hands. His hands were warm now; he let the radiance flow through him into their bent, shaking backs. So frail. They all were. . . . "Gentlemen, please." He cleared his throat.

The men pushed themselves to their feet and stood, looking expectantly at Herbert. "It is time to begin." Herbert lowered himself into a chair. He indicated the other chairs. "Be seated, I beg of you." The Quartet sat down instantly.

"Coffee," said Helen as she put the cups on the table in front of Herbert.

"Thank you, dear lady," he said. He turned his kind, illuminated gaze to the men, looking at each one in turn, their lined faces, their troubled eyes. "Now," he commanded softly, "tell me."

There was sudden silence in the cafeteria. Herbert could hear the clanging of the morning sunlight outside, above the narrow streets, scraping against the sooty buildings with sharp, harsh sounds. He heard early-morning traffic, laboring. But all this was far away. "Tell me," he said again, even more softly. "Tell me." He whispered, as to a child or a lover. His lips were papery against each other.

Without a word, each man, as if offering a gift, placed his left hand, outstretched, upon the table. These hands—the ones used for fingering—lay on the table, palms up, vulnerable. They gleamed like newly netted fish.

"Look, Herr Doktor," whispered the first violinist. "Observe."

The hands, which had a life of their own, lay mute under Herbert's examination, unprotesting. They quivered a little. They were gnarled and muscled and sinewy from years of pressing themselves against strings. Herbert looked. In an instant, as when a puzzle is completed, he understood. On each hand outstretched in front of him, the final joint of the smallest finger was missing. The hands, ashamed, lay in front of him. They trembled with the effort of trying not to hide their disfigurement. The stumps of the little fingers, which wanted only to creep away under the others, now, obedient to their masters, allowed him to see their painful embarrassment. They twitched but lay still.

"But what?" Herbert questioned incredulously. He looked into the eyes of the first violinist, then at each of the men.

Their leader answered for them all. "Yes. They took our fingers. We can no longer play." The hands, the mutilated fingering hands of the Quartet, lay suspended on the table. "And so the Tolstoi String Quartet is silent."

The instruments in their cases began to throb, their noise swelling next to their owners. From the dark cases came discordant deaf-mute sounds, a cacophony of scrapes, the meaningless tonalities of deserted music. The violins sobbed like sick women; the viola and violoncello howled.

"Ach . . ." The four men put their right hands on the instrument cases. "Be silent." And at that, the sounds subsided into moaning, and gradually into exhausted sighs, and then diminished slowly. "Rest," the men admonished their instruments.

They turned their dark eyes toward Herbert. "We have no more tears," they said. "But they are different."

The instruments were silent again in their cases, except for an occasional hiccup. "They still have hope," the men explained.

Herbert thought of the harmony of these instruments, and the look of rapid fingering hands, the left ones, dancing and twisting against the strings. He remembered the courtly sway of the right hands as they bowed the music forth. Music curled out of stringed instruments as the musicians birthed it.

"You will help us," the first violinist said to Herbert. The four men nodded in agreement. Herbert could not keep from looking furtively at the mutilated stumps of the final fingers. "Yes," said the leader. "That is why we come to you, Herr Doktor. That is why we asked you to meet with us. It is for the sake of music that we come to you today."

"What can I do for you?" Unwillingly, Herbert felt he was being forced into the piano part; that what was being played here was no longer a quartet, but a quintet, with the guest artist—himself—obliged to participate.

The first violinist nodded, as if Herbert had come into the music at the right place. On one breath, on the exact same beat, all four men answered him at once. "You will find for us our fingers." There was a brusque, brisk silence, a silence thrumming with sound.

The little fingers began to twitch on the table, their stumps dancing in exasperated rhythm. "You can do it." coaxed the viola player in a honeyed voice. "Our fingers. Ours," the violinists said. The cellist said only one word, but it came from the bottom of his vocal register. "Please," he implored softly, looking into Herbert's eyes.

The instruments in their cases now also began to twitch and scrape, and once again sound rose from their dark coffins.

A cacophony of discordant, jumpy agitations, warnings, confused like the shrieks of an ambulance or a police wagon or of men being tortured. The air was filled with suffering. "Find our fingers!" screamed the violinists. "You can help us," the violist coaxed. "Please. Please!" groaned the cellist, wringing his hands.

Herbert could not stand it. He rose to his feet and clapped his hands over his ears. "Stop this noise!"

"Ah," breathed the four waiting men at once. And with a sigh of relief, they sat back and removed their mutilated hands from the table, putting them discreetly into pockets, where the naked fingers could lie again in safe darkness, curled around one another, taking whatever comfort that remained in one another's presence.

"They do not like to be reminded," explained the first violinist to Herbert as the left hands relaxed into safe pockets. "It hurts them too much. We prefer to let them be quiet, to forget a little."

And each man placed his right hand soothingly on the instrument case next to him and, bending toward the hinged closure, whispered a few quiet words. "They, too," said the leader, indicating the instruments. "They were with us. They saw it all."

The hands twitched a little in their pockets. "Shh, my little ones," the first violinist said, admonishing the fingers. "It is all right." He looked at all four men intently, then nodded, raising his head and staring directly at Herbert as he spoke. Herbert listened, as if in a trance, as if he already knew it, to the first violinist's song.

For twenty years, the Tolstoi String Quartet had lived as one. They had traveled, playing the great concert halls of Europe. They had even, once, come to America. They had met at the conservatory, married one another's sisters, but their first loyalty was to music. And to one another. The violist and the cellist were, additionally, first cousins.

Each night, in some dank hotel room somewhere, they lay next to their instruments and counted themselves the luckiest of men. When they were not playing together, they were preparing to play together. Each went home and practiced day and night, embracing his instrument and thinking only of the harmonies he made with the others. Because of this, they decided to live as close to one another as they could. After several years, two flats came vacant in a building next to that of the first violinist. There was a bit of a skirmish about it, but eventually the violist and cellist took the flats next door. The second violinist moved himself, his violin, and his wife into the parlor of the first violinist, where the two men lived happily, practicing their parts until the wee hours of the morning. So really, they were never separated, if they could help it.

The men did not even need to speak to know one another's thoughts. Critics spoke of the unity of the Quartet, as if one person, one larger God perhaps, were breathing. And the Quartet, if they spoke at all, it was only of music.

At night, after a day of playing, each man wiped his instrument with a soft burgundy velvet cloth and kissed it tenderly. The soft beds waited for them, gleaming. Sighing, perhaps under the breath still whistling the theme from *Death and the Maiden,* they turned back the covers. They laid the instruments beside them on the adjacent pillows. Gratefully, each man slid into clean sheets, embracing his instrument. And there they slept, the satisfied sleep of a part of God, until morning, when they would resume music together again.

Even the cellist refused to have a special bed made to accommodate the larger violoncello. "I like big hips," he explained, and he caressed his instrument all night.

Sometimes from the adjacent houses would emanate soft

noises, something forgotten: the instruments playing a fragment of Haydn, perhaps, or of Mozart. The instruments, happy, sang in the arms of their masters. "Shh," whispered the men. But the instruments could not help singing out, so deep was the ecstasy in unison.

"And your wives?" asked Herbert. "What of your wives?"

The four men looked at one another, and the second violinist took up the story. "They were good women," he said. "They could not help themselves." The four men nodded thoughtfully. "Yes, they were good." The four men sat back, as if the wives, and the goodness thereof, were not of great importance.

For fifteen years, the wives served the Tolstoi Quartet. And for fifteen years, neither the musicians nor their wives questioned that arrangement. The wives of the men were the handmaidens of their music. They cooked the meals, served cakes when the Quartet practiced at home, kept quiet and behaved in an exemplary fashion. The men were clean, well fed, laundered, and their tuxedos and shirts were always spotless. "But," added the cellist, "it was our fault. We simply didn't realize."

"Yes," concurred the second violinist. "We should have seen it coming. It seems that they were jealous." There was a thoughtful, regretful silence.

"Jealous!" That dark word cast a somber C minor shadow over the narrative. Herbert's heart set up an answering vibrato. Dark wood, an ache like Pernambuco—the wood of a cello bow. His breast ached with the word and the overtones resonated throughout his body.

"Yes," echoed the cellist, "jealous." The word scraped in the air harshly.

During these fifteen years, the wives slept on the rugs beside their marital beds. For, of course, the musical instruments were in the beds, lying on the connubial pillow, beside their owners, where, all night, the men caressed their instruments and both man and instrument cried out in ecstasy.

"But we thought they had accepted it," explained the first violinist. "We thought they understood. After all, they said they loved music when we married them."

"Well," said the second violinist, "my Gudrun did." "And my Ludmilla also," said the violist. "Not really." The cellist sighed, being realistic. "*Ja,* that is correct," the men agreed in unison. There was a four-measure rest in the conversation as they contemplated this phenomenon. For the wives finally came to resent their sleeping places on the floor.

One morning, Gudrun and Ludmilla got together to discuss the situation. Gudrun had arthritis, and she no longer wanted to hunker down on the carpet while the violin slept on her fine feather bed, the high one with the big pillows, between the sheets she had embroidered. And Ludmilla also was having problems sleeping; the throaty whimpers of the viola, expressing ecstasy in the middle of the night, disturbed her. And then they spoke to Olga and to Inge.

"This is too much," the four wives agreed. Olga, it turned out, wanted to smash the belly of the violoncello, which sang with such pleasure its part in the Brahms quintet each time its owner laid his cheek against its smooth wood. And Inge was jealous of the second violin.

One day, while the men were deep in a rehearsal of the Mozart Quartet in F Major, the four women decided for the first time to enter the room. "It is enough!" said Olga.

The four men played on, oblivious. "Do you hear?" demanded Inge. "It is enough, we say."

"Shh, my darling," her husband replied mildly, not taking his eyes from his score. "It must wait till we are finished."

Gudrun spoke for all four women. "No. It can't wait another moment."

Alarmed by this, the four men put down their bows and turned their mild, astonished faces toward their wives. "But darlings, we are rehearsing," protested the first violinist.

"We don't care about your rehearsals. We are fed up!" the women shouted.

"Tonight we play in the concert hall; tomorrow we talk," suggested the cellist reasonably.

"To hell with the concert hall!" shouted Olga boldly. "Yes," said the other wives, emboldened. "To hell with music. To hell with the Tolstoi Quartet. We want to lie in our own beds!"

The men were astonished by this outcry, so astonished that the violoncello gave a small involuntary scrape of the open G string. "Forgive me," the cellist said to the instrument. "What is it you wish, my darlings?" he continued, turning to the women, who stood, arms akimbo, hair flying out straight from their heads, glaring at their husbands.

"We want to lie in our own beds," repeated the women. "Where we belong," Inge added.

"But, my pets, you know this cannot be," protested the viola player.

"We know no such thing," said Gudrun grimly.

The instruments began to whimper, but the men stroked their smooth sides. "Shh." They turned to the women where they stood blocking the light. "But haven't you been happy? Haven't we all been happy together? Don't we exist to serve music?"

"No!" said the wives together. "We hate music." At that they took up a little chant and began to prance around the room, shouting, "To hell with music. To hell with music!"

The four men looked at one another. They could not imagine such a thing. "But . . . ," expostulated the viola player. For fifteen years, they had all lived happily together—the players, their instruments, and the wives.

"You can suppose, my dear Herr Doktor," confided the first violinist, leaning forward into Herbert's gaze, "how surprised we were."

"We must continue our rehearsal," the first violinist had finally interjected. "Dearest women, we will discuss all this later. But for now, we must rehearse, for we have our concert tonight. Please." He turned to the other players with iron in his voice. "Gentlemen, measure number one ninety-nine." At the authority in his voice, the wives subsided, and the four men picked up their instruments and resumed, albeit a bit shakily, where they had left off. "Don't forget the mezzo forte," reminded the violinist, and they continued the rehearsal.

"But it didn't go so well," recalled the violist. "And the concert that night, it didn't go so well, either," added the cellist. "No, we didn't play well. And I broke a string," he recalled. The instruments were peevish and bad-tempered and the men a little off. "It happens," the violinist said to Herbert. "But I remember this night particularly."

After the concert, the men returned to their homes. Their beds were turned down as usual, and after kissing and polishing and again kissing their instruments, they all slept. The instruments lay in the beds and the wives lay meekly on the rugs beside the beds. All seemed to have been forgotten, and soon this episode receded in everyone's memory.

But the wives stopped going to the concerts. Where before they had occupied a box of their own in the concert hall, chatting among themselves companionably at intermissions, and, during the performances, knitting endless sweaters, even sweaters for the instrument cases, now they no longer attended. All of Vienna wondered what had happened. But it was supposed that perhaps they were tired of hearing the Beethoven late quartets after fifteen years of faithful attendance. Or perhaps, so used were they to exquisite rehearsals of the works at home, they did not need to be present at the lesser fare for the public. Or maybe, more simply, there was more work to be done at home as the Tolstoi String Quartet became more famous.

And at night, after the concerts, it was different, too. "Good night, my dear friends," each man would call to the others, as they parted at the street corner in front of their houses. "Good night." But upon their return, the musicians found no warm supper, no clean towels waiting for them. All was silent. At night, when they entered the bedrooms and prepared to wipe down their instruments, they found their wives, already undressed, stretched out on the beds. "But my darling," each musician protested to his wife. Without a word, but with a look—oh, a look that carried far more than words—the women got out of bed, naked, and stretched themselves upon the carpet beside the beds, where they would, with cold, passionless eyes, observe the men's caressing of the musical instruments.

"Turn off the light, Ludmilla," protested the violist. "It is not decent." But Ludmilla would not; she would watch and watch and say nothing. The musicians laid their instruments upon their pillows and turned off the lights themselves.

And then Olga, or Inge, or Ludmilla, or Gudrun would whisper into the darkness, but in a sforzando, "I hate music!"

"Shh, my little one," replied the husbands, stroking the bellies of their waiting, faithful instruments. "You do not know what you are saying."

"I hate music, I tell you."

The musicians could not respond; they merely grazed the soft curves of the stringed instruments beside them gently with their lips, and the instruments shuddered with a slight ping of the open G string.

"Furthermore," added the wives, "I hate *your* music!"

The men did not respond to these provocations, but their enjoyment of their instruments at night was slightly curtailed. No longer did the instruments sing out with joy; they sang in furtive whispers now.

"I want to sleep in the bed," the wives whined all night long. The men could hear them turning over on the floor restlessly. "I want the bed! Listen to me," they complained. Where before the men went to sleep listening to the strains of the Brahms or Schubert they had just finished playing, now their concentration was disturbed.

"Ach, there is dust here under the bed." The wives thrashed. "Why did I never see it before? Why must I lie here on the floor looking at dust while she—the musical instrument—gets to sleep on the pillow? On my mother's sheets. Does she think I am just her maid, hmm?"

The violins, viola, and violoncello said nothing to this unfair attack as the men pressed their cheeks to the smooth necks of the instruments and curled their fingers around them. But the next morning, at the rehearsal, it was hard to feel their customary joy.

Somewhere in the recesses of the first violinist's flat, four discontented women threw pots around the kitchen, and the sounds of quarrels and complicity filled the air.

"Again," commanded the first violinist in rehearsal. He had been distracted. "The first movement again."

"But why?" The second violinist questioned.

"Silence."

All four men laid their instruments aside. Never in the history of the Tolstoi Quartet had the authority and decision of the first violinist been questioned. "Because . . . ," the chief finally stuttered. "Because . . ." He could find no reason. Silently, he took off his glasses and wiped them, laying them on the music stand. All the men looked at one another. "My friends . . . ," began the first violinist with difficulty. "Oh, my friends . . ."

"Oh mein Gott!" the second violinist cried aloud in an agony of remorse and shame. "Forgive me! Forgive me," "Shh," said the cellist, laying a restraining hand on his knee. "It is normal," added the viola player soothingly. "We begin again."

And then, as if the interruption had never happened, the four men took up their instruments and played the first movement from the top. But the heart had gone out of them, and the instruments sounded dispirited.

"My friends . . ." The first violinist sighed as the four men put down their bows, and before they could turn the page and essay the second movement. "Nothing is normal," muttered the cellist. He looked at his watch. It was almost time for lunch, that savory mixture of soups, dumplings, breads, and apple strudel that sustained the men through long rehearsals. "Maybe we should stop for the day." The four men took out their cloths of red velvet and rubbed down their instruments, which lay inert and silent as little children. For they, too, were depressed at their rendition of the first movement. "It is nothing. We will play it again after lunch," the men promised one another. But the instruments did not gleam with their usual luster, not even after their rubdowns.

Laying the instruments in their cases, the men did not shut the lids, but left everything as it was, the bows on the music stands, the pages of musical notes still gesturing wildly to them, and headed for the kitchen, where, as usual, they would sit down and eat amid the cheerfulness of scented steam.

As they trooped in single file, the men rubbed their hands in anticipation. "Here we are, my darlings!" sang out the first violinist, as he had every lunchtime for fifteen years. But silence greeted them. The kitchen was tidy and cold. No pots bubbling merrily on the stove. And the enamel kitchen table was unadorned. No tablecloth, no deep white bowls awaiting soup and gratitude. Nothing. The kitchen stood bare and clean and cheerless. Bewildered, the four men looked at one another. What was this? What was this terrible void?

"Where are you, my little dumplings?" the men sang out, as if playing a little game of hide-and-seek. They tiptoed around the room, into the pantry. "Where are you, our little mice? Our dearest ones? Our little strudels? Our sweet little legs of lamb?"

But there was no answer. Clasping their hands in front of them, the men coaxed. "Come out, come out, little darlings. Are you hiding from us, silly ones? Oh, come here our succulent pork chops, our sugar buns."

Again, nothing but cold silence greeted them. "Now, my dearest ones, be reasonable," said the first violinist, trying a sterner note. "You know it is lunchtime. And we must eat. This is enough of joking." Still no answer. The men looked at one another. Their eyes widened and they began to feel frightened. "Come now, our *Lebkuchen,* this has gone on long enough." The cold kitchen gave no answer, and the instruments, waiting in the parlor, were silent also. A vacancy filled the house.

Chapter 11

WHAT IS MISSING?

Soon all of Vienna knew the wives had gone. But where? That was a mystery. The men continued to practice as before, to give their concerts, and to travel together, sharing rooms. They could be seen walking together as a single body, each carrying an instrument, as if nothing had happened. Only—at night—some joy had gone from their sleeping. Although they lay freely now with their instruments, although beautiful music resounded at full voice from the bedrooms, there was something missing. It did not have the same sweetness, perhaps, as the piano sobs in the muffled nights attended by their wives.

And yet they would have said, if asked, that they were now happy. They could play music freely; they could rehearse until the small hours of the night—no one to complain or shout "I hate music!" at embarrassing intervals.

Only, there was the problem of food. Musicians, like everyone else, must eat. Or maybe they must eat even more. "For after all," as the violist used to remind his wife at mealtimes, "I must eat for two." Although some of the good women of Vienna, the same women who swooned over the men and their music in the grand concert hall, left casseroles at the violinist's door, and although sometimes there would be found a large tureen of good chicken soup, there were many times when the men were obliged to live only on Sacher-Torte and *Apfelstrudel* purchased from the Café Mozart or the Hotel Sacher or one of the establishments that produced good strong coffee and cake. "Man does not live by cake alone," reminded the cellist jokingly. The men grew nervous and thin.

"Gentlemen, something is missing," the cellist announced gravely as, after a nearly spirited rendition of the third movement of a Brahms quartet during rehearsal, the men sat back for a moment and returned their instruments to their cases. Without music, the apartment was suspiciously quiet, and each man sighed, remembering the good meals that had awaited them so often at moments like this in the past. "Ach, how I miss Gudrun," said the second violinist. "And Inge," said the first violinist. "And I, too, my sweet little Ludi," added the violist. "And Olga," the cellist said. The men sighed, and their instruments shifted restlessly, twanging a bit awkwardly as they did so.

"Yes." The violist sighed. "We must face this. Gentlemen"—he leaned forward portentously—"we are getting stale."

"We are getting old," whispered the second violinist. "Old!" Could it be true? Startled, the four men looked at one another in wonder. Yes, these dear faces were now lined. They all wore spectacles now to read the music. Hair, formerly tumultuous and passionate, was now almost white, thinning, and in the case of the cellist, it had gone completely. Their kindly faces were wrinkled, especially at the smile lines. How had this happened? Four ardent young men had, in the course of years, grown old.

"But we have always made beautiful music together," said the first violinist. "Yes . . . And we will make more beautiful music." The men smiled fondly at their instruments and patted them. "Don't worry, my darlings, you will stay young forever." The instruments preened, but the men looked at one another again.

Their final concert of the season was approaching, and only a few months were left to prepare it. As if one person, the Quartet regarded one another. "Yes . . . ," whispered the second violinist, already reading the thoughts of the chief. "Yes . . ."

"Gentlemen, it is time for the Tolstoi Quartet to change. We must show the world that we are young and alive, that we have not grown tired and stale. The public demands this," declared the first violinist.

"Music demands this," stated the violist boldly.

The first violinist leaned forward, impulsively snatching the score of the Schubert quartet they had been playing—a score that, by the way, he knew by heart—off the music stand. Fishing in his violin case, he brought out the program of the season's concerts. "Gentlemen, we must change. We must be flexible. We must grow." He waved the program before the men, the program that announced that for its final concert of the season, the Tolstoi Quartet would present the works of Haydn, Mozart, Brahms, and Schubert. "We must change! We must become avant-garde!"

At first, it was difficult, preparing this new secret concert for the public. For one thing, new music was unfamiliar to the musicians' ears. The instruments shrieked and groaned and protested each note. "Come, my darlings, sing!" exhorted the men to their instruments, and the stringed instruments tried to oblige. In secret, the men had obtained, by dint of many hours in the coffeehouses and dank halls of the conservatory, scores from the new composers—there was one called Schoenberg, there was the upstart Stravinsky, and, of course, already known but heartily disliked, Alban Berg and his music.

From the windows of the little apartment on Strëverstrasse issued forth squawks and shrieks and dissonances that caused even the birds to fly away from adjacent gardens. Eager women, bosoms heaving, hesitated at the front door. Then, clasping their throats and muttering some sort of quick prayer, they turned on their heels, casseroles still in hand, and left.

The practicing continued. The men sawed away at the instruments, trying to make sense of the strange notes. Sometimes they had to stop and wipe their eyes, they were laughing so hard. "I confess, I am bewildered," declared the first violinist one day, putting down his bow in the middle of the phrase.

"The first violinist bewildered?" At this, all four men looked at one another. Their laughter was an even stranger sound than the music itself, so unused had they become to it, that even a pigeon pecking bread crumbs in front of the sidewalk flew off in alarm.

Soon all of Vienna knew that the musicians of the Tolstoi Quartet, whose wives had left them, were planning a sort of comeback. Or else they had gone quite mad with grief. The postman no longer left letters for them, so strange were the sounds coming from the flat. The gas man, the maid—all stopped coming. Only the Sacher Hotel sent its delivery boy still, a young kid who had no choice but to leave cakes upon the doorstep. Meanwhile, inside, the men practiced this strange new music. The instruments cried aloud in pain.

At night, the men polished their instruments with renewed tenderness, so that even the musical instruments were forced to realize they would not lose anything by cooperating with their masters; no, indeed, they were doubly loved for their willingness to accede to the new positions the men put them in, the contortions of the men's hands upon their necks and bodies, the strange quivering sounds they uttered from their polished bellies. It was not altogether disagreeable, shivering to Stravinsky, or resonating, perhaps, to a musical sound they had not felt before. The instruments, too, were growing younger, more modern in their outlook. But secretly, all eight of them, men and instruments, still loved their dear old Brahms and Schubert most of all. It was necessary, perhaps, to be able to play Schoenberg, although they all doubted it. Nevertheless, the thought of change—of a second youth perhaps—encouraged them.

The concert itself began badly. As the men took their seats onstage and once again, discreetly, tuned their instruments, there was a sudden interruption. A group of latecomers entered the concert hall from the back and proceeded loudly down the aisle.

The audience turned away from the stage to follow the procession as it moved down the aisle and into the front row, which had been kept empty with a large RESERVED notice until that moment. The group entered the row but did not sit down. The audience shuffled impatiently, annoyed. The members of the Tolstoi Quartet froze at their instruments, bows in hand, their heads turned, incredulous. "It's my Ludmilla," whispered the violist. "My Olga." "My Inge." "My Gudrun," the others said in turn.

The wives, their hair marcelled, inclined their heads toward their husbands. Their cavaliers in military uniforms affixed monocles to their eyes and took the wives, hands tenderly. The most distinguished, who was the most decorated, turned on his heel and faced the waiting audience. "Heil Hitler." The audience rose to its feet. "Heil Hitler."

The leader turned to the musicians onstage and fixed them with his monocled eye. But the Quartet did not move. The musicians sat in silence, waiting. Under their hands, the silky feel of the instruments. Not even a twang of an open G.

The officers took the arms of the wives, and all those in the front row seated themselves. A sigh filled the hall, the bumping of chair backs, and then coughing, lots of coughing.

"Let us play," said the first violinist quietly to the others. The musicians looked at him in silence; the audience subsided, a large creaky animal. The first violinist drew his bow across the strings. The second violinist entered. Notes quavered in the dusty air of the theater; then the viola came in, and finally the violoncello. The members of the Tolstoi Quartet breathed in unison.

All through the Alban Berg quartet, the audience sat silent, waiting for it to end. There was uneasy applause when it did, and the audience settled back. For now that the "new music" was over, they would be able to relax into their beloved Mozart, perhaps, or Brahms. Enough excitement for one night: they hoped for a little rest.

The first violinist barely gave the other members of the Quartet time to acknowledge the reaction to the Berg. He raised his instrument to his chin, his bow to the strings, and nodded to the others. The instruments wailed and gnashed and cried their way through Stravinsky, Shostakovich, and finally, for the last was the worst, the Schoenberg. Strange sounds pierced the air, and glass fell from the chandeliers throughout the hall.

Indignant rustles rose from the audience. Husbands had been unable to snore peacefully beside their wives throughout this concert. Disturbed, they sprang to their feet. "Can't one even get a good night's sleep in Vienna anymore?" one asked. Casting an angry glance at the stage, they left in haste, dragging their horrified—though fascinated—women with them.

The Tolstoi Quartet played on, forgoing the customary intermission. As they played, defiant sounds bubbled in their chests, and their musical instruments laughed dissonantly. The fabric in the velvet curtains gave way and shredded under the impact of strange sounds. The cushioned seats in the house burst open and the stuffing hung out in limp, exhausted trails. The famous concert hall was a wreck.

The Quartet did not hear the genteel screams of dismay, did not see the hands clapped to ears, the hats pulled down. They did not notice the general stampede toward the large outward-swinging doors of the concert hall, the outrage as the Viennese rushed toward the exits and into the streets, running away from new music.

The four officers in the front row sprang to their feet. "Stop this," commanded the senior one. "I command you to stop this noise immediately."

The powdered faces of Gudrun, Inge, Ludmilla, and Olga cracked in dismay, and their lip rouge ran from the corners of their mouths. They looked haggard. "Stop," whispered the women. But the Tolstoi Quartet played on. There was no stopping them. The officers took the women by their arms and firmly raised them to their feet. "Oh!" The four women's mouths crumpled.

"Come, my dears." They were dragged from their seats into the aisle, through the hall, and out the door. The women turned back in dismay, looking at the Tolstoi Quartet. But the musicians played, triumph and rebellion rising from the musical instruments that fiddled and scraped and scratched and twanged.

The Tolstoi Quartet played until finally, mercifully, a lone stagehand noticed that they were still there and lowered the tattered curtain. He clapped his hands over his ears as he did this. But it was too late. By the time the curtain, in shreds, was fully lowered, the man was deaf.

The Tolstoi Quartet played till the end of the final movement and put down their bows after the last flourish. They looked at one another, pleased. Alone on the darkened stage, they could still hear glass falling from shattered windows.

"Now, gentlemen," the first violinist whispered in satisfaction, "it is time for an encore."

Eine kleine Nachtmusik filled the now-empty concert hall, the notes falling like sunlight after a hurricane. The men played gravely; the notes were a poultice. They played in harmony, breathing as one man. Warm notes filled the cavities of their chests. The hall restored itself; even the draperies seemed to take on a new sheen. The instruments relaxed under the caressing hands of their owners. The strains of the Mozart soothed. And when it was finished, that music, the men looked deeply into one another's eyes. "Oh, my friends," they whispered in unison. "Oh, my children." They kissed their instruments reverently.

They left the empty stage. The final notes of Mozart hung in the air and blessed them as they walked home.

"Don't tell me any more," Herbert said. He already knew the end of the story. The early-morning sunlight had given way to noon as light crept into the front section of the Automat on Forty-second Street, the usual bustle of day. Steam rose from the cafeteria, the yeasty smells of gravy and mashed potatoes. Herbert pulled his scarf closer to his body. Near the entry, Helen, the waitress, seemed to pause in her cleaning, and the counter boy and she stood silently together, wreathed in pale light. That winter New York noon light sang like an organ even within the dim cafeteria. The weak coffee had long ago grown cold. Herbert sighed. He looked at all four men, the question in his eyes. But perhaps it was no longer a question.

"Yes." The four men looked down, cradling their hands in the folds of their coats. "Next morning they took our fingers," said the second violinist.

"They wanted our hands," the first violinist said. "They wanted to take our hands. The whole hand. The fingering hand. But at the last minute, our wives prevailed."

The morning after the concert, a large black police van drove to the little flats of the Tolstoi Quartet. The musicians were allowed to take their musical instruments with them, but nothing else. The men were questioned gently, but there were no real questions, and no real answers to the questions. It was to be only a partial execution. Their hands were forced in front of them. At the last moment, a woman's voice cried "No. Not the hand."

"No!" said Olga, Gudrun, Ludmilla, and Inge with one voice.

"Fine," said the chief officer. "Take only the little finger, then. Just do it." He wanted to get it over quickly. "Just do it now."

"But why?" asked Herbert. "Why the little finger?"

"Well, you see," explained the first violinist. "The little finger, it is the revolutionary one. It is the one that stretches, that produces the most difficult sounds."

"The pinkie," explained the cellist, "whose reach exceeds the grasp."

"The little one, he tries the hardest," added the viola player. "He is the risk taker. He strives."

"It is the little finger that played the high notes that drove them mad," said the first violinist. "All this music, it cannot exist without him. When they took the little finger, they took the music, you see. They wanted to make sure we would never play such music again." The men seemed in agreement about that.

Afterward, the men were—through the intervention of perhaps the wives, or was it the Ministry?—driven to the station, where, with instruments in hand, they were banished from Vienna forever while a military band played "Hänschen Klein" repetitively, out of tune. The four officers stood at attention as the train carrying the musicians pulled out of the main station. "Oompah, Oompah-pah," went the gleaming tubas, thrusting the little song forward loudly, mockingly. At the last moment, the four wives ran out from behind the military guard, babushkas hastily tied around their curls, fur coats thrown in a panic about their bosoms. But they were thrust back again behind the watching crowd.

The members of the Tolstoi Quartet raised their bandaged left hands toward the women in a last, sad farewell gesture. The tubas yowled their sardonic notes as the train pulled out, carrying the men away forever.

Now the afternoon was darkening, and the Automat was empty after lunch save for a few lone men sitting morosely in the front, their hands cupped around warm mugs. A chill wind blew in the air.

"Ach." Herbert sighed, pushing his chair from the table. He was preparing to leave.

"And so, our dear Herr Doktor, we come now to you." The Quartet looked at him with mad, beseeching eyes. "To find our fingers." The fingers, the Quartet knew, were still there somewhere, waiting for them in a dark box, waiting to be rejoined with their owners.

Herbert tightened his lips. His beaky shoulders hunched nearer the floor. The Quartet waited, but Herbert did not speak. He looked down at his own outspread fingers, which were resting quietly upon the table; his hands, gnarled, liver-spotted, stumpy. "Ah, my friends," he said, as if half to himself. "Ah . . ."

"Please, Herr Professor, Herr Doktor. We implore you," breathed the four men in counterpoint, and the instruments shivered next to them. Herbert could visualize the scene at the police station: the generals, the musicians' wives, their sudden cry, and then the fingers. Those fingers, caught: did they still exist? Where?

"Gentlemen, forgive me. But I can do nothing for you." Exhausted, Herbert longed to prepare his getaway.

Aah Oh Eee Uuu. The high ululating voice of a soprano

practicing somewhere pierced the air. Did he imagine it or hear it? The voice rose and fell, wailing and climbing the scale, note by note, then rose another octave. *"Aaa Eee Ooo Iiii Yyyy Uuuu."* It climbed upward confidently.

Herbert pushed his chair away. Already he was putting the Quartet's story behind him, moving on to the next and then the next impossible plea.

Herbert listened as from the tombstone street a piano accompaniment began under the soprano's voice. Somewhere roses opened in a sunny garden. A woman came to a balcony, watering pot in hand. The soprano voice rose and fell with pleasure. Herbert shivered. The notes of the piano anchored the voice firmly. "Aaahhhh . . ." The strains of a quartet tuning up before a performance could be heard. Adeline was putting on her best dress, and downstairs, maids were laying white linen upon the long table in preparation for the reception to follow.

Adeline! Herbert closed his eyes, vanishing instantly in his mind from the Automat. He was somewhere else, in his own home. All was in readiness. The rented chairs were set in proper rows for the concert, and his friends were slowly coming up the stairs into the house and handing their coats to the old maid, then walking into the main salon, where Adeline, radiant in mauve silk, greeted them. At the front of the room, under the curved bay windows that looked out into the garden, the grand piano waited, dark and mysterious, like a lover looking into the moonlight. Outside, the roses preened their last as dusk tinged them and their scent unfolded like the open arms of women toward the windows.

There was a rustling in the room, hushed as the Tolstoi Quartet entered, carrying their instruments aloft. They smiled at Adeline, who seated herself at the grand piano. Herbert's heart swelled; he would ache with pride and pleasure. As the first notes of the Schubert piano quintet laid themselves on the waiting air, Herbert felt the tears startle forth from his eyes. There was not a sound during the playing, not a sound afterward.

Adeline came up to him and took his hand. She led Herbert to the front of the salon, where, held in the loving gaze of his wife and his friends, he watched as the Tolstoi Quartet led the room in applause for his presence.

"My dear Herbert," Adeline said, holding out her arms to him for all the world to see. "Thank you, Herr Professor," whispered the Tolstoi Quartet. The instruments shone under the soft light in Herbert's house. His friends had never looked so beautiful. The dinner, the white drapery, the silver, his guests—all gleamed with a beauty of a still life now held in his memory.

"Your dear wife . . . ," murmured the leader of the Tolstoi Quartet reverently. "Tonight, she played like . . . like an angel. . . ." Yes, that had been true. . . . Herbert's gift to himself. To her . . . That she should play one piece with the Tolstoi Quartet in his home. His birthday gift to her. And she had thanked him for that night. Yes.

Herbert thought of Adeline now, a strange feral creature, crazed with what she had and had not been forced to witness, stretched out in bed, in an asylum, a stranger almost even to him. And the Quartet, how sad they looked. Where was their music now? Their mutilated hands?

Herbert gathered his scratchy coat about him. "My friends," he said softly. "Do not grieve any longer. We will find your fingers." As he said this, Herbert, who had not the slightest idea of whether this was possible, felt a lightening, a resolve. "With God's help, gentlemen, we shall find those fingers. And the Tolstoi Quartet will play again together." Giddy inspiration entered Herbert. He wanted to be done with the whole thing. "I promise you. You shall play again together. In New York. Our new home." Herbert's ears stuck out from his gilded head. He poked his chin forward. "You shall play again. In Carnegie Hall."

The four men looked at one another as if confirming their faith in Herbert's magical powers. One last swoop of daring and hope entered Herbert's heart. "And you shall play once more the Schubert piano quintet. With my dear Adeline," he added.

"With the gracious Frau Professor Doktor?" the men exclaimed. "In Carnegie Hall?" The Quartet sprang to its feet, almost alarmed at such presumption. "We shall play again with Frau Professor Doktor? The Schubert? In Carnegie Hall?" They peered intently into Herbert's face. "You will find our fingers?" they queried anxiously, as if not believing that their mad request would so foolhardily be met. "You are sure? You are sure, Herr Doktor?"

Chapter 12

HERBERT IN A HURRY

Now Herbert was in a hurry. He was flying through the air, rising up on the tails of his oversized tweed overcoat, bounding over the poisonous streets in a great whoosh of dark intention. Automobiles stopped, and passersby gaped, their mouths open, making large gray O's of wonder as he flew over their heads, pursued by the beast of the night. Propelled by relief, a desire to escape his own recklessness, he gulped the cold air and hailed a taxi. He would make it to the hospital before the end of visiting hours.

The hospital doors flapped open and shut behind him. Herbert dropped his shoulders, forcing himself to appear relaxed as he entered the ladies' ward. "My darling."

Adeline lay in bed, unmoving, but she pushed herself to a half-sitting position when he entered. Her face was dirty with tears, her unkempt hair tangled. Thin strands of it lay upon the pillow, where the invalid had pulled it out.

"My little flower!" Herbert cried when he saw her. "But what has happened?" Seeing her, even like this, made his heart dance, and he floated past his own dread and put himself gently next to her. "Tell me."

"Oh, Herbert!" Adeline cried suddenly. Throwing her arms

around his neck, a gesture unusual for her, Adeline clutched him to her. Her breast heaved. Herbert felt her racked body as if it were his own. He patted her ineffectually, pushing back her tangled hair from her hot forehead.

"Herbert," Adeline cried, "they took him. My Michael." She could not speak further; her hands twisted around him, clutching first her hair, then his neck.

Herbert cradled his wife. "Our children."

The wraith of Michael stood in the corner of the ward and watched them both. He tried to suck some breath of life from their wheezing presences. There were ashes in the air. White-boned, Michael stood, glowing as he watched his parents' grief, then faded into a small, thin ash of himself.

"And what of David, who saw his brother taken?" Herbert did not permit himself to think about it. David was married now, and had the children. His precious grandchildren. Herbert was weary.

"Adeline, listen to me." Herbert wanted to get away, but he took her face in his. Fearful, his wife regarded him. "Listen," said Herbert. "I have seen the Tolstoi Quartet."

"The Tolstoi?" Adeline suddenly stopped crying.

"Yes, my darling," said Herbert. "They are here in New York."

"Can it be true? Here?" Adeline made a convulsive movement, as if to throw Herbert off.

"They asked for you," added Herbert.

"Ah, I am nothing!" she hissed. "Herbert, look at me," She indicated her ravaged face. "I used to be something. Now I am nothing." Her voice rose.

"Shh." Herbert held her thrashing body. "Listen to me. You must, my dearest." Adeline twitched, but less strongly now. Herbert continued to talk, although she twisted her face away from him. "They want you to play with them." Adeline gestured angrily with her head, her mouth curling. "Yes," said Herbert, not knowing whether he was lying. "In Carnegie Hall." He sounded desperate, even to himself.

"Carnegie Hall?" Adeline's mouth gaped.

Herbert continued more bravely now. The inspiration of a liar was oiling his tongue. "They want you to play the Schubert. Yes, my darling, the Schubert. In Carnegie Hall. They wait for you."

"When?" asked Adeline.

"When you are ready," replied Herbert, stroking her hair. Adeline started to sob again. As she continued to cry, Herbert tried not to laugh, so relieved was he at finding something to placate her. Boldly, he added, "The concert is planned for the end of the year." *Planned*—he heard the word echoing after he said it. Casting a quick glance into the corner of the large room, where he assumed the spirit of Michael still watched, he tightened his arms around Adeline. "Planned already," he repeated defiantly.

"But darling, you are mad. I am sure of it." Adeline said.

"No, my little flower," her husband answered. "Hurry and get better now. The Tolstoi Quartet is waiting for you."

"Herbert," protested Adeline in her normal preemptory voice. She sat up abruptly, removing his arms from her body. "How is this possible? I haven't played for years."

"Never mind," said Herbert bravely. "It is too late to think of things like that. The concert is already advertised."

Adeline was silent, thinking this over. "But . . . ," she began again.

"Shh," commanded Herbert, holding her. She was calmer now. The steam pipes hissed in the corners, but they were only steam pipes after all.

After a silence, Adeline said softly, "Herbert?"

"Yes, my darling?" He stroked her hair into a semblance of smoothness.

"Herbert?" She plucked at his sleeve questioningly. "What shall I wear?"

"Why, your best silk dress," said Herbert practically. "You know the one I mean."

Chapter 13

DAVID IN NEW YORK

Herbert's elder son, David, was absent from this story and perhaps from all stories. He was a cipher, working in a Washington basement, trying to decipher other ciphers. Because of his job as a war decoder for the U.S. government, his eyes were swollen, red, and scratchy, almost granular. But he could sleep on trains, and on the night train to New York, he let himself sink into the smoke-imbued night. He slept, and sleep renewed him. The weather changed along the way and the sky lightened gently. He would arrive before anyone in the family was awake, as he did one weekend a month.

The first signs of spring had come to New York. They came suddenly, stealing into the city and breathing their soft breath against the cheeks of sleepers, as if to remind them that they were here. Fists of magnolia blossoms opened furtively in the dark, revealing their pink centers. The frothy cherry trees, the soft green of leaves stirring, the fingertips of trees along the avenues: remember me?

David noted their outlines. Perhaps this had been happening in Washington, too, but he had been too long underground, immersed in papers, to notice. Spring had returned. He crossed New York on foot, his nose and skin picking up the fresh odor, the stirring wind. The sounds of the city had become more muted, baffled by the petals that appeared everywhere.

David entered the building, passing the sleeping elevator's cage. At the top of the stairs, he took out his key and entered the room furtively, silently. He sighed, letting his coat fall off him in a heap. The curtains stirred in welcome.

At that moment, spring entered the room also and woke his wife, Ilse, kissing her eyelids. She stirred and moved her dampened thighs, half-aware of her body's surge. A dream perhaps? What had she dreamed? Her husband stood beside her awakening form, standing there as if waiting for something.

Ilse sat up suddenly, pushing the blankets aside, only her nightdress sheltering her body. "Shh," said the figure.

"David?" cried Ilse sharply, questioning in a whisper.

"Shh," he said, and sat carefully on the couch where she slept.

"David," she whispered. No one else in the room stirred. Herbert's snores fell rhythmically from his corner.

"My darling girl." David slid under the sheets beside her, pulling up the bedclothes. "I'm here." He took off her nightdress gently as she raised her arms to him.

Suddenly, they were together, warm, naked. Ilse's body opened in many little mouths, soft velvet lips. She was ready for him. She arched her body toward his caresses as if feeding. His hands glided over her silky skin and smoothed it. It became fluid, as water, as transparent chiffon, silvery in the spring dawn. Ilse parted her legs. For one moment, she felt as if pierced, and he slid inside. His hotness rose in her; she could feel herself swelling in bloom to meet him, an answering opening and response. "David," she gasped. They held their breath together and lay fused, as if one. Ilse's body trembled with involuntary spasms as she pressed deeper, further against his. He moved slowly, more deeply inside her, but at the same time, he waited, growing larger. And opening her legs, she grasped and accommodated him, an answering opening as he moved deeper, coming to rest somewhere in the region of her heart, or so she imagined. They lay together in the soft spring air. And in that moment, merged, they were complete.

"David," Ilse whispered, wrapping her legs more tightly around him and drawing him in even deeper. Their bodies trembled, and streams of spasms ran through them, involuntary, hardly noticed, so deep was their fusing.

Spring wrapped her gauzy curtain around them both as they lay together, a curtain that obscured them from the others. Ilse's eyes were closed in ecstasy, and for once she was not aware of the little family that had become her responsibility. There was only that large, delicious darkness penetrating her body, the swelling warmth.

"David?" Ilse half opened her eyes and saw his eyes looking deeply into hers. She closed her eyes again, feeling their bodies' slow, liquid acceptance of each other. They rocked as they lay together, answering shiver to shiver till finally breaking in a long crescendo, almost regretful, a soft, strong, dark good-bye, as the largest wave took them both.

"Just one moment longer. I'm only here for a little while," muttered David against Ilse's dark hair. "I can't stay. Just till tonight. I need you so." A surge of despair, even then. He sighed.

"I know," whispered Ilse, raising her breasts to him. He kissed them, as if wanting to nurse, to be comforted by their round, soft beauty.

"No one knows I'm here," he said. "I had to see you. You and Father." In his mind, he was already going back to Washington.

"My darling," she answered softly, "we'll be together soon."

"When the War ends. For it must end someday."

This they thought, they hoped, but didn't say aloud. There was so much to say; yet so little really mattered. Each turned a bit; David hastily regrouped, becoming his shabby, buttoned-down self again.

"I must go now," David whispered to his wife, feeling for his spectacles. "Tell Father I'll be waiting for him. The usual place. I have news." Ilse moved away, loosening her hold.

"Yes, of course," she whispered, already half-asleep. David left hurriedly, leaving the door half-closed behind him. The whoosh of spring air caught it, slammed it shut.

Ilse slept until the morning light woke her. The room looked as usual, small, dark, and drab, but something had changed.

At first light, Herbert woke. A moment to register that dawn had a slightly lighter look than before. He dressed quickly.

"Father, David's here," Ilse whispered to him as she served his tea.

"David?"

"Yes, he has news." Herbert appeared to be his deliberate self, but there was alacrity as he put on his coat. Ilse brushed the lapels for him, and he was gone.

Beethoven's "Ode to Joy" played itself through his head as he hurried down the stoop and out into the streets. New York had been transformed overnight. The first leafy fronds of tree branches, delicate fingers, arched toward the sky. They thrummed to an imaginary Pastoral Symphony. "David, my darling boy!" Herbert thought, skimming the sidewalks quickly, floating without interruption across intersections. No taxis honked impatiently this morning; no crowds barred his way. Effortlessly, he entered the Automat. "Be quick, old man!" he told himself. An expectant joy. "David, my love, my life." Herbert remembered his two little boys, one dark, one fair, as they stood on the stairs of his house, watching the musicians in the parlor. One of Adeline's soirees—they all merged—and the two little boys were delighted to be allowed to watch from the outside. The men and women festively dressed. The music. The Tolstoi Quartet at its prime in those days. And Adeline, how her eyes had glittered as if with fever, as if with delight.

Herbert sighed. His boys. Michael—but instinctively his mind recoiled from the memory. Best not to think—but he was the one I loved best. No, how can I say that? Don't even think that. My David—whom I love best—can I forgive him for living? Can he forgive himself? The story of Abraham and Isaac came to the old man's mind. The pain almost stopped him in his tracks.

From the dark corner of the Automat, already metallic with morning sounds and smells, David rose. "Father?"

Herbert looked with wonder at this stooped, balding man, his son. David's skin was faded with living and weariness. David took off his glasses, rubbing his reddened lids. His eyes were permanently tired and strained from looking endlessly at old German newspapers and microfilm. For a moment, Herbert did not recognize his small, shining son in this stooped and tattered man. "My David," he said, for he knew something was expected from him. The two men took care not to embrace.

"Please, Father." David gestured to a chair.

Herbert longed, as did David, to run to the other, pressing him forever in his arms, stroking his thinning hair, his strained, suffering face. But next to them both stood the specter of Michael, a wraith in a wreath of smoke. "Think of me always," insisted Michael with his sad gaze. "I will not permit you to think of anything else." Michael was as prevalent as air molecules around them.

"My son," said Herbert, not knowing exactly which one he was addressing, "I am so happy to see you."

"Father," said David. Michael stood by his side, breathing his dead breath into David's living one. "I was at home earlier. But I wanted to see you here."

"Of course," Herbert replied, approving.

David got to the point without preliminaries. "I have perhaps some news, Father," he said. "I have brought copies. No one else knows."

"Did anyone see you come here?" asked Herbert.

"No. No one has followed me here." David stopped, then asked in a lower voice, "And Anna? How is she?"

"Fine," replied Herbert.

"Good."

The two men sipped the watery Automat coffee for a moment in silence, no hurry, as if over their own breakfast table at home in Vienna.

"Father," said David, putting down his cup. "I think we have found a link. I have seen ads in the German papers—and for a long time I could not understand them. But now I think I do." David paused, and Herbert settled back. He knew it would be better not to ask questions; that if he did, in any case David was constrained not to tell him the answers. The less he knew the better, Herbert supposed. He and David, by implicit agreement, never shared anything they did not absolutely have to.

"Look at this, Father," said David. He pulled an envelope out of his pocket and took out the small bits of film. In the darkened restaurant, Herbert could not make out anything but brownish rectangles.

David produced a small pocket light. "I came across this the other day in the *Berliner Morgenpost*." He had been scanning the Classifieds section of the newspaper.

"Develop Your Tonality Potential," it read. "Have you ever wanted to be more intelligent, more creative, more musical?" The ad went on to promise success. "For only a small price, Perfect Pitch can be yours," it concluded. Underneath was an address in Germany to be called to the attention of a certain unnamed "Herr Professor Doktor."

Herbert put down the little piece of film. "So it is true."

"No question, this is it." David pocketed the envelope.

"The Tolstoi Quartet?" asked Herbert. "Do you think . . ."

"Yes," replied David, "quite possibly."

Herbert looked down quietly at his own intact hands. Their five stubby fingers functioned perfectly. He took a long moment. "And Michael? Do you think that perhaps Michael . . ."

David looked away. "Father, I don't know," he said.

"You're a good boy," Herbert said mildly.

David looked at him gratefully. "Father." He seized his father's hand and pressed it to his lips, feeling the cold metal bite of the large ring. David kissed his father's ring respectfully.

"No, my boy," said Herbert firmly, trying to avoid his son's display of emotion. "This does not do."

David looked away. He had already put himself and perhaps his family in danger. "We shall say nothing," he reminded Herbert. He reached across the table, grasping the older man's wrist for emphasis. "I have already made some inquiries. We think the link to all of this is in New York."

"New York? But how can it be possible?"

"I don't know for sure," said David. "I have friends, you know. Or rather, we have friends. Old friends, Father." He saw that Herbert wanted to speak. "Don't say anything. I cannot tell you, and don't ask." Herbert stopped his thoughts. "They know of us, of—Michael."

The air sprang back, shocked at having heard that name

uttered aloud, and rapidly David continued, as if to cover up the fact that he had spoken his brother's name. "Never mind, Father, friends of yours and—Mother's—"

There was impassive silence; the atmosphere shuddered just a little this time. Herbert showed no emotion. "But you are not to worry about that," David continued rapidly. "Let us just say that we have friends helping us. And that we know for a fact that the link to all of this is in New York." David leaned forward, still grasping his father's wrist, and dragged the older man into a half-leaning posture across the table. "Father"—David looked down at the brown Formica table, avoiding his father's eyes—"we have reason to believe that he may be one of us."

Herbert's heart thudded wildly for a second, then lapsed back into its ho-hum rhythm. Surprise! But yes, why not? Of course, it was obvious.

David got to his feet. "I must catch the train back. I do not want the Archives to know that I have been away." David was due back in Washington the next morning. "Tell Ilse and the children good-bye for me," he said. "Tell them I love them."

"David, one thing . . . ," Herbert said, faltering toward the departing body of his son.

"Father. What is it?"

"David?" Herbert did not want to seem to be begging. "Your mother . . ."

David's face assumed a sharp, impatient outline. "Yes, Father?" he asked, but his voice was brusque.

"David," pleaded Herbert, "she is longing to see you. Will you go and see her before you leave?"

David's face turned into a mask of despair and irritation. "Don't ask that of me," he snapped.

"But David . . ." Herbert's eyes watered, the eyes of an old man.

"No, Father," said David sharply. He could not bear to see his father plead, and he hardened himself against this state. "Don't ask that of me. You know it is impossible!" Abruptly, David turned from his father and walked quickly, almost running, toward the door. "I am sorry," he muttered, "but I just can't."

Spring reached David, embraced him as he parted the door and entered the light, gauzy streets. "You selfish bastard," David thought, reproaching himself, even as he ran toward the train station. David saw no beauty as he ran, only the bitterness in his heart, the veiled, dark gaze of his father, his mother's madness, and, through it all, his own guilt at still being alive.

"It's all right, I forgive you," whispered a ghost, wafting beside his brother as he ran for the train. But David, hot dark liquid rising in his throat, heard nothing.

Ahead of him in the brightening spring air, Grand Central Station squatted, a yawning hulk. David felt for his press pass, the one that allowed him to travel for free. The early-morning newspaper hawkers were grouped beside the flat open mouth of the station, and the shoeshine boys had already set up their thrones for customers inside the door. The light shifted and changed in the doorway, reaching in striated bands through the gloom. The building clanged with activity—the sharp heels of impatient people clattering against the stone floor, and the information rotunda ringed with light and flurry like a pulpit.

David stood for a moment, his eyes adjusting to the changing light and sound. The station opened its dank mouth, and its bad breath soared toward and enveloped David. A dragon, ready to roar flames from its menacing mouth. In his mind's eye, David saw the station as if hit by a bomb, crumbling suddenly to rubble. The scurrying figures rushing toward trains looked like ants to him, and he saw their twisted limbs, heard their suffocated cries. An acrid smell of flesh burning. David turned on his heel as the choking sensation overwhelmed him. He knew where he must go now. He flagged down a taxi.

There was morning activity at the psychiatric hospital, and David waited for a moment in the hopeful light of Adeline's ward before being able to make out which bed was hers. The hospital echoed with hustle—the hopeful chirping sounds of trays, the shoes of the nurses whispering along the floor.

From a distance, David observed his mother, her thin hands picking at the sheets. She lay, her gray hair in a tousled aureole, staring at nothing. David was shocked to see her thin, frowsy face and form; he had never before seen his mother so untidy.

Before he knew it, David found himself kneeling beside her bed. "Mother," he said. Adeline did not respond. Bitterness flooded his throat. There was dust under the iron bed, and parings of nails and scraps of adhesive. Disgusted, David got to his feet. "It's me, David," he said, clearing his throat.

Under the iron bedstead, a thin, flattened heap of bones, an imagined watching skeleton shifted slightly. What was that rustle that only David seemed to hear? Perhaps Adeline heard it, too, for she stopped her endless fingering of the sheets and held out one hand to David. As if blind, her hand walked about his face. "Michael?" She queried vaguely. "Is that you?"

David felt the impatient anger welling up in him. He knew he shouldn't have come. "No, it is I, Mother. David," he replied.

"Remember how you use to love my clothes?" said Adeline longingly, ignoring his self-identification. "Sit down, my darling boy," and she pulled him to her side on the bed. David sat down reluctantly. The familiar hatred for her welled in him, but he tried—no, willed himself—not to show it. "I loved to see you dress up in my clothes," Adeline said again, and a smile came to her ravaged face.

"No, Mother, that was not me," David said cruelly.

But Adeline seemed not to hear. "They always said you looked like a girl, like me. Remember, my darling?"

David uncrossed his legs, standing up. "I just came to see you, Mother, but I cannot stay. I must get back to work."

"Oh no," cried Adeline suddenly. "Please don't go. Stay with me awhile. Please." Tears came into her eyes.

"Self-pity," David thought disgustedly.

"I am so alone here," she said. But it was too late for personal revelation. David deliberately looked at his watch.

"I must go, Mother," he said again as cruelly as he could. He hated himself for his moment of weakness. How had he ever thought he could find tenderness with her?

Anger, deprivation, and mourning threatened to rise to his eyes, too, as he felt his brother's presence among the dead.

"But where is Michael, then?" Adeline asked thinly, as if reading his mind.

As David did not answer, she quavered again, more loudly, "Where is my Michael, then?"

"Lie," the ghost of Michael whispered. "Lie!"

"He's fine, Mother," said David weakly.

Disgusted by the answer, Adeline turned her face away.

David sat down again. "Mother, listen to me." He gripped her hands as if to breathe his own life into hers. "You must try to think of something else. You must try to live." Adeline gave no sign that she had heard him. Leaning forward, David hissed into her ear. "You must, for Father's sake. You owe at least that to him."

"Don't speak of what I owe him," Adeline retorted, suddenly catching fire in fury. "What do you know of it? How dare you presume to tell me what I should and should not do!" It was the old Adeline for a moment, imperious, arrogant, impossible.

David did not know whether to laugh, be relieved, or feel angry about how difficult his mother could be.

"I have every right," he said. Her eyes flashed and a bit of life came into her skin. "It's selfish of you to keep on like this," he continued.

"How dare you say this to me, David," she retorted, proving that she had recognized him all along. "You! David! After everything that's happened."

"Especially after everything!" David responded. "Exactly." He was impatient with her, did not approve of her, had never approved of her, he realized in an instant. He was too practical, disliked her airs and aspirations. It was Michael who had been close to her, the girlish one, the artistic hope of the family. Michael had loved dressing up in Adeline's lace things, had loved the smell of perfume and flowers. Michael had Adeline's nervous, delicate temperament, her love of music. David, the practical one of the family, was Herbert's son. In that moment, David saw and accepted this. Darkness fell away from him; his old jealousies over his younger brother's relationship with Adeline slid off him. They fell to the floor and his shoulders straightened, lightened.

"Let it go, brother," Michael breathed from the dead space beneath the bed. "This is good." Deftly, Michael scooped up the dark, useless pieces of David's discarded weight, and with a thin, bony hand, he carefully piled them alongside the heaps of dust he had collected.

As if sensing this, Adeline's mood suddenly changed, and she sat up in her bed. "David," she said, addressing him directly and patting his hand, "I am so happy to see you." She spoke to him now as one lucid person to another. "Sit down. I have something to tell you." David sat tentatively again, and she looked into her remaining son's eyes as if seeing him for the first time. "It is so good of you to come." David waited. "You have always been so good, my dear David," said Adeline directly to him. "To all of us."

"She sees me! She knows who I am!" David's heart grew wings.

"Thank you, David," whispered Adeline, as if the effort of clarity had exhausted her strength. She sank back after giving this benediction, and David's eyes glistened.

"Mother," he said, this time respectfully, and raising her small hands to his lips, he kissed them.

"Did your father tell you the news?" asked Adeline. "The wonderful news?"

"No," David said, waiting for her to go on. Or to lose the thread of her speech.

"The Tolstoi Quartet," she said. "They are here in New York." David did not tell her that he already knew this. "And when I am better, I am going to play the Schubert piano quintet with them in Carnegie Hall. Think, David, Carnegie Hall!" Adeline's eyes shone. "So you see, my darling, I must practice. A lot."

David realized that what he had seen when he first entered Adeline's hospital room, the unending restless movements of Adeline's hands on the sheets, were the movements of a pianist's hands upon a keyboard.

"Do you remember your part?" he asked.

"In fact, I remember most of it. I am surprised," she said proudly. "But I have asked your father to get the score for me, as I must rehearse. There is not much time to lose."

David thought of the Tolstoi Quartet, that brave group of aging men. How fondly they had treated him, walking into the family house, carrying their instruments ahead of them. Frankly, David had been bored when the music started, and he had amused himself by watching the people in his mother's living room. His brother, for example, who was taking it all in with large, rapturous eyes. David was frightened for his kid brother when he saw that swooning look. How could they ever communicate? Was it possible two such different souls could be brothers?

Allied with Herbert, his father, outside that soft, delicious circle, David felt as his father often did. Foolish, loving, practical, a taken-for-granted balance to the family.

The Tolstoi Quartet, like everyone else, not seeing the tensions, treated both boys as one. They smiled at David/Michael tenderly, nearsightedly as they left. "Such fine boys," they said vaguely as Herbert and Adeline stood at the doorway, thanking them. Herbert paid them handsomely. "Good night." The cries fluttered back into the apple-scented garden. David saw the family house in Vienna, solid, bourgeois; the garden, the garden wall, the street, the streetcars running on curved tracks, taking him and his brother to school each day.

"Good night." The Quartet struggled into their coats and, embracing their instruments, descended into the soft night. "Fine boys," they said again mildly as Michael stood pressed against his mother, regarding them gravely with great eyes. David, standing by his father, manfully shook their hands.

As if reading his memories, Adeline sighed now. "Ah, my David. Shall we ever hear such fine music again?"

David shook himself out of the past. "I don't know, Mother," he replied, forgetting to lie this time. "I don't know."

Both mother and son were silent. The spring air hovered somewhere, wafting to the far-off strains of music. Was it Mozart? No, it was a popular song on a tinny radio, down a gloomy corridor in a place where institutional food was being prepared.

"Well," said Adeline, for once practical. "We must act 'as if.' And for that reason, I am rehearsing, even as I lie here. In case they should need me. In case, indeed, they meant it when they said we would play together in New York. It's always best to be prepared, son." The organized maternal side of Adeline, which occasionally surfaced, showed itself now. David felt the old moral lessons starting again.

"Of course," he replied meekly. Then, more kindly, he said, standing up, "Of course they will play again. And you with them. It will be grand." He put his hands in his pockets. "But now I must go. And you must practice. I will see that you get the score," he promised. "And I will be back for the concert, you may be sure."

"Good-bye," Adeline replied absently as he quietly left the room. But her eyes were staring at something else, and her fingers were already beginning to move in chord-seeking clawlike gestures upon the folded edge of the sheet. She was humming to herself, humming so quietly that only Michael, lying close to her, pressing his very ashes against her living body, could hear.

Behind him as he left, David felt rather than heard the music going through Adeline's mind. He was startlingly angry with his father for giving his mother such false hope. But since it was unthinkable to be angry with Herbert, David stopped the thought immediately, hurrying, now running with long, relieved strides through the streets of New York City toward the arms of Grand Central Station, which this time welcomed him joyously. The train was waiting when he arrived at the tracks, waiting just for him. And the old train sang on its rails, singing to the rhythm of Schubert, carrying David back to Washington, where he would spend days, weeks, and longer, hunched like a mole over old newspapers, magnifying glass in one hand, sorting carefully through all the old newspaper ads of Europe for those that advertised, in code, yet proudly, for additives: elixirs that, when ingested, would somehow deliver the attributes someone, a geneticist, for example, might crave.

"Be Smart." "Get Lucky." "Think Positively." "Improve Your

Memory." "Develop Your Muscular Potential." "Grow Hair in Only Twenty-one Days." "Learn to Play Music in Twelve Easy Lessons." "Enlarge Your Bust." "Become the Master of Your Fate." "Find True Love."

These were the kinds of advertisements David scrutinized. What did they offer? What did they really mean? And who was profiting from all this in the end?

Somewhere, right now, people were doing experiments. In Europe, clearly, but the pills and powders that made it possible, the ground-up substances supplying these laboratories, were, David knew now, coming from America.

Chapter 14

RASPUTIN'S MARK

Each night after she had satisfied herself that all the others were sleeping, Anna, the Rat, undressed carefully under the heaped bedclothes in the darkened room. But this morning, she woke early. Spring light moved across the room. But the family slept, Ilse as never before. Herbert had already left. The Rat wondered what time it was; perhaps time to wake Ilse and the children.

Spring caressed Anna's cheek as she regarded the still-sleeping figure of Maria, tucked in so tenderly beside her. Painfully, the Rat managed to shift herself into an upright position, which is to say a semicurled sitting one. Her spine ached. Anna drew aside the blanket where it weighted her. And in the soft first light of the morning, she peered at her body as she pulled her nightgown aside.

Anna's spine, curved in a semicircle, condemned her to stare forever at her own lap. Because of this, she always, even to herself, even in the dark, kept herself covered. But now she took a look.

There it was. The handprints were still there. A sulfurous burn of a hand mark, each long finger articulated on her withered white flesh. The hands were etched into the flesh of each upper thigh as strongly as the print of a leaf can etch itself into cement or stone.

"Oh." She sucked in her breath in dismay.

She forced herself to look closely. The bony, determined fingers, the emblazoned palms, the hands gripped her thighs and moved them forcibly apart. As she looked, a smell of quickly struck phosphorus rose up from her body. She felt herself on fire, scorched again and forever by the rapacious hands of Rasputin.

"Unspeakable things," she murmured to herself, now tracing the outlines of the cadaverous hands on her body. She ran her own small, soft hands over the large marks. "He did to me unspeakable things." And even while she said this to herself, even while she experienced anew the shame and horror, a little spasm, the beginnings of wild excitement, began to mount.

The hands flickered into flame; the flame ignited. Anna melted into her memories, confounded of shame and excitement. "Yes!" she cried to her now-dead lover. Unwillingly, yet at the same time gladly, the sigh rose up from her silent body. Rasputin seized her, looking into her beautiful eyes, entering her once more. Her body throbbed around his. And Anna gave way, rapturous and horrified.

"Dear lady . . . ," Rasputin had said ironically. "Would you do anything to save your husband?"

"Yes," Anna had replied. "Little fool," she thought now, looking back.

She saw herself once more in the dark room alone with the Mad Monk, a candle flickering. His savage, sensual face stared at her, the head hooded, partially hidden by his cowl. But nothing could veil his fierce desires.

"Very well," he had commanded, not even bothering to look directly at the woman as she stood, a supplicant for her husband's lands and money, a bent figure bowed before him. "You shall be my companion for two weeks. And after that, I shall intercede with the Little Father on your family's behalf." How quickly Anna had agreed. Even then her heart had pounded with dread. Her body itself was a hooked question mark. She waited meekly. Rasputin took her roughly by the hand, blew out the candle, and led her through a hall.

A cold wind swirled around them. And suddenly, there was an ignited odor in the air. Perhaps it was the odor of fresh air after lightning; perhaps it was the Devil himself. But always, forever after, no matter how often she washed, the Rat was to perceive that odor. It would accompany her everywhere. Like night fog, it swirled about them, and her body was forever after impregnated with it.

"Look at me," Rasputin commanded. Rasputin parted the skirts of his robe. His mad eyes fixed on hers; he drew from his skirts his enormous member. It throbbed and weaved toward her, pointing toward her body as surely as a dowser's stick. It quivered. "Look!" Anna tried to look away, down, up, anywhere but directly in front of her. "Look. Behold the Rod of God!" There was moisture on the end of it, a shiny, pearly drop hanging from its tip. The enormous branch of flesh moved toward her; it appeared to be drooling lasciviously. Despite herself, an answering river of liquid ran through her body, down her thighs, a shining river on which to travel inward.

Rasputin stared at her fixedly as his member grew and swelled. "Down on your knees," he commanded. "Down on your knees before your God!" He grappled for her hump, held it, clawing, palpating. Roughly, he pushed her head against him. The oversized penis grew and found her mouth. "On your knees. Pray," commanded Rasputin. "Pray, my little Countess." His head was thrown back; he was staring fixedly at something far away. He began to rock in her mouth. "Pray."

On her knees, with Rasputin fondling her hump, Anna was trying to pray. "Please, God," her heart cried. Her mouth choked around his huge organ. Above her, Rasputin spasmed, whispering strange sounds, fingering the heavy rosary. The beads swayed against Anna's face. There was a rank smell rising up from his robes and his body, from the enormous searching organ, with its mysterious forested hillocks below.

"Pray, my Countess. Behold thy God," Rasputin commanded. "Say it aloud. Let me hear you."

"Please, God," Anna choked.

"Oh God," said Rasputin at the same moment. He tore the clothes from her hump, and his hands forced themselves downward. Suddenly, he drew his huge throbbing penis out of her mouth. He grabbed her and in one motion ripped the clothes from her body. "You were praying then," he muttered. "Now I will give you something to really pray about." He turned her around and around in his large hands, the smell of incense and unwashed male musk mingling together. "Ah, let me take a good look at that little body of yours." Anna tried to hide with shame, but Rasputin carefully examined her hump, her deformed spine. Then he once again tipped her face to his. "Look at me, little Countess," he commanded. "They call me the Devil. Do you think I am the Devil?" He grasped his enormous penis in both hands. "Some may say I am the Devil, but in fact I represent the only true Christ. I come to you as the only true Christ. The living God, do you hear me?"

Rasputin pushed her down on a rough bed. "*Your* God, do you hear me? I am your God." Grappling in the dark, the Rat tried to defend herself from his sudden cruel hands. "Say it," he whispered. "Let me hear you say it."

Before she could say anything, Rasputin grasped her mouth

in his. He bit her savagely. A taste of salt . . . He bent his head toward her thin breasts. A searing pain shot through her body. "Say it." Anna smelled his sulfurous odor mixed with sweat and wine.

Rasputin pulled up his monk's robe and fell upon her voraciously. "Pray, dear lady," he hissed sardonically.

Anna began to cry piteously. "Have mercy," she pleaded.

"God has no mercy," replied the monk. Inexorably, he held her legs apart and gazed at her sex.

"What a pitiful thing a woman is," he mused. "They give us life. And they can destroy our lives as well." He seized the huge silver crucifix dangling from his rosary and pressed it to Anna's bluish lips. Then he held it to own lips and kissed it. "Blessed Virgin Mary, I do this in your name." The words were drawn out of him, thick and slow. "I do this for you."

Shrinking, the Rat lay exposed under his gaze. "A poor sad creature, you are, eh, Countess?" He burned her with his eyes, which changed color, green to fiery, as he looked at her. "And a poor sad creature is your husband, the so-called Count," he added. Anna tried to curl herself up, to really become the small protected shrimp. "Remember your duty to the Tsar and the Holy Family!" Rasputin roared.

Then he fell to his knees, grasping his swollen upright penis as if it were a candle. Or a crucifix. He held it between both hands as it became a shining fleur-de-lis. The monk bent and kissed its blazing purple tip, taking it reverently between his lips. He fingered his rosary, rubbing it against the organ. "Lord, I give myself to you. Take my ornament; take my bright sword. Use it as thou wilt against thine enemies." His penis flared; a shining aureole surrounded it.

"Lord, I am prepared to do thy will." Grasping her firmly

by each thigh, Rasputin forcibly tore her body open. A searing pain—the wrack of Anna's fused spine cracking open. There was a sizzle of flesh, an imprint of his large hands forcing her body apart, an imprint so strong that she did not even notice it under the greater pain of her body's deformity giving way. He entered her and the hot light of his organ pierced her. Rasputin forced deeper and deeper, his penis growing so huge it reached to her heart. And there it penetrated, stayed.

"Let us pray together," he said. The hot organ became a burning fer-de-lance and drove itself in farther. Her flesh sizzled. He grabbed her hump and forced her head back. His eyes rolled up and she saw only the whites. He rammed his member into her again and again, until finally he was sated. First light was leaking through the high wainscoted windows. She swooned.

When she came to, Rasputin was already retying his robe. "Clean yourself up, dear lady," he said. "I shall expect you here at the same time tomorrow night." He pushed her aside with not another glance. Small, naked, broken, the Rat lay in her violation. She heard heavy-booted footsteps receding through the stone corridors. It was the hour of Matins.

The Rat lay there dry-eyed. She did not weep for the rough violence that had entered her. She did not weep for her own insignificance. What, after all, was she offering Rasputin? Hers was the body of a woman who had never known sexual pleasure. The reluctant advances of her husband had never aroused her. "Anna?" he had pleaded wetly, once his mother had given him the idea of what to do. "Anna, tell me. Is it all right?" The more her husband had asked her permission, the more she despised him, lying inert. The Rat could not remember how they had managed to conceive their children.

As she found her clothing, pasting it over her humped body,

the sound of monks chanting was rising from the chapel on the other side of the building. She made her way out, shamefully. Now, like a dog, the Rat dragged herself home through the streets of Saint Petersburg. It was not yet dawn, and finally she managed to find her carriage, the coachman sleeping peacefully, in front of the palace beside the frozen Neva. She stumbled painfully, spots of blood staining her passage, into the large house, and then to bed. There she lay all day, her eyes closed.

She dreamed of Rasputin, his huge organ, and of her total surrender. Anna was in a state, climaxing again and again. She could not stop the strange sensations overtaking her. She refused to see anyone, even her children. She could not live until she would be with the Mad Monk once again. "Your mother has a headache," her mother-in-law said, shooing the children away.

The next evening, the Rat once more summoned her carriage when the others were asleep, and returned to the covenant she had made.

Rasputin looked at her directly, his somber eyes burning with knowledge. "So, my dear lady," he murmured, "you will come to like this. Even this."

The words, the realization of truth, sent Anna into an immediate panic. "No . . . ," she pleaded on his bed, naked, curled up around herself.

"My dear Countess . . ." Rasputin smirked. He raised her small clawed hand to his lips and kissed it sardonically. His large hands were gentler this second night. They prayed together.

The same smell of sulfur, the same searing of large handprints on her thighs. But this time, Anna ignited also. A strong burning smell rose up from her flesh as her body met his. There was a green sizzle in the air. Rasputin poured his hot spurt into her again and again. His enormous organ throbbed. "My sword of

Christ," he called it, forcing it into her till she thought she would burst. His hands seared her body. He touched her everywhere. She swooned. But her body's mouths cried *More!*

His hand grasped her hump, and he forced her over the bedpost and took her one last time from behind. "On your knees, Countess," he hissed, "on your knees!" He rammed her again and again, reciting the liturgy as he did so. Blasphemies and exhortations. He recited it backward and forward. He took her both ways, too.

At dawn, Rasputin pulled out of her as quickly as before. But this time, Anna wanted to keep him in her, to know this man. She tried to hold him with her body, squeezing against him as he withdrew. He laughed ironically. "So, perhaps you are changing now, my fine little lady?" She opened her eyes just long enough to see him close his monk's robe about him once more. A glimpse of something strange and hairy—was it a tail?

"Dress yourself, dear lady," he said. Anna's torn-open body lay meekly, still throbbing with desire. All of a sudden, she longed to put her arms around the monk, to kiss his large sensual lips with a passion she had never felt before. "You will come to like this, to crave this," Rasputin murmured cruelly, as if reading her thoughts. "Already you are developing the appetite. You see, dear lady, even a countess is not so high-and-mighty." He mocked her as he left the stone-flagged room, his rosary clicking, his robe swirling about his legs.

Anna managed once more to get herself to the entry and then into her waiting carriage. The monks' chants rose mournfully from their stone crypt. By now, the Rat had become obsessed. All day she lay in her bed at home, not speaking to anyone. She thought without stop of the moment when she would rejoin Rasputin and her pact with the Devil.

The sulfurous handprints on her thighs throbbed with desire, seeking again their owner. They would not be still. Her body twitched and jerked, as if now it had become a phantom body desperate for completion—Rasputin's hands on her thighs, his large entry into her, his blazing sword. Anna felt she had come into her real life. Everything before had been unreal, uninteresting. She burned only for her nights with Rasputin.

As the two weeks neared their end, Rasputin began to be tender toward Anna. He kissed her hair, moved her body toward his more gently. He still came as many times, sometimes even more. He would not let her move from him; he lay in her body, hardening again and again, coming without end. "Now I am truly lost," he murmured. He caressed her private parts. "The source of joy . . ." He spoke aloud to the Holy Mother and then he came in Anna again.

She arched her body to receive him; she could not contain her cries of joy or the large tears that welled up in her beautiful eyes. Her body was not large enough to contain it, their passion. He saw her arousal. He played with her. He watched her again, her angelic eyes and mouth, her consumed expression. She bore down on his organ, and they lay together for hours and hours. A throb, a vibration, an answering one. "Pray, my little Countess," he murmured to her as her ardor rose toward his. "Christ is risen." Tears came into his furious eyes, and he let them fall, his large head heavy on Anna's narrow chest. "Our two weeks are almost over," he murmured. "Let us pray." Anna stroked his bulging forehead; she had always known they would part.

Rasputin put his hands into his handprints, which lay like large silver leaves on Anna's body. "You shall have something to remember me by, eh, my Countess?" he said. "You shall always remember thy Lord, thy true God."

And then Rasputin took her again and again without stopping, as if he would slake a mad thirst by consuming her. Anna, crouched like a dog, endured his repeated entries. A mad lust rose from her body, a wild, bitter scent filled the room, and the flowers outside the window in the garden withered instantly. Anna's body was an opened red poppy,

Rasputin kept Anna with him until after the first dawn's light. The monks were already chanting their dirgelike sounds, but he did not seem to heed them. With half a mind, Anna worried about the hour. But this thought was pushed away by her body's answering desire. This time, Rasputin did not come; he thrust and, quivering, thrust again. He held his rosary, watching her come almost to the brink of satisfaction, then withdrew pleasure again. Anna writhed, biting her lip. He watched her, brought her to the brink again, and then watched her body twist, pleading for more. His eyes were still abstractly focused. He made her kiss his crucifix. He made her kiss his penis. "Kneel," he commanded. He entered her again. He held himself back. He watched her spasms, impaled upon his penis.

Finally, he threw her down disdainfully and pushed her away from him. "It's over now," he said. It was time to leave: the end of her two weeks' pact. Anna lay in an exhausted heap. She thought she would expire from her own heat. Rasputin swung himself away from her. "Well, my Countess?" he said quizzically. But his face and voice were tender. He tied his robe once more around him. "Now you shall remember me."

"No. I beg of you, my Little Father." Anna held her arms to him, imploring.

Rasputin threw back his large head and began to laugh. "So," he said. "So it has happened. Good, then. Now I return you to your husband, the Count, and your house and land. But money, house and land, and a poor figure of a Count for a husband, all that is nothing, my lady, nothing." He hissed, his dark eyes glowing, putting his face close to hers. "We know that now, don't we, little lady?"

Anna's body burned. "I implore you," she said softly.

"You made a bargain," he reminded her. "And we have had the best of it, both of us." He scrutinized her naked, unprotected body. "Something you'll never forget, eh, Countess?" She looked at him. "But it's over now. Over and done with. Never let it be said I broke my vows." He threw back his head and laughed, a deep, rusty laugh that broke the pitcher beside the bed. "Pray for me," he commanded. "If you dare." Rasputin turned on his heel and, without another look at Anna, left her forever.

Anna pushed herself to her feet, a large, passionate, sorrowing cry rising, even as she stifled it. She tottered after him a few steps, but Rasputin was gone. Only the smell of brimstone lingered— a smell that was never to leave her flesh thereafter.

The weak Count was never returned to his grateful family, weeping and slobbering with the miracle of it all. But the house and lands and money were once again returned to him. "The Tsar pardoned us," his old mother kept repeating over and over in dazed wonderment. And though no one ever spoke of unpaid gambling debts, the Rat was never to have peace of mind again.

Over and over, she replayed the two weeks with Rasputin in her mind. Her head burned; her ears rang. She could think of nothing else. Although sensible to the world around her, the Rat merely went through the motions of her life. Her children did not move her, and her husband, whom she realized she despised, seemed a little stuffed doll to her, propped up in the Crimea, which she imagined as a painted cardboard panorama: *The Tsar's Officers at Rest.* Complete with tents, horses, cannons, binoculars, gaming tables, and outspread maps. Like hand-painted wallpaper.

Obsessively, the Rat remembered the scenes with Rasputin: the pain, the terror, the excitement. Wildness rose up in her. Each night, she regarded her body, putting her small, wondering hands against the large, passionate handprints burned into her flesh. She thought of Rasputin's gleaming organ every time she prayed. The Rod of God. She climaxed each time she knelt in church. She bit her lip so none could hear her cries.

As if at a distance, as if it were happening to someone else, the Rat lived through all the later ensuing horror: the complete disappearance of her husband, the flight from Saint Petersburg, the loss of her children. She heard, as in a distant dream, news of the slaughter of the Holy Family. Of Rasputin's fate, no one knew. But even this did not move her as one would have thought—she merely thought of his large face, the hooded face, the hairy body, and what looked like a tail. And she touched her body and dreamed of the time when she would meet him again.

But something finally cleared in the Rat's mind when she was reunited with her beloved cousin Herbert and his grandchildren. Dumped unceremoniously on the floor of a large, vacant, echoing space, the New York Public Library, Anna came to. Suddenly, she snapped out of the obsession—that obsession for sexual experience, for union with evil, that had managed to cloud all subsequent suffering. That obsession that had silenced her during her flight through Europe, the long wait in detention camps for passage to the United States. The long, silent wait, while she kept herself sealed in her own thoughts.

The Rat was freed from all this, and although she remembered dimly, as if at a distance, all her losses, once carried home in Herbert's arms, she returned to herself, as if all were washed away.

The Rat was once again the earnest young girl she had been, arguing seriously with her cousin about the meaning of life. She and Herbert looked at each other as if no time had passed. They did not see the age upon their faces, only the simple joy of being.

Watching Maria and Philip, the Rat knew happiness. She dreamed, and her dreams were gentle ones, not the hot, tortured sexual ones that had carried through the long years of a heavy life.

In this stuffy room, rejoined with the little family, Anna knew once more a simple purity of being. She was content to sit by the window, hearing the sounds of New York rising up, and watching the faint rays of sunlight cross the room. Everything here made Anna happy; she was a simple Rat after all.

Anna watched the little girl in bed beside her, her breath rising and falling as she slept peacefully. Her hair caught the light. Anna drew the bedclothes about them both more snugly. She had entered another time of her life, the easiest time.

Anna adjusted her small aching body. She knew there were modern ways of getting rid of marks. She had heard already that doctors were voluntarily removing tattoos—one did not need to be marked forever. In conversation, Herbert had told her that Felix, their friend from the old days, was one such doctor. Compassionate, humane, Felix treated only the escapees from Europe. The Rat remembered him from the old days, their fierce intellectual discussions. Yes, she would offer to go with Maria to her next appointment with the old doctor, and there she would ask him to help her. Almost regretfully, the Rat stroked her own marred thighs. It would not do to go to her Maker with the mark of evil on her. She knew her time was coming; she was already preparing for it.

Chapter 15

DEAD A LONG TIME

Maria did not know then that she would not be dead a long time. In 1945, when the war ended, she would be ten. Inexplicably, her visits to Uncle Felix stopped before then.

But until that time, each week on Saturday afternoons, Maria was taken to his office, where Uncle Felix would give her "vitamins." Often before the visits, Maria lay on her cot in the family room, stiffly, passively, refusing to respond to her mother's pleas. "Maria, put on your coat. It is time to leave now." Then, more forcefully: "Come, Maria, you must." Maria tried hard to make herself even more dead; with a little effort, she could almost tune out her mother's existence.

But inevitably, she didn't know how, these refusals would end. Larger than death, her young and beautiful mother would win. For her mother was helpless and angry. And it was somehow Maria's fault.

Years later, Maria was to read about Gandhi and the principle of passive resistance. She had almost invented it, she felt. With just a little more time, she might have perfected it. She read of swamis lying on beds of nails and not feeling anything. She read of people staring at the sun. Maria practiced all this, or the equivalent.

At night, she stared into the darkness of the room and pretended not to hear little Philip when he cried. She found she could tune out the grown-ups when they talked to her. Later, in school, she practiced not moving at all, although sometimes she would blink when her name was called.

Maria practiced being clean. She practiced being good. She was a top student. She practiced being invisible. "How good she is," the adults marveled. "Maria is always so polite." Maria liked this; it gave her more time to be herself beneath the facade. But there was no self. Maria practiced and practiced being dead. It would become a useful skill.

Maria felt most herself, that is to say, most dead, when lying on Uncle Felix's examining table, her hand forcibly pressed to Uncle Felix's "broken leg." She let herself float out of her body, up near the walls among the photographs of the angel children. Had they, too, been in this room? She wondered, regarding their grave little faces. They all seemed so clean, so purified. Maria knew that she would join them someday; Uncle Felix was making her ready for that other life. She longed to wear white.

Somewhere in the room, far away, Maria listened to the sounds of water running. Felix washed his hands. Maria lay before him, naked, meek, and sacrificial. She thought of heaven.

Maria encountered another little girl waiting in the entry, a child also accompanied by a nervous, fussing mother. Maria did not want to think about this too much. The two girls would, in passing, lower their eyes in shame and confusion, avoiding each other's too-careful scrutiny. Did they share the same experience with Uncle Felix? Did the other girl need "vitamins" also? Maria wondered, turning her head in sudden, sharp, unbearable pain.

After her sessions with Uncle Felix, Maria sat outside the door on the little sofa and waited for her mother. Did her mother need "vitamins," too? Maria heard, through the door, her mother's hypocritical laugh, and a growl that seemed to come from Uncle Felix. She buried her head in Schatzie's neck. Sometimes, as the door closed, she saw, in her mind's eye, her mother's beautiful slip, her blouse, flung over the top edge of the yellow Chinese screen.

When she was older, her mother stopped going with her to Uncle Felix's. But this was after Maria's father, David, had returned to the family. "You're old enough to go there by yourself," Maria's mother said.

Maria was too thin, with deep bluish circles under her eyes, and an anxious expression, which she tried to tame into impassive calmness. She didn't protest too much, had long since given up protesting. The dead feel nothing, after all, so what did it matter? Meekly, she went.

Felix's room was always warm, and with a certain voluptuous dread, Maria partook of his rituals. His "broken leg," her "badness," all these she accepted. After Felix was finished, he stroked her forehead, her hair. She was his "good girl" then. She felt loved and soothed. Maria imagined that at those times she heard the angels singing. Yet, immediately after, Felix dismissed her with a brusque dislike. She could see she wasn't good enough yet; and each time, between the visits, Maria was a "bad girl" again.

Maria wanted to stop eating. She wanted to stop going to the bathroom. She ate less and less, and although the family did not have much food, she gave half her share to little Philip. Maria's mother, noticing this, began to scold the girl. "Can't you see how hard I work for our food? Be grateful, you ungrateful child!" Maria held the tears back from her eyes and stared at her mother while at the same time trying to make her vanish.

"You must eat." Irritated, Ilse steeled herself angrily for this new development in their lives. "The child does not eat." Maria's mother expostulated to Felix during one of their visits the following month. With frustration, she regarded her wan girl.

Felix bent down and scowled at her. "What is this, you bad girl?" His brows beetled. "Now you worry your poor mother? She has enough already to worry about. You must eat, my child! Otherwise," he hissed, "you will go to the hospital. And do you know what they will do to you there?" Maria shrank back. She did not want to know. "Do you know what they do to little girls there, hmm? They make them into liverwurst!" he exclaimed, his voice a dramatic whisper.

Maria tried to cover her ears. "Yes," he insisted. "Liverwurst! Do you want that?" He stepped back a pace. "So . . . ," he said in a low, threatening voice, "I want to hear no more of this nonsense, hmm?" He flipped a sugar cube to Schatzie. "If you do not eat, you will come to me every day." His voice rose to a shriek. "And do you know what I will do to you?" Maria tried to shut him out, but his hot breath was close to her face and his voice at full volume. "Uncle Felix will beat you, bad girl! *Ja*, every day! You will come to Uncle Felix every day and he will beat you."

Felix looked up at Maria's mother for emphasis. Then his tone changed again. He fixed Maria's mother with his black hypnotic eyes. "Authority, my dear madame. What this child needs is some authority! You are much too lax." Maria's mother unloosed the silken scarf from her neck. She looked down at Maria. Maria could see in her mother's eyes fear and determination, as well as the sense of being utterly alone. Felix seized both Maria's and her mother's hands in his own. "Now," he said, "this is better. We will be a good girl now, yes, and eat for Mutti?" He stroked Maria's hair. "And Mutti will be happy." Maria nodded. "And you will make your old Uncle Felix happy, heh? He does not really want to beat you."

Maria nodded and shrank back. He took this for assent. Felix pressed her mother's hand. "You see, dear lady, all that is needed is authority. A man's authority." He looked significantly at Maria's mother. Maria despised them both, but she did not show it.

"Mutti will tell me if you do not eat," Felix warned Maria. He took her into his office then. His hands spent a long time with her, but they were not so nice. "Remember, you promised." He was angry with her, impatient as he pressed her against his lumpy leg. He was eager to be done with her that day. But with her mother, he took a long time. Maria sat on the couch outside, waiting, and pondering her sins. Her stomach gurgled. She felt suddenly ravenous with hunger.

Chapter 16

ROMANY

Herbert walked quickly through the early-morning streets of New York, the image of David's dear strained face in front of him. The balm of a spring morning touched Herbert with a new sense of hope. "My son," he whispered to himself, not knowing of which son he spoke. "My son!"

The air was heavy with a perfume of early blossoms, and the sharpness of the blue harsh light cutting into the ravines between buildings was weighted with a new freshness. Herbert strode quickly now, propelled by the spring wind toward the dank-breathed mouth of the New York Public Library. He hurried up the steps past the waiting stone lions he loved, and into the entry, where the day's work—intrigue, the sorting of refugees, the passing of false papers, false money, false promises, and false news—awaited him.

The Tolstoi Quartet was already expecting Herbert. As he approached the staircase, the four men prostrated both themselves and their instruments, the noble violoncello bowing facedown on the marble floor along with the rest. Herbert felt annoyed, but he suppressed that feeling.

"Herr Hofrat, it is a great honor to see you again," the first violinist spoke for the other men. "Please forgive us for disturbing you." The four men, attired in their concert costumes—trousers, black tailcoats, and carefully shined shoes—lay in front of Herbert like spokes of a Celtic cross.

"Not at all," said Herbert mildly.

"We thought . . . ," began the second violinist in a higher pitch, but then silenced himself.

"Please rise, gentlemen," said Herbert, spreading his hands, palms down, fingers open, in a gesture of peace and blessing. The men seized his hands, and before they rose, they kissed his ring passionately.

"We thought perhaps," said the violist, "you might have news."

The cellist added gravely, "Yes, news!"

In their jar, far away across the city, the four little fingers drummed impatiently on the glass. "News," cried the men, their hands twitching.

"Well," said Herbert slowly, "perhaps I do." The instruments began to wail and clamor from within their heavy cases. "Shh," Herbert cautioned them, "this is a library."

The men stroked their instruments as if to gentle them. "Be still, my children." "Tell us!" went around among the men and their instruments. "Tell us." The soft urgency of the syllables fell on the still air.

Herbert bent forward and cleared his throat. "Nothing definite, I am afraid," he said in a low voice. "You know my son David has been working on this. . . ."

The first violinist cut the air with a high imperative. "Yes?"

Herbert was reluctant to say too much. "He thinks we may be closer to the solution." There was a crashing sound from the instrument cases, discordant, in unison. Herbert put his finger to his lips. The four men looked at each wildly. Silence? A half-note rest was possible. But silence? That would mean death.

"Please, my friends, say nothing about this," Herbert cautioned. The pause shivered before his firm note.

"We understand," the men said in fifths.

"We must wait." Herbert turned brusquely on his heel and left the astonished Quartet, the men, their faces slack, holding their instruments. As Herbert mounted the huge stairway, his footsteps deliberate and his back turned against all further questions, the men prostrated themselves again on the floor under the great rotunda.

"Herr Hofrat," they whispered. There was a faint cinnamon scent in the air. If they had looked up at that moment, they would have seen how the spring sunlight, poking its way into the great rotunda, gently caressed Herbert's large ears and liver-spotted scalp, coaxing him into the great hall and reading room. But they did not look up until Herbert had mounted the staircase and disappeared. Now they scrambled to their feet again. Straightening the tails of his waistcoat, the first violinist announced to the others, "Remember, not a word now. It is time for a slight intermission."

Herbert's steps were hardly audible on the expanse of stone floor as he went toward his next meeting. A whisper spread through the library. "Herr Hofrat comes." Quick fingers rustled the pages of dusty books, and in the periodical rooms men looked up from the outspread newspapers in foreign languages. Not wanting to appear too eager, the small old eyes seemed to skim the headlines again. Then nervous hands, trembling, smoothed closed the newspapers. Books were carefully shut, the precious page numbers marked. Humbly, Herbert entered the Rose Main Reading Room, sighing to himself as he saw the dim green line of lights and the thick walls that shut out all the joyous clamor of the city streets. He drew his overcoat more closely about his shoulders. As if counting the customers, he noted all the old people waiting to talk to him, the nervous, destitute petitioners.

In one corner, not even bothering to look as if he were reading, one shabby man awaited him. Manfred looked more like a garage mechanic, his alleged occupation in New York, than royalty, Herbert thought. The King of the Gypsies in exile slouched casually. As Herbert approached, Manfred straightened and faced Herbert. His black pupils were striated like those of a hawk, and his fierce gaze locked with Herbert's. "My master," hissed Manfred as his gaze demanded answer from Herbert's mild, watery one. "Manfred has not been tamed," thought Herbert.

In his gaze, Manfred held the entire Gypsy nation in flight. He himself had found his way from the lands of the Roma to New York, escaping prisons and nets and roadblocks to do so, hoping to get to Washington to plead the Gypsies' cause. Herbert sighed. For the Roma were a fierce wild species. How many would survive their cruel captivity?

"Your Majesty," Herbert replied. He bent low over the Gypsy's brown calloused hand and pressed his lips to the Gypsy's ring. "Noble master."

"So the news is bad?" King Manfred queried anxiously. His fine, sensitive pupils quivered, but he fixed his hawk's eyes upon Herbert's face insistently. "Tell me." Herbert would have liked to choose a tactful answer, something indirect and open, leading perhaps to hope at the end, as he so often answered the refugees who beseeched him. He could contain knowledge of hopelessness and suffering if he had to.

"Tell me the truth," commanded Manfred. "It is no use hiding it. The truth. And then I will handle the rest."

Herbert tried once again to avoid answering, but under the Gypsy's penetrating gaze, prevarication was impossible. Seizing the Gypsy's hand in both of his, he said, "I cannot conceal from you the fact that it is hopeless."

The Gypsy's gaze flickered, then resumed its fierce, commanding expression. "Are you sure?"

Herbert looked away sadly.

"As I thought," the Gypsy said.

"You must tell your people to try to escape at all costs," Herbert said. "There is no diplomatic help for the Romany people."

Manfred nodded in understanding. "As I feared."

"We are still trying," Herbert said. "But so far we have not been successful." He looked directly into the Gypsy's face, something he would never have done under other circumstances. The Gypsy was a proud and secretive man, and to stare was to assault.

"Have we been refused everywhere?" asked Manfred, quickly assessing the worst of the situation.

"So far, the President of the United States has refused all our requests," replied Herbert sadly.

"We cannot hope for much, then," the Gypsy responded. "We have been betrayed." Herbert was silent. He could feel the Gypsy thinking quickly, plotting escape of all sorts, his heart beating like a wild bird, caught. Manfred darted forward, and in one gesture, he cupped Herbert's head between his hands. He drew his face near and, quickly, almost harshly, kissed the old man on the lips. It happened so suddenly, Herbert had no time to react. The Gypsy's kiss was soft and tender, a quick extravagance of feeling upon Herbert's mouth. A Judas kiss. "Say farewell to the Romany," Manfred whispered desperately.

"Not yet, my friend." Herbert raised a restraining hand.

Dropping to his knees, Manfred, doomed, kissed Herbert's ring. "Your Majesty, Your Majesty," Herbert tried to protest. He thought of the Gypsies behind bars, condemned to the concentration camps of Europe, traded and betrayed, their wild hawks' natures languishing.

"Everything that we can do, we will," Herbert promised Manfred. "False papers. Money. Everything we can do. You have my word."

"Yes," Manfred replied. He seemed not to be listening, his mind already looking for chinks of light elsewhere.

"We cannot do more. Warn your people. Tell them."

Manfred, in a hawk's trance, nodded. His face almost appeared to be asleep. But Herbert knew it was merely gathering its strength.

"Everything official has failed," continued Herbert sadly. "But we will do everything we can in unofficial channels."

Manfred, as if in a dream of understanding, registered this information, gripped Herbert's hand once more, and was gone.

Herbert sat down heavily on a bench. His day was just beginning, and already he was exhausted. From the corner of his eye, he watched those in the reading room watch him, the petitioners straightening their shoulders in resolve, preparing to line up and speak with him. Herbert knew that every person in the reading room understood what had just transpired. The room slanted into sadness and despair, and a mourning rose up from within each heart.

Chapter 17

FUROR/FÜHRER

Guten Morgen. Good morning, my darling. My dearest one. My adored Father!" Felix whispered, picking up the photograph of his Führer from its altar. "Good morning, my dearest sweetheart." Felix brushed back the skirts of his silk dressing gown and fell to his knees, still holding the photograph. "Oh my darling, my beloved," he whispered passionately. He pressed his lips against the glass over where the lips of Hitler might have been, concealed beneath a firm and manly mustache. "My beloved one," whispered Felix, kissing Hitler's photograph square on the mouth. The outline of Felix's breath still misted the glass when he put the photograph back on its stand. He masturbated deliciously; he exhausted himself. Felix rose to his feet a little unsteadily and went into the kitchen, where Schatzie awaited her breakfast. "Sausages today, my little one," Felix announced to the dog, who, sausagelike herself, wagged her body enthusiastically.

From within the refrigerator, the severed specimens in little jars thrummed, but neither Felix nor Schatzie paid attention. Only when the sounds of the fingers grew more insistent did Felix cry out, "Quiet!" and at his voice, the sounds immediately ceased. "Authority, authority!" Felix told Schatzie. "That's what the world needs. A firm hand." Schatzie wagged her tail in response. Felix rolled a few more greasy sausages into her dish and carefully wiped Schatzie's jowls with a napkin. Felix checked his watch. It was almost seven o'clock in the morning, and that meant he had only one hour to prepare for his patients.

"Cleanliness," Felix told Schatzie as he cleaned the kitchen. In his office, he quickly remade his bed, folding it back into a couch and firmly planting the large Chinese screen in front of it. "For the ladies," he said. Schatzie whimpered but lay down beside rather than on the couch. Felix washed his hands and then washed them again. He put out his instruments. He was almost ready.

Felix surveyed the gleaming metal and rubber. He was the best children's doctor in all of New York. "I am a genius, you see," he told Schatzie. She seemed to agree. Felix looked at himself in the glass approvingly: the three-piece suit, the vest pocket, the monocle on its string, and the stethoscope in his upper pocket. He took a little brush and brushed his eyebrows. He clipped a mustache hair. Then he went once more into his laboratory and reviewed it with satisfaction.

On the homemade shelves, all was silent in the specimen jars. The refrigerator hummed, but no other noises uttered forth from it. The small snips of flesh in their brine lay subdued, at least for the moment.

"Yes," murmured Felix to his open closet. "You shall have your breakfast now." Carefully, he prepared the brew on the small hot plate: two parts oatmeal to three parts liverwurst. The mixture heated, and Felix hummed to himself. He affixed his monocle to his eye socket. Then, carefully with an eyedropper, Felix fed each of his jars. Some he did not dare open, but instead inserted the food through a small hole in the top. But others he opened quickly. The specimens twitched a bit as the nourishment entered their briny bath. But they posed no danger; nor did they try to escape.

Only the fingers of the Tolstoi Quartet remained intractable and scratched at the sides of their jars impatiently as Felix approached with his brew. "Good," Felix said. "So you can still play, my pretty ones, hmm?" The fingers drummed madly in response. *"Gut."* He passed quickly on to his own preserved scrap of scrotum. "Was it growing bigger?" he wondered. Felix fed it an extra drop of the mixture, even as he felt guilty for doing so. This was something he had never written to Helmut about.

"This is strange," he told Schatzie as he carefully put the rest of his mixture away again. "I have not heard from Helmut for almost a month." Schatzie looked sympathetic but offered no response. "Strange," murmured Felix. He wondered how things were with his old friend. But Felix didn't really worry. The experiments were still going on, he knew, and Helmut was no doubt too busy just at the moment. It had been nearly a month since Felix had received a new shipment of test tubes from the great drug companies of Germany. But such delays were common nowadays. "Here, Schatzie, come here," said Felix, tightening his monocle. The dog approached, and Felix carefully caught a bit of the dog's saliva onto a slide. He put the cover on it and inserted it under his microscope. "Would you like to see?" Felix picked up the squirming dog and held her near the microscope. Schatzie's eyes looked wide and terrified, but she adored her master and would let him do almost anything with her. "This is what your spit looks like, Schatzie," Felix told her, holding her toward the eyepiece of the microscope. Schatzie wiggled and finally Felix put her down. "Hmmm, interesting," he said, taking a look himself.

How he regretted not having taken more of Marthe with him to this new world. She had been a beauty. But stupid, he reminded himself. What other part would he have taken if he had thought of it in time? Not her nose, that definitely Jewish nose. Maybe a piece of her ear? Her hair? Her breast? Felix felt a bit revolted.

He picked up a scrap of paper with Herbert's writing on it and let it drift down into a waiting formaldehyde-filled jar. But the writing did not grow bigger or more clarified to his gaze. The ink ran; the letters were more inscrutable than ever. "Aaach!" he said in disgust.

It was eight o'clock in the morning. The doorbell rang. The first patient of the morning waited upon Felix's ministrations. Doctor and dachshund moved toward the entryway, past the photographs of beautiful children in white pants and dresses, with dark beseeching eyes. The doorbell rang a second time.

Felix opened the door. There Maria stood, heart heavy, holding the hand of the Rat. "The child's mother could not come," said Anna meekly. "So, my old friend, here I am."

Felix's heart stopped. He made no move.

"My friend," said Anna sadly, "do you not recognize me?" She stood in front of him, her eyes downcast, her spine bowed into a complete question mark.

Anna entered humbly, and Maria, shrinking, followed. This was not her idea, this visit. Her mother had gratefully allotted to the Rat all the tasks she really had no time for. One of these was the visits to her children's doctor so early on Saturday morning. Ilse was already out at the grocery store, doing the shopping, the haggling for the family for the week. It was her only day to try to catch up with their lives. She had had no time to think during the week, not of the children, nor of her husband. She and David were working in parallel, working so the family could survive. Ilse pushed all further thoughts of him from her mind.

"I won't go!" Maria had protested.

But her mother, impatient—what is wrong with this child?—pushed her toward the door. So oversensitive. So selfish. "Nonsense. Auntie will go with you. Mummy is too busy." Maria tried to resist. "Come," said Ilse, trying not to let her impatience show. "After all, you are a big girl now; Mummy cannot always go with you everywhere."

"Come, my darling," said the Rat, grasping Maria's hand in her own firm small one. "It is early, and your mother must do the shopping. Afterward, we will come back and I will teach you a card game. A special card game," she promised. "It was taught to me by the Tsar's valet himself." Maria could not resist the efficiency of the two women.

Now Doktor Felix did not even notice the presence of the little girl. Which annoyed Maria further. She removed herself from the scene, wafted up near the ceiling, where, along with the hypocritical photographs of angelic children, she could survey with superiority the adult scene below.

"Can it be?" asked Felix in a hushed voice. Schatzie padded in from the examining room and stood silently behind her master. Felix's voice rose. "After all these years?"

"Yes." The Rat nodded.

Felix seized her little hands. "My dearest Countess," he murmured, pressing her hands to his lips. Felix loved nobility. Imagine, the Countess in his own New York office. "Come in," he said, gesturing. "You see, I am quite installed in the New World." Felix was beside himself. "May I offer you a cup of tea? I was just finishing breakfast myself."

"We just had breakfast, but thank you," replied the Rat, hastily surveying, from her bent position, the parquet floors and worn carpet of Felix's rooms. "Ah, Schatzie!" she cried with delight.

Upon hearing her name, the dog wagged all parts of her body and shuffled forward, licking Anna's right foot. "Can it be the same Schatzie that I knew? Is she still with you?"

"The same!" replied Felix proudly. "She was permitted to escape with me. Special permission," he whispered in a conspiratorial way. "Special permission, hmm?" He crooned to the dog, grasping the rolls of flesh about her neck. Schatzie appeared ecstatic and drooled happily. "But she's old now," he told Anna.

"Who is not?" the Rat said, sighing in response. She looked at Felix sharply. "And Marthe?"

Felix shook his head.

"My dear, forgive me," said Anna, taking his hand in hers. "I am so sorry."

Maria tugged impatiently on Anna's hand, but neither of the adults noticed her.

Felix shook his head again. "And the Count?" he responded in a low, hoarse voice.

Now it was Anna's turn to shake her head. "Gone," she said. "And the boys also."

"Both boys?" echoed Felix in a low, horrified voice. The Rat looked away. She squeezed Maria's hand more tightly.

"Alas, dear lady," said Felix, "we must speak no more of such sad things." He could not stop looking at Anna's curved spine. It entered his mind like a huge force field and drew all his attention toward it. He tried to pull his mind from its magnetic field, but his mind instantly slid toward it again, attaching with an almost audible click.

Felix bent down, putting his face close to Maria's. "And what of this bad girl, hmm? How has my bad girl been?" Maria shrank from Felix's bushy face. "Have you been eating your porridge for Uncle Felix, hmm?" Maria did not answer. She pressed her body more closely into itself. "Has she been eating her oatmeal like a good girl?" Maria was tongue-tied, as usual, before the two adults.

"Look at this, my girl," Felix growled, pulling his eyebrow up and down with the string. The bushy eyebrow wiggled like a centipede on his face. "Look at this!" Maria did not dare raise her eyes. "This is a bad girl," Felix told Anna. "Have you been doing everything Uncle Felix told you to do? Everything?" he demanded angrily.

"Don't be afraid," whispered the Rat hastily. "He is making a little joke, that is all." The two adults laughed in a condescending manner.

Maria felt furious, abashed, and betrayed. Could not her beloved Anna see how terrifying Uncle Felix was?

"Come now!" cried Felix jovially. "Let us see exactly what this bad girl has been doing."

Maria cast a last look for help to the impassive photographs above her. But, unlike Ilse, the Rat did not sit down in the hallway outside, under the angelic photographs of grateful little children. She followed Felix, who had now taken Maria's hand in his grasp, into the examining room. The table gleamed as always with a fresh white sheet on it, the instruments lay ranged in the sink, and Maria felt the familiar sense of shame in the deepest center of her body. Felix's room was, as always, immaculate, the screen ranged artfully in front of the velvet couch.

Schatzie followed the three of them into the room. "My dear Countess," said Felix, "there is no need for you to accompany us. Perhaps you would prefer to wait outside."

Anna made a small protesting movement with her head. Felix's bowed chest swelled with something like pride. "Well, then, that is fine." He gestured toward the room, which lay pristine in its expanse before the arrival of the days' patients. "And afterward, if we have time, perhaps I shall show you my experiments, my notes." He turned to the Rat proudly. "Since we saw each other, my dear Countess, I have been engaged in much important work. New breakthroughs in science," he continued. "The face of mankind is going to change, must change. There are advances possible now that you and I have never even dreamed of." Anna looked interested.

Today, Felix did not spend much time with Maria. He was excited at having the chance to share his work with the Countess, known even during his youth for her intelligence and interest in new ideas. She turned her beautiful deep eyes toward him. He could hardly keep his attention on what he was doing. Perfunctorily, he lifted the child onto the examining table. He unbuttoned her dress and laid his hairy ear on her narrow chest. He breathed heavily for a moment or two, then took out his stethoscope. "Have you been eating?" he asked fiercely. "You see," he said to Anna, who stood waiting, her spine bent and eyes downcast beside the examining table, "I am quite busy here in New York. There are so many children who have need of me."

This time, he did not fully undress Maria. This time, he did not place her hand on his "broken leg." This time, "Hänschen klein" lay quietly, obediently in his little house. He did not stare at her fixedly. As Anna watched Felix sympathetically, Maria squeezed her legs together very tightly under her candy-striped little dress and let herself float toward the ceiling. She tried very hard to be dead.

But no one was noticing this. Maria was somewhat piqued to see that Felix's attention was not at all on her. His eyes were fixed on Anna. The Rat was watching him with a rapt, admiring expression. Her eyes held an odd sheen. And Uncle Felix, he was staring at Anna's face, and at her deformed spine as, absently, he palpated the spine of the child. Maria squirmed away from his hands. But he didn't notice. He appeared hypnotized by the White Russian Countess.

Maria twitched angrily under his hands. "Good girl," he said, rearranging her dress. Quickly, he palpated her stomach. Maria let herself float up to the ceiling of the room, near the large light, big as the eye of God. Then Felix was done, his hands tucked again into themselves, and Maria was restored to herself as well. He smoothed her dress and lifted her down. "Fine; getting better," he muttered. To Anna, he said, "You must bring her back, of course. She needs treatment once a week. So many problems. Her mother . . ."

The Rat nodded, and the two adults locked eyes for a moment.

"But perhaps, my dear lady, you might come back again yourself?" suggested Felix. "I would like to show you all I have been doing." For the doorbell was ringing, and Felix padded quickly out of the room, Schatzie in tow. "Come in," they heard him say.

Anna seized Maria's hand in hers, adjusted her coat, and walked toward the front door. "We must not keep you," she said. "I know how good you have been to Ilse and the children."

Felix bowed his head modestly. "Will you do me the favor of dining with me, my Countess?" he asked.

The Rat nodded. "With pleasure."

"Perhaps this Sunday next?"

"There is nothing on my calendar," replied Anna. "It will be good to sit with an old friend again."

Felix started to close the door gently behind them as they left. But just before the door closed completely, he suddenly cocked his head and, catching Maria's eye, grimaced, raising one eyebrow, and stuck out his tongue. It happened so quickly that only

Maria noticed. "Bad girl," he hissed. "Uncle Felix will be watching you."

A veil of shame flushed over Maria's body and she cringed, clinging to Anna's hand. She felt something in her chest that closed; something that might be called "heartbreak." But why? She didn't understand. Hatred for the Rat came over her. She understood in the gaze between Felix and Anna that her doctor preferred another. "They look at each other like two sick cows," she told herself, despising them both. She didn't know how two sick cows might regard each other, but she liked that disdainful phrase, "Like two sick cows!" Maria had come, in a way that even she knew was perverse, to crave her visits with Doctor Felix. Now she saw her power was nothing compared with the power of Anna's eager face. Maria felt hot all over. "I am dead," she whispered to herself fiercely. The more she said that, the more her body betrayed her. She felt nothing, she told herself, nothing at all. It was only the grown-ups who pretended to be alive, walking around and laughing. The stupid grown-ups. "I am dead," she told herself. And the sensation of those words, repeated, was delicious.

Chapter 18

THE SPINKZ MOVE

A month later, Herbert leaned over the table and took the hands of his son David in his stubby, gnarled ones.

David was tired and rumpled and impatient. This time, he hadn't slept well on the overnight train from Washington and had gone immediately to the Automat from the station. Herbert waited, regarding his son with both affection and a surprising distance, as if he hadn't recognized in this man the boy he had been.

"We found this," David said, "in a letter." From his pocket he carefully pulled a wrinkled page, then smoothed it out under the greenish cafeteria light.

Herbert leaned forward. There was something oddly familiar about the crumpled page with the small spidery markings upon it.

"Look at it, Father. Do you not recognize it?"

Herbert looked more closely. Then, peering at David for affirmation, he looked again. "But it is my writing."

"Yes," David replied. "Read it. What does it say, your mixture of Esperanto and chess?"

"So that's what happened to it," Herbert said. "I was wondering what had happened to the rest of the game. Maybe I had mailed it. But then I never got an answer."

"I recognized it immediately when they handed it to me to decipher," said David. "But then I thought, 'What is it doing here? Why here? And what is he telling us?'"

"'He'?" asked Herbert. He had not imagined that all his correspondence would be intercepted.

David brushed aside the comment. "And then I saw it was my father, up to his old tricks again. A chess game. A flirtation with a lady, is it not so?"

Herbert smiled, not bothering to hide his crafty delight. "Of course. It was my move. The famous Spinkz opening."

"And then I thought," continued David, "'Why does he write in Esperanto? Why now? There's only one lady in the world who might still be interested in Esperanto.'" He sat back, proud of his own cleverness.

But at this, Herbert protested, laying his hand upon the arm of his impetuous and wrongly informed son. "No, David, there are many. And, you will see, soon there will be many more. It is a world language. You will see. Like chess. A universal language for mankind."

"Father," said David, cutting in impatiently. He had heard this all so many times before. What did the old man know? Look at the state of things right now. Why did his father, his irritating, idealistic father, so insist on clinging to his idealism despite all evidence to the contrary? David swallowed his impatience. Let the old men carry on; the young would make the changes.

But Herbert would not be quiet. Toward his son, he poured all the humanitarian ire. Also, he was fueled by the humiliation of having his mail intercepted. And by his son, of all people. "To have been so careless, so confident," he thought but did not say. His mind raced. Had there been anything implicating in the letter?

David regarded him, authority in his reddened, watery eyes. He was tired. "Father, please. We do not have time."

"Time, David? If we do not have time for language, then we do not have time for the human race."

"Yes, that's exactly the point," said David in an irritated voice. "There is no more time."

"Always time for chess," mumbled Herbert. "There is always time for chess, David. There is always time for a language like Esperanto, which will allow us to communicate with one another. Think of the Tower of Babel. Do you want a world like that?"

"We have a world like that," groaned David. "Old man," he thought. But instead, he said, "Father, I know. And," he added slyly, "there will always be time for the ladies, no?"

"Exactly." Herbert leaned back and beamed. A truce! "Now, dear boy, tell me where you got my little Spinkz move? You know, it was meant to reach the Rat."

"Yes," said David, "I managed to figure that out. But," he continued, smiling at the old man, "you had all of Washington going out of its mind, trying to crack your code."

"And did they?" asked Herbert.

"Well," said David, "I was surprised. And you will be, too, when you hear how this paper came to me. But the code, no."

David, hunched in his basement cubicle in Washington, had been shocked when the letter first appeared on his desk. "This is your specialty, old boy," his boss had said. Almost immediately, David had recognized the chess, the Esperanto, his father's writing. Then, of course, he had realized that the paper was meant for the Rat, his father's cousin, the mad White Russian Countess. The king protecting the queen. The Spinkz move.

"It was that Spinkz move that gave me a hint," David explained. Herbert smiled. "Well, I didn't know exactly what the next move would be," he bragged. "I had to sacrifice the castle, the knights, everything. That was inevitable, but not before she had taken her turn at the board."

"And if she hadn't?" David asked.

"Well, my dear boy, you know this is just an exercise. I do it to keep myself sharp. In the end, chess is a game one plays against oneself."

David laughed. He shook his head. The fox trying to hide.

"Don't you remember?"

"Of course." David remembered the chess game under the linden trees in summer. How many times he had cried with frustration. And yet, he had loved the game. Loved spending time with his father. "But I never won, not even once," he reproved Herbert.

"Ah, dear boy." Herbert sighed. "I know. Your mother used to scold me. 'Humor the child,' she said. 'Let him win.' But I thought you would never learn the game properly if I babied you."

David did not agree with that philosophy. He had resented his father's hardness with him.

"Now chess," reminisced Herbert, "that was something your brother would never play."

David heard his father's stern voice in the garden. "Pay attention," Herbert said as David frowned, looking away from the chessboard. The air smelled sweet, the branches swayed in a slight breeze, and the notes of Chopin floated out the garden doors; inside, perhaps tea was being prepared. With delicious mouthful-size cakes. "What kind of cakes?" David wondered. "The little chocolate ones with whipped cream? Or maybe the ones with the raspberries?" Cakes and music and perfume wafted toward David in his mind, all borne under a silver cover. "Pay attention, David," Herbert warned in a strangely soft voice. He looked at the boy with piercing attention.

David forced himself to focus on what was, he saw, already a hopeless position.

"There is still time," Herbert warned from under the linden trees. *Time, time, time,* the first notes of Beethoven's *Appassionata* wafted, each note carrying its own weight toward David's hungry ears. "Pay attention, my boy."

What were the trees saying? What was the music saying? David looked at the squiggly figures, black and white, on the board in the garden. What was his father trying to tell him? In the background, the sounds of the tea service, and the sounds, farther away, of shouting, of cries, of each held breath, each breath of beauty, turning desperate. "Pay attention."

David forced himself to return to the board, to return his gaze to the dark figures. What were they supposed to be telling him? Herbert drew on his pipe. In the distance, the shouts of terror, the sounds of beatings, a crowd being captured, herded somewhere. But for that sweet moment—sweet, how sweet, David realized in retrospect—he fastened his gaze on the board. "Try," murmured Herbert.

"Try, dearest boy, to understand." David hunched his shoulders. "Take your time," counseled Herbert.

Time stood still in the garden, the late light of the autumn afternoon filtered through the linden trees, and Adeline's clear voice wafted through the doors onto the terrace. "The lindens, the lindens," she sang. And the joyous, girlish spirit of Michael, like a wraith, buried its face in her skirts, overcome by the unbearable beauty of the afternoon.

"Take your time. Your opponent will always wait," Herbert whispered, his little eyes concealed in hooded elfin calm. Beyond the garden, in the streets of the city, in the secret squares, and even at the railroad station, the commotion was already mounting. If David could only understand the game, perhaps he could hold it all safe, at least for now. "It's your move, dear child," reminded Herbert.

David grasped the figure of a pawn and tentatively, then more firmly moved the black figure two steps ahead. He slumped back.

"Good." Herbert approved.

Now, across the table, framed by the clangor of the steamy Automat, Herbert regarded his son through half-closed eyes. He waited. He could wait forever if necessary.

David shifted, exasperated. "So of course we wondered how your letter had happened to find its way to my office."

Herbert waited. How tedious, all this chasing about.

"But it is only normal. All letters must be opened," David said. Far away, he heard Adeline singing, her raucous fingers drumming on the counterpane.

David continued. "And then we put it together. Your contacts, somewhat unexpected. An agreement you made. Shipments from Germany; your letters intercepted. Spies in New York and Berlin. The Rat in that latest exchange. Safe passage. 'In exchange for what?' we wondered. We were able to trace it."

Herbert raised one hand. "I don't want to know. Better not to know. Secrets, David, should remain secret. Better to know as little as possible."

David was determined to continue, pressing forward insistently. "We traced it to a certain person. A certain family friend. So-called. A trusted one. Be careful." David hesitated. How could he hurt his father more than Herbert had already suffered?

"Yes?" asked Herbert rather indifferently.

"A friend well known to the family," muttered David. Then, with a kind of malicious, darting pleasure, he leaned forward. "A certain doctor."

To his surprise, his father did not seem in the least dismayed.

"Is it true?" was all he asked his son mildly. David nodded, feeling deflated, deprived of his moment of triumph. He had hoped to shock his father, or at least surprise him. But the old man betrayed nothing.

"So . . . ," Herbert said, half-closing his eyes again, sinking into his own reverie. David realized his father was exhausted and saw Herbert's age upon his face. The thin winged shoulders, the faded overcoat, the sagging, wrinkled demeanor—but wait, wasn't that deceptive? Even as David watched, Herbert seemed to gather his coat about him, seemed to gather force. And, still immobile, it was as if a faint pulsation of light surrounded Herbert's creased dilapidation.

Herbert muttered to himself, then deliberately changed the subject. "Have you seen your mother yet?" He looked his son directly in the eyes.

David sighed with exasperation. He had traveled all night on the train to bring his little moment of triumph, dropping the letter like a bone at his father's feet, wanting approval, wanting to be noticed. Wanting to hear, "Very good, my son. You have done well." Wanting to be acknowledged. Instead, he felt his weariness: small, useless, stupid. The old man probably knew it all along anyway. Why had he bothered? Would he ever be free of this family? Hopelessness swept over him. Couldn't his father ever let him rest?

Herbert called the waitress for two more cups of coffee. He leaned toward David. Herbert allowed his son to see into his opaque weariness, the sunken eyes, the brows curving downward in immense fatigue. Then, as David watched, the eyes took on their keen liquidity again, small, red-rimmed, and piercing. "Felix, did you say?" he questioned, looking intently into David's face. Like a blow, like a wake-up call, David felt the force of his father's personality upon him once again. He straightened, invigorated.

"Very good, my David," Herbert said approvingly. And the small boy, reaching for the first move of the first pawn, glowed.

"Does anyone else know?" asked Herbert.

"No," David said. "I wanted to talk with you first."

"Ah." Both men sat now in companionable silence, drinking their coffee.

"I am not surprised," said Herbert softly. It always seemed too easy. Deals made in secret with anonymous persons. Too simple for the Countess to get out. "Yes, it fits," mused Herbert. He wondered how Felix had gotten his hands on his letter to Anna. But that was not important now. "Did Felix read Esperanto? Probably," thought Herbert.

"We know he has been receiving shipments from Europe," David said thoughtfully. Both men looked at each other. Of course. "The net will be closing now."

"Ah yes, checkmate."

"But not right away. We must be patient."

Herbert nodded, his eyes fully closed now.

Chapter 19

DON'T LEAVE

Across town, in their jar, the severed fingers of the Tolstoi Quartet musicians were going wild. It was always so in the evenings, when they sensed the beginning of music time. In the dusk, driven to a frenzy by the vibrations in the air, the fingers started their undisciplined dances against the sides of the jar. The urge to feel—anything. Even glass. As Adeline danced upon her bed linens, so the fingers, more sensitive for being their severed selves, began to twitch. The familiar rhythms, sound without voice, those faint tremblings in the air, became intolerable. The fingers knew their parts by heart. Adeline thrummed, raising the presence of her dearest child. And the fingers thrummed against the sides of their pickle jar: "Let us out!"

With one accord, they sought again the frequencies of Schubert's *Death and the Maiden. Da, da da duh da,* they played, each in his own part. The chemicals in which they lay sloshed to the music. They hammered against the sides of the glass. They would play as if compelled. For they were summoning now, summoning David to come and find them. "Come, save us," they played to David. "We are here. We are waiting. Come to us. Hear us."

But David did not hear them that night. He couldn't sleep, sharing the uncomfortable cold couch with his wife. He twitched restlessly; he stared at the ceiling.

"Don't leave," Ilse begged, although she knew that he would have to go.

"It's only for a little while," he promised. He sensed a moment of irritation; something crossed his concentration. Were they never to have time enough together, never space of their own? "We are together always."

"Always?" questioned Ilse. She thought of the distance between them, her job, the children, the problems of money and food and health.

David remembered the stale basement in which he worked, the temporary lodgings he shared with three other tired, impatient German refugees, all deciphering and translating what was for the most part nonsense, useless print. "Yes," he said, against all evidence. "We are always together; you know that. Even when we must be apart."

"Especially when we're apart," said Ilse thoughtfully.

Michael watched from the corner. "Love her. Be happy. Nothing else matters." He uncoiled himself into smoke. David and Ilse drew in their breaths. Michael entered their mouths, kissing them both as he allowed himself to be inhaled. "I am with you."

"He died for us," thought the lovers. Then, quickly, as if to drown that thought, David kissed his wife deeply.

"My darling," Ilse whispered. Was it to Michael or to David that she gave herself? It did not matter. Her love flowed toward him, out of the past they had lived together, all of them.

"Yes," said the watching spirit of Michael from both within and without. Pressing himself inside their bodies, he felt the force of their lives' pulsation. He sighed, expiring again, this time in ecstasy. He panted; he could not breathe. But it was all right, this not breathing.

The orgasm took David and Ilse, and at the crest, right where the wave curled, they saw the pale floating face of their skeletal beloved. David gasped as he took his wife in love.

"Help me!" begged Michael as he clawed at the jar of their memory.

"Oh," cried David and Ilse in one hoarse whisper to each other. And spent, they lay upon each other while a black despair came over them. They held each other and tried to brush despair away. They would never succeed; it lay on the underside of every happy moment they were to have. Shaken by the depth of their love, they lay, not needing to speak, gazing into the bare room, each holding the precious body of the other.

"We will find a place for ourselves as soon as this bloody war is done," David promised, kissing her. He stroked her strong hands, which lay softly opened toward him still. "We will find a little house, one with our own room."

"Yes," agreed Ilse, curling herself around her husband's body. "David," she whispered. "How I love you; I've always loved you. Yes, right from the moment I saw you."

"And I, I, too, loved you," David lied. For in fact, he had not noticed her in his university classes at first, this quiet girl. "But I love you more now than ever." This was truly spoken. Quietly, they lay while the interchange softened their bodies, and finally they gave themselves together in sleep.

Was it Adeline who was dreaming this whole story? Adeline, who lay in her crazy bed, far removed from any action? Adeline drummed her fingers on the edges of her sheets and blankets, as if her blind fingers could find their way home through music. Her fingers found their way through the scores her brain half knew. Schubert, Brahms, Mendelssohn. "My son, I am calling you. From my bereft womb, I am calling you." Michael sat beside her. His breath wreathed about her, and his parted lips still held, as a kiss, his last denied breath.

"It was always you whom I loved best," Adeline's fingers sang silently, reminding him. Adeline kept her eyes open. For it was she who controlled the world's appearance. If only she could remember enough, go crazy enough—yes, even further than she had already traveled—all might be well again. "Herbert, I am trying to get well," her fingers sang. "Herbert, I am trying to believe." "Silly man." Adeline's fingers tapped in counterpoint.

While to the rest of her family Adeline lay, inert and unkempt, in a crazy house for old ladies, to Michael his mother was as beautiful and fresh as ever. They stayed in each other's regard as if time had never happened. Adeline's last moment of lucidity was when Michael was taken from her. "I shall never look beyond," she promised herself and her dream boy firmly. Michael curled his smoke self beside her. "Play for me, dearest Mama." So Adeline played on the sheets.

Anna, lying awake in the dark next to the sleeping Maria, smiled to herself and curled around Rasputin's heavy handprints. She smelled the sleeping warmth of the little girl next to her, and, having enjoyed to the fullest the sounds of the young couple's lovemaking, she gave herself to the languor that follows love. "Be happy," she whispered into the dark toward the couch where the parents lay. Oh, to have known such relations. But Anna had her own memories: the dark side of the unspeakable. She lay there, her body throbbing. Something parted her thighs, placed rough hands on her, and, with a little moan—was it one of pleasure, or terror?—Anna allowed it, quietly, her breath held against the waiting darkness of the room, the delicious pulsations of release that took her body down its own river.

Da. Dah duh duh . . . thrummed the fingers: *Death and the Maiden*. The Rat's body burned and stirred. The air thrummed about her. The handprints vibrated. Something was calling her, summoning her body out of the darkened room. Her flesh danced with the ache of curiosity, a devil's dance. Paganini? No, it was more than that, more sonorous. She lay on her bed, a sudden excitement animating her body. The orgasm, almost a seizure, left her, and her eyes shone with resolve. Across the city, the fingers were thrumming like mad, calling. But it was Anna who heard them; or rather, in some primitive way, it was she who sensed already the outcome of her story.

"We are playing. We are singing. We are calling. Here we are." The fingers thrummed as never before, all longing and intensity.

The men of the Tolstoi Quartet woke suddenly to the sounds of their instruments still in their cases. The men wrapped themselves around their instruments. "Shh," they whispered. In their dreams, they were playing Schubert perfectly and their instruments responded to their commands as if united with one another and with them. The men did not wake, or if they did, it was only to believe themselves dreaming. Each man closed his eyes and dreamed himself a part of a perfect quartet that was playing perfectly, the varnished musical instruments gleaming and swaying. And they were swaying, too, under the linden trees to the music of Schubert and perhaps Mozart as well. The linden flowers breathed their odor into the afternoon air and the men's bodies vibrated with the music. The music took its crescendos and decrescendos, breathing through the dark, curved bodies of the musical instruments and so into the sonorous, resonating bodies of the men who embraced these instruments. The piano, insisting on skeletal structure, floated through French doors. The linden trees turned yellow. Leaves drifted softly onto the ground in the garden, where, seated at a glass table, a father and his elder son were playing chess. They were bent over the chessboard, seemingly intent. Did they hear the music? Did they breathe in the sweetness of that acrid air, that moment? Kristallnacht was waiting to shatter that perfection. *Dah, dah du deeh,* sang the Quartet in exaltation. The garden held its beauty; the young boys sensed the odor of the moment. Michael, overcome by the music, pressed his face into his mother's skirts and the Quartet played as one. "Your move," Herbert said to David.

Chapter 20

PASSION

W hat happens when passion is "spent"? Where does it go? Is it like money, always circulating, finally ending up, after passing from hand to hand, as a dirty, wrinkled bill in some unlikely eager fist?

All the cries and sighs of lovers, wreathing upward in a kind of urgent smoke: what happens to them? The precise moment when one first recognized the lover? The precise moment when one began to suffer? Do those moments stay in the universe? They wait, like parasites, for another host to come by, attaching to them as fixedly as if their former source of blood had not already existed. Then, something happens; those moments of passion take a little rest. But look, it is not for a long time, for passion is merely waiting somewhere around the corner, unlikely but determined. Passion is just waiting to steal silently into one's sleep.

Or maybe it is like the laws of continuous conservation of energy. Nothing goes away; it just changes. So evil stays in the world, perhaps only lying dormant for a moment, in a heap, its black wings folded. But nothing is ever lost—evil stays, and so do passion and suffering and love cries and the tenderness of parents for children and the children's pulling away from it all and then the beginning of life all over again. Nothing is lost.

Passion transmutes itself if necessary, rising from one person or another, sometimes from a couple at the same time. And then . . . and then . . . the smoke of its urgency wreathes itself away into the general passionate universe. But sometimes, when it goes from one person to another, it leaves a little mark.

So on Anna's flesh, the imprint of Rasputin's hands. But it was not merely her flesh that was seared; this was just the external mark of it. Rasputin, when he took her, forced his mark not only on her small white thighs but on her heart itself. Even as he himself expired, in all senses of the word, his imprint remained. Somewhere in the world, still vital, still hot with its own fire, as his last breath left, spiraling upward to become part of the general world breath, perhaps to find its way into another's body. But the mark of his passion remained behind. It was the fate of the Rat, small, hunchbacked, to bear it.

In the early hours of the morning, Felix, in an ecstasy he could not describe, cleaned up his rooms and then, in his dressing room, fell on his knees before his altar to the Führer. Clasping his hands, he rocked back and forth. "There are no words," he murmured, pressing his lips to the glass-covered photograph. The Führer, glassy-eyed, stared back at him. "Oh, *mein Liebchen*," Felix murmured.

Putting the photograph down, Felix, still in his silk dressing gown and his stockings, moved quickly to his desk, where he began to scribble a few notes. "My dearest Helmut," he wrote, unable to contain himself. "I think I have discovered . . ." Here Felix paused—would his old friend understand? He must not say too much: ". . . the secret of life!" Felix underlined the last words and put the pen down. He went into the kitchen and opened the refrigerator door. Yes, his precious jars were still there. Everyone was sleeping. He looked into the cupboards. The jars were quiet and peaceful, taking nourishment from the universal brine of sleep and renewal. Good. Felix sat down once more to his letter.

"Can you imagine? Perhaps we have not only the capability of keeping alive that which is best in humanity. Perhaps we can even do more than that." Felix wrote quickly now, covering that which had been written with one hand as if to protect his thoughts from other prying eyes. "We had thought to improve on what was imperfect in man. We had thought to build a new race, a splendid new race from the fragments of our own. Such had been our dream. Do you remember?" Felix paused, then bent again to the letter. "But now it has been revealed to me—I dare not say how—that we can do much more. Oh, so much more." Did he dare tell Helmut how? No, Felix decided, the authorities were no doubt everywhere. "I can say no more," he concluded. "Only that I see a way—perhaps it is possible—to re-create the best and the greatest human possibilities." "Nothing is lost," thought Felix, "only transmuted." Never had he felt himself so close to God.

To regenerate Rasputin. And after that, who knew? Felix's mind swam at the possibilities. "Let me be worthy," he prayed aloud. "Let me be worthy."

But how to convince Anna to allow him to try? It would mean taking a bit, just a bit, from her thigh. Felix thought rapidly. Yes, if his laws of cellular multiplication were to be proved correct, one bit would be all he would need. Provided that Rasputin had indeed placed his imprint there. One cell, that is all it takes, one human cell. Felix thought with excitement of the specimens he had already collected. He had watched the Schatzie tail specimen now for nearly three months, and the particle showed every sign of wanting to regenerate itself. A supertail of a superdog. And the fingers of the Quartet. Felix planned to regenerate from them an entire quartet, better than the Tolstoi, less interested in modern cacophony, more interested, as in the past, in the classical compositions of his beloved composers. And his own sexual parts—was he not in the process of creating from that part of himself a supersex, a man of beauty and passion and supreme sexual confidence? In time, mankind would be able to create the exact shape and form of the most desired human attributes. Meanwhile, Felix had before him the possibility of working on this most cherished project, of re-creating the dead genius of the past from scraps that had been left on the flesh of others. For it was only through the dead genius that hope lay.

Felix thought of the troubles in the world, those that had led to mass exodus, displacement. Even he, Felix, servant of the Führer, had been forced to relocate himself. A victim of mankind's folly. Now there was a chance to call upon the past with the aid of Rasputin. Maybe he wouldn't have been Felix's first choice. But the man had, after all, been the adviser to Tsars. And his hands lay almost beneath those of Felix.

The doctor realized that he had been working all his life just for this moment of revelation. "Schatzie," whispered Felix, stroking the dog, who lay beside him on the couch. "We will see great things, you and I. It is not too late, hmm?" He shook the scruff of Schatzie's neck affectionately back and forth, and Schatzie looked up at her master adoringly. "Great things lie ahead, my little one." Schatzie thumped her tail sympathetically.

Chapter 21

PRECIOUS WINE

It was dusk. Time for milk, time for bedtimes and clean hair and the minty toothpaste kisses of tired children. Time for Ilse to stretch out and rest her sore legs on the sofa. Time for David to bend once more to the microfilm, trying to forget the scratching pain of his eyes. Time for Herbert to walk tiredly home. No, time for Herbert to visit his wife. Tonight belonged to rest. Perhaps he would prefer a simple supper—tea and toast—with his old friend Anna. But he would not let himself think about that.

For once, Anna was not sharing anyone else's sadness. Even her own had been forgotten. It was dusk. It was Sunday. And she had been invited to dinner.

She crawled naked under the blanket and patted lotion all over her body. Her hands caressed the handprints of Rasputin.

In her best dress, her brooch at her neck and her little coat of mouse fur drawn tightly about her, she stood on Felix's doorstep as the doorbell sounded somewhere far away in the reaches of his rooms.

"My dearest lady." Felix beamed as he opened the door, an apron about his waist, and Schatzie, a welcoming little sausage, at his feet. He ushered the Rat inside.

Anna's beautiful eyes gleamed. As Felix took the coat from the

Rat's shoulders, his eyes strayed furtively to her curved spine. He longed to see it, to touch it. "Come in."

The table was already set, and flowers stood in a large vase next to Felix's examining table. "Tonight we do not eat in the kitchen," Felix said. "Tonight Schatzie and I welcome you, my good lady, with our very best."

Anna looked around appreciatively. Felix quickly darted into the kitchen. "Quiet, be quiet!" he hissed as he opened the refrigerator. The Tolstoi Quartet was making a silent racket—nothing Felix could hear, but the agitation was visible. The fingers continued to play their one-note parts. "Quiet, children!" hissed Felix once again. "Do you want me to silence you, hmm?"

At this threat, the fingers stopped their restlessness, waiting until Felix closed the icebox before resuming their mad music.

"Yes," hissed Felix. "If you are not good tonight, Uncle Felix will have to make sure you behave." He thought of the vial of chloroform, wondering vaguely how much would silence, but not deaden, a specimen. It could be an interesting experiment. Perhaps he would write Helmut about it. An inquiry. Helmut would be interested.

Felix prepared the little plate of sliced rutabaga, poured the vinegar over it, and carried it into the next room. The wine stood ready on his desk, precious wine smuggled out of Europe. Courtesy of Helmut. An exchange of favors.

From the cut-glass decanter the doctor carefully poured the elixir into glasses. The two raised their glasses to their lips. As the wine entered Anna's mouth, her eyes filled with tears. She swallowed; an inexpressible sweetness rose through her little body. She looked at Felix, a misty nearsighted gaze. "What is this?" her eyes seemed to ask.

"A present, my dearest lady. I have saved it just for this evening with you." "Ah, thank you, my dear Helmut," he thought. For was this not indeed the elixir of life? Felix spoke his thoughts aloud. "It is the elixir of life, is it not?"

Anna nodded. At the first sweet swallow, her body, arced, sang like a bow for its arrow.

Felix's narrow chest swelled, too. "Ah, my dear lady." He sighed. "We must try to be happy."

"In spite of everything," the Rat murmured, looking at her host significantly.

"Yes, exactly. In spite of everything. We must try to create happiness."

"I had thought . . . ," Anna began tentatively in her melodious voice.

"That happiness was forever lost to the world?" asked Felix, finishing her sentence.

"Yes . . ." The two old people lifted their glasses again to their lips. The evening began. The candles, which Felix had set upon what had been, in daytime life, his examining table, shimmered, casting their shadow on the sheet that covered it. In the mouths of the dinner companions, the wine transformed itself.

"Please, dear lady." Felix offered the first course. Anna politely took a piece of bread, a slice of turnip. Felix liked root vegetables. Anna did not. She waited for him to begin.

"It is we who are the guardians of happiness, is that not so?" Felix broke a piece of his bread.

"This wine . . . ," Anna murmured. "I had forgotten."

"The blood of Tsars," Felix explained as he refilled her glass.

"Ah, yes," murmured the Rat. Nothing would surprise her tonight.

Felix returned to the kitchen for the next course. "My children," he whispered quickly. Hastily, he poured a few drops of wine from his glass into Schatzie's dish. The dog lapped and lay down quietly, sighing with pleasure. "Be still tonight, I beg of you," Felix murmured into his laboratory shelves. He opened the refrigerator, where his most recent acquisitions, the fingers, were still playing like mad. "My children, the night is mine," he crooned. He opened the top of their large jar with delicately probing fingers. "Share my happiness!" he whispered. Felix poured another few precious drops into the Tolstoi fingers' brine. The fingers thrummed softly, then curled and relaxed.

"I shall be with you in just a moment, my dearest lady," Felix sang out from the kitchen. Felix slid two lamb chops, his precious ration, into the pan. He turned the meat and took out the potatoes he had boiled that afternoon. "I'm coming."

In the other room, Anna waited. An enormous passivity warmed her. She felt herself relaxing—whether it was the wine, that exquisite liquor, or whether it was the presence of an old friend, she did not know. She had made her decision. Now she had only to enact it. As Anna regarded her long, slim fingers, the longer fingers that bejeweled her thighs began to tingle. Warmth surged through her body. At this moment, the handprints of her former life did not sear; instead, they caressed her thighs. Memories rose through her body, memories of lascivious nights. She regarded them now not with fear, but with lost longing.

Anna's hands caressed her torso as Felix cooked in the kitchen just beyond. She placed her hands where she knew Rasputin's prints to be. Anna stroked her burned thighs through the material of her skirt. "How I have loved you all these years." Soon it would be time to say farewell.

"Now, my lady, what do you think of this?" Felix beamed as he carried in the meat. Behind him, Schatzie stumbled to her feet. But she sank down, inebriated, beside her dish.

It was the first time the Rat had smelled meat in an age. Her little nose twitched with pleasure; her whiskers trembled. She looked at Felix meltingly. That gaze.

Felix felt as if her glance struck his heart. He staggered, then set the meat down on the examining table. "Ah, dearest lady." Never mind that he would go hungry for the next month. Just that look, that greedy, grateful look, was food enough. "Please. Eat. You must be hungry."

Hungry! The Rat controlled herself, though in her mind she was already tearing the meat off the plate. Tentative and ladylike, she put out a claw. Yes, she was hungry. After all these years. "I told myself I would not eat as long as my children could not," she said to Felix in a trembling voice.

"Is it true?" he asked.

The Rat nodded; her delicate nostrils quivered. She could not trust herself to speak further.

"Eat, dear lady." Felix broke off a morsel of a lamb chop with his hand and held it out to her.

"But no," protested the Rat, laughing, picking up a fork.

"My dearest lady," Felix cajoled as he held the piece of meat, sizzling, dripping, steaming with warm, salty life, toward her lips. The Rat opened her little mouth. "Eat."

"This is my body which is given for you . . ." Those words, those strange words from the liturgy, heavy with sadness, freighted from Orthodox religion, came to the Rat's mind as she ate from Felix's hand. The somber chants in Russian, the incense, the dark skirts of a man. "This is my body . . ." She closed her eyes.

"Why, this is exactly like feeding Schatzie," Felix thought in surprise. Anna's velvety lips nuzzled his outstretched hand. Felix tore off another morsel of dripping meat. As the little Rat chewed, her eyes closing in ecstasy, Felix poured more wine into their glasses. He held a goblet to the Rat's mouth and watched her throat as she took a delicate drop. A flush slid down her body, disappearing at her neckline, a trail of delight. Felix imagined the rest of the path of that flush, making its curved way downward. He imagined licking her, the whole length of that drop of wine. Downward, downward. "Dear lady." He longed to see her entirely; he was obsessed. To fling himself on her, to see her completely naked, submissive before his gaze. "Will you be mine tonight?" But this he did not say aloud.

No need. In the kitchen, the fingers of the men of the Tolstoi Quartet moved languidly, deliciously. The gentle rhythm of Brahms's Liebeslieder Waltzes encircled the old rooms. Felix gently placed a piece of potato into Anna's mouth. "Take, eat; this is my body."

There was dinner; there was darkness. The candlelight flickered on the remains of the meal. No need to say anything more. Had everything already been said? Now is the moment, thought the Rat. "My dear friend," she began.

Felix put out a warning hand. "Ah, my dear lady."

"There is something," the Rat said firmly. "Something only you can help me with."

"Yes, gladly. You may ask anything of me."

Slowly, the Rat got to her feet. Silently, her eyes fixed firmly on those of Felix as she gauged his reaction. With a sad pride, she drew the hem of her dress upward. Felix fell to his knees.

"We have both drunk too much," whispered the Rat in caution.

Felix pressed his abdomen to the ground, and reaching out, he touched one of the Rat's small feet. "My Countess."

"Observe, dear friend," commanded Anna as the cloth of her dress slid upward.

Felix pressed his lips to the arch of the Rat's unsteady little foot. He smelled and tasted black pores of boot leather, shined and waxy. He moved his lips upward toward the stockinged ankle. Stockings, ladies' stockings! He inhaled joyously.

But the Rat was not thinking of him. In a kind of oblivious trance, her eyes commanding his to look, she unclasped her stockings and, with small, determined, agile hands, rolled them downward toward her knees. "Look."

By now, Felix, rolled into a Schatzie-like bundle of delight, was whimpering softly, kissing his way up Anna's leg. With one groping hand, he reached upward to caress her hump. "Dear lady." He writhed. Schatzie, hearing her master, shook herself awake and came stumbling out of the kitchen to sit sympathetically beside him, licking his bent head from time to time, and regarding the Rat with alarm.

"Don't be afraid," murmured the Rat, drunk both with wine and with her own courage. "It is for this that I come only to you." She gave him her most ravishing look.

"Come," whispered Felix to her. He was licking the Rat's knee by now.

Anna lifted her petticoat as Felix's rough face traveled her leg. His whiskers brushed her skin; he put out an experimental tongue. So far, it was permitted. She swayed. "Look carefully," she commanded. Reaching down with her little claws, she pressed Felix's face against the soft crepey flesh of her inner thigh.

Felix's nostrils contracted as the sharp odor of sulfur assailed the room. There was a sizzling noise as he approached that part of Anna's body. "Let me see," he crooned, but it was of the Rat's hump that he was thinking. "I must see it." He tried to move his hand surreptitiously to her spine.

"Oh, my friend," cried the Rat suddenly. She fell into a dead faint beside his crouching body. She lay as if stone-cold at his feet.

"My lady!" cried Felix in alarm. Hastily, he began to scramble for his doctor's bag. His point of view immediately shifted, and, mustering whatever sobriety was possible, he found the tube of smelling salts and broke it open.

The ashy scent of ammonia entered the room, commingling with that of sulfur and smoke. The whole formed a cloud and, blowing into the kitchen to join the repellent odors of formaldehyde and pickle juice, caused the entire company of Felix's parts collection to begin twitching nervously.

Felix did not know whom to care for first. Leaving the prone Anna on the floor beside the examining table, he rushed into the kitchen and opened the doors of cupboards and the refrigerator desperately. "Quiet at once!" he shouted to all his specimens. But all—the parts of women and intellectuals and even his own scrap of scrotum—were flailing about, trying to escape extinction.

The poisonous cloud encircled Felix's head. With a last supreme effort, he managed to fling open the window, and the diaphanous danger, a greenish coagulation, exited. The specimens began to subside as the fluids in the jars returned to normal. Felix scanned each one quickly, paying attention to the Tolstoi fingers. But they were drooping quietly in their jars; they were gradually resigning themselves to their prison.

He closed the refrigerator, then reentered the room where the Rat still lay, now weakly lifting her head and smiling. He recalled with fascination what he had but dimly perceived in all the commotion that had ensued. The memory of his lips on her flesh, the soft feel, that odor.

"Are you feeling better, dear lady?" he asked.

The Rat nodded. And, regarding him again with her expressive eyes, she once again reached down and drew her dress upward, commanding him to look.

"Ach!" cried Felix as he began to comprehend. He dropped to

his knees beside her, his eyes fixed with on the handprints burned into her flesh. "Yes," Anna's eyes seemed to say to him. "Yes, it is true. The Monk."

"Rasputin's?" Felix asked, his lips almost numb.

"Exactly," the Rat replied, and her head fell back, her body twitching.

Felix stared at the large burned-in handprints on the little Rat's withered thighs. The prints seemed to vibrate, to sizzle ferociously even as he looked. A sulfurous steam rose upward, smoldering. "Look elsewhere, everywhere. Feast your eyes on her. You have our permission," they said. "She is almost unconscious. You can do what you want with her. She is already corrupted; take her now!"

Gently, although he did not wish to do so, Felix smoothed Anna's dress once more over her body.

She lay curved like a fishhook and concealed before him. "I have come as a supplicant," she murmured. "It is I who beg of you." She reached in a small convulsive movement toward the built-up toe of Felix's heavy reinforced shoe to press her lips against the leather. She now desperately wanted him to seize her in his arms.

"No!" cried Felix, dragging her to her feet. "I am a doctor. I am a scientist," he cried. It was enough. He recalled the kitchen, his laboratory, the specimens. They needed tending; he must not forget responsibilities. "It is enough. Enough for one night." He half carried the Countess into the entryway.

Anna blinked, seemed to come to her senses. She allowed Felix to find her coat. He wrapped the mousy fur about her shoulder, found the armholes, the sleeves, closed the lapels, and buttoned them tenderly. She did not resist. "Come, dear lady, the night air. It is not good. I shall see you home."

Out on the street, the cold wind hit them both, reviving them.

A taxi darted toward them, a winged dragonfly in the night, and stopped, quivering, at Felix's call. Then it bore both passengers away.

Felix held her little hand in his own, patting it from time to time.

"May I come to you again? Another time?" the Countess asked timidly.

Felix's body swelled with pride. He squeezed her hand, then kissed it in answer. "We shall manage. Come to me again next week. Without the child."

Chapter 22

BLESS ME

B less me, Little Father," Anna murmured to Herbert. She
hadn't slept all that night. Now, still in her best dress, her
temples throbbing, she stood at the threshold. She handed him a
cup, his morning tea, milky and sweet. In her other hand was a
crumpled wad of papers.

"Perhaps you would like to come with me today," Herbert
suggested. He was going to the Automat. His normal routine. He
found Anna's mouse-fur coat and put it around her.

Maria, waking lazily on her side of the small cot, lying in the
still-warm imprint of the Rat, watched sleepily. What were they
whispering about, those two old people? She stretched, sighing,
the length of her body falling back into sleep like the scent of
apples. In that sleep, she felt kisses on her face, like apple blossoms. "Sleep, my little girl," the Rat whispered. And she bent also
to kiss Philip.

Herbert waited, watching. They walked outside, and the fresh
morning air hit them, waking Anna and soothing her headache.
Anna turned to him. "You know what I am going to say to you,"
she began. "It is my time." She looked at him deeply. "I am ready.
Thank you for saving my life," she continued, looking at him
firmly. Herbert tried to avoid her gaze, but met it finally. "Yes,
you saved my life," repeated Anna. "But now it is enough."

She turned to him, unable to say more. Her velvet gaze looked long and deeply into his rheumy eyes. "Here, my oldest, dearest friend," she said. "This is for you." And she handed him the packet of papers, the scratchy marks on yellow lined paper, the codes and false names and numbers she had stolen back from Felix, who had taken them from under Herbert's mattress long ago. "Here, this will tell you everything. It is my last gift to you. Act quickly."

"My dear little Rat," Herbert said, pocketing the papers immediately. And he knew he must let her go. He recognized her desperation, had seen such cases before. People, rescued from the jaws of death, so to speak, rescued from the most horrible suffering, would, after a time, find it unbearable to live in a halfway normal manner again. Survival affected particularly the women. They would manage heroically, despite all loss and deprivation. The men might perish right away. But the women, living on, were broken forever. No matter what might happen. They could not later survive the ordeals they had undergone in a numbed dream.

"Can you not at least wait a little bit longer?" Herbert asked mildly, taking her arm as the two rounded a corner. The wind shook them and they staggered toward each other. "Can you not wait just a bit more?" Anna looked at her friend but did not answer. There was no need. In her eyes he already saw resolve and clarity.

"I understand," said Herbert. And that was all. The Rat released her cramped breath with gratitude. She squeezed Herbert's arm, "I won't ask any questions," he said. The two old friends walked in companionable silence.

"And Adeline? How is she?" asked the Rat finally.

"Improving," replied Herbert without much conviction. Adeline had refused to see anyone not of the immediate family. Would the Rat's visit help her at all? Herbert doubted it. "She thinks now only of her music."

The Rat drew in a breath. "But that is good."

"That I cannot say," Herbert confessed. "She is determined to play again with the Tolstoi Quartet. And unfortunately, I was stupid enough to promise her a concert in Carnegie Hall if she recovers quickly."

"Oh, I see," Anna said thoughtfully. "But that is marvelous. And the Tolstoi Quartet?" she inquired.

"Yes," Herbert said. "They are here."

"Here? In New York?"

Herbert nodded again.

Anna said nothing to this news, though she began to turn it over in her mind. But of course. Why not? Why shouldn't the Tolstoi Quartet be here in New York under the aegis of Herbert? "All of them?" she asked. "All four?"

"Well," said Herbert, "Not quite all of them. You see, my dear Countess, something is missing, it appears." He took her arm firmly, steering her toward the doorway of the Automat. When they were both seated, watery coffee in front of each, he leaned forward and explained the situation.

"The little fingers of each of them?" The Rat pondered this. "I see."

"Yes," said Herbert, sinking deeper into his chair. "They are here in New York. And the fingers, it appears, are also here somewhere in New York." His eyes hooded over and he appeared to be staring not at the Rat but through her into faraway scenes. Then he came to himself. "You see, my dearest Anna, this time I am truly worried. This time I cannot work the miracle. My power is leaving me."

"Power?" asked Anna.

Herbert did not answer for a long time. Finally he said, "Countess, this is my curse. I can help everybody. But I cannot help my own family."

"It is often so," agreed the Rat, touching his hand gently. "It is usually that way, my friend."

Herbert looked away. "Yes, it is often so."

Anna touched his tattered coat sleeve. "My cousin, do you not know how we all love you? Do you think that we do not see what you do? Who you are?"

"Aah." Herbert sighed, a groan from his oak depths.

The procession of those he had not been able to save marched across a background. Herbert thought of Manfred, the Romany king, and of his failure to help there as well. He saw the Romany, their sad, wild eyes, their quick, dark bodies caged by the closing doors of railroad cars. "I can do nothing," he said. "Forgive me, Your Highness. I have tried."

Manfred, hawklike, proud, and silent, did not answer. His imperious gaze held Herbert's in its own, challenging.

"The President has refused," said Herbert in self-justification. "What else can I do?"

"Yes," answered Manfred's gaze. "But it is my peoples who will be exterminated. You have not done enough, my friend."

"Forgive me," said Herbert, closing his eyes.

"Father, I forgive you," whispered the wraith of Michael from the shadows. His cavernous eyes watched his father with dispassion. Michael at least was calm now. Or was he?

"Forgive me," Herbert sighed to Anna, who stroked his hand. "Shh, Little Father."

The guards closed the doors of the railroad cars, beating back the prisoners who pressed their emaciated bodies against the aperture for a last desperate attempt at freedom. "Father, help me!" cried Michael. Where were they taking him?

"You, with all your connections. You could have done something!" Adeline's silence reproached Herbert.

"I have tried everything." But it was too late. Herbert was doomed to live forever now with these memories. Why had it not been he who had been chosen? The "Chosen People." Yes, he had been chosen to live the hardest life of all: that of the survivor, the savior. Who could not save those whom he loved most.

"It was Michael whom I loved most," Adeline cried silently to Herbert. "It was never you!"

For this, Herbert was condemned for the rest of his life. Condemned to hear the petitions of others, to ransom everything—his remaining family, his health, his life—to assist others in escaping their fates. Only in this way could Herbert expiate his own sense of helplessness. And he had connections—that, too. He had been accustomed to power: the manipulation of it. But even power had its limits. There were others more powerful. "Bless your people," Herbert said to Manfred silently. "I pray for them."

Manfred regarded his old friend with scorn. "You are worthless in this, Herr Hofrat. Worthless. I believed when I came to you."

"What?" cried Herbert. "What did you believe?"

"In you, in your philosophy."

"In my philosophy?"

"The Romany knows only his horses. But the Jew seeks to question further."

"Better to stick with the horses."

"Ah yes, there you are right." And a glint of humor flashed in the king's steely eyes. "But the Romany believes in more than just the horses. The Romany believes in freedom. Must have it. Will die without it."

"Freedom. The right to sleep under the open sky."

"You, with your ideals. Your Esperanto. What have you accomplished?" challenged Manfred.

Tired of being chided like a child, Herbert gathered himself together. "I have helped many. And there many more yet who will be helped."

"But not my own," replied Manfred sadly. "And not your own, either, old man."

Herbert bowed his head under the burden.

"And I also," said Manfred more softly. "I also am unable to save, even with all my connections. I am also now a useless old man, do you not see?"

Herbert saw the eyes of the Romany king regarding his steadily. Within the dark wild pupils he saw terror and sadness. "How can we live with this knowledge?" Herbert murmured sadly. The Gypsy was silent, contained in his own grief.

To Anna now, Herbert said softly, "How can we live with this knowledge?" She pressed her benefactor's hand. "Tell me, my dearest Countess, how can we support such sadness?"

"I do not want to add to your burden of grief."

Herbert raised Anna's hand to his lips. "My dearest Countess, it was always you I loved," he whispered to her. "Forgive me! It was always you. I should have married you; I always loved you."

"Don't say such things," Anna soothed. From the darkly circled eyes, from their furrows, arose the slight faint odor of brimstone. The after-scent of ashes. "We have suffered enough."

"Yes, it is true, it was always you whom I loved." Herbert sighed. The two old friends regarded each other. Was this true? "You are the only one I could ever write to," said Herbert. "The only one who was interested in Esperanto."

"It is true," whispered Anna, and she laughed.

Herbert, too, began to smile. "Is this not true?"

"Yes." The Rat nodded.

"That cursed Esperanto," said Herbert. "It never did a goddamn thing." His smile broadened. "And worst of all, it never got me the girl."

"Of course it got you the girl," whispered the little Rat. "I am here now, aren't I?"

"Yes, but not for long." Herbert sighed.

"But here I am just the same."

"It is Felix who has the fingers," Herbert burst out suddenly. Now, gathering himself together, he leaned forward across the table, grasping her two hands in his. "I know you have seen him. Has he told you anything?"

"Felix?" Anna asked, brought sharply out of her gentle, foggy, romantic moment.

"Yes, the Tolstoi Quartet. Their fingers. I am sure of it now," Herbert said, his eyes focusing away from his own concerns to the job at hand.

"But . . ." Anna was confused. She would have much preferred to continue on, the two of them, in their nostalgic daze, the love not shared, the romance not expressed, and so forth.

"David told me. And I see now that he is right. Has to be right. There is only one person in New York. As far as we know . . ." Herbert paused, looking thoughtful.

"Felix?" repeated Anna stupidly.

"Yes. Now I see. We want you to help us."

"You can ask anything of me. You saved my life. Ask anything, my cousin. It is yours. What is it you want me to do?" The queen, protecting the king.

Chapter 23

LAST WALTZ

The Rat hurried onto the street and darted into a taxi. Soon she stood once again outside Felix's heavy oak door, her head bent, spine curved, as always. Her little heart was beating quickly.

It was early in the afternoon. Not the appointed day. But she knew it was his Wednesday afternoon off, that sacred afternoon Felix reserved for himself and for his research. An immediate resolution brought her here a few days after her talk with Herbert. She was ready: the Rat knew what she must do. She hoped Felix would be ready, too.

Back at the apartment, nothing had been prepared. She would have liked to have left a moment or two for the children, but that didn't matter now. She would have liked to have spoken some final words to Ilse. Too late. She must seize the opportunity that had presented itself, and act quickly. What was most important: her words with Herbert. "I love you," uttered in Esperanto. The most important words in any language. "Farewell. It has always been you I loved best."

Crashing music thundered against the big door and penetrated, through its cracks, the entire building. The Rat pressed her hand on the bell and rang again, firmly.

But there was no answer. Within, the music swelled, like a river of hot lava, throbbing through her concave chest as well. It was Wednesday afternoon, a respite from the time when Felix saw his little patients. His time, his own private time to do as he wished. Felix did not emerge.

"Yes, it is Strauss," thought Anna, listening. "The naughty one." The music, demonic in its energy, beat against the door, desperate to be let out. "I never liked the Strausses. Neither one of them."

The Rat preferred the throbbing passion of Brahms. Her hands, trembling under the weight of so much sound, nervously smoothed the front of her coat. She patted her hair and then, once again with all her force, leaned into the doorbell.

"Aha!" The door swung open suddenly, to present a surprised Felix. The music rushed out in a great draft and hit the Rat with full force. She recoiled but stood her ground. "Aha!" cried Felix again.

Felix was wearing a frilly apron, and on his head sat a conical birthday party hat, held in place by an elastic under his chin. Beside him, the silent but enthusiastic Schatzie waddled, wriggling her wrinkled hindquarters and tail. Schatzie, too, was wearing a hat—a birthday hat—also fastened with elastic under her immense jowls. Both dog and master looked surprisingly alike.

"My dear Countess," said Felix, hesitating at the door. He had not expected any visitors. When he saw it was her, hope rose in his chest. But he had no right to hope, did he? He stepped aside to allow Anna to enter. "Please, I beg you. Won't you come in? To what do I owe . . ." He cast a hasty glance backward toward his laboratory.

Anna held out her hands, clasping the doctor's between them. "My dear Felix," she murmured, "I know you do not expect me today. I hope I am not intruding. I have come to tell you some-thing important. I count upon your understanding." Her voice quavered a little as she said these words.

Felix and Schatzie cocked their heads together and regarded her. They looked surprisingly like twin wizards, with their conical little hats. Above the crashing of the music, Felix said, "Schatzie and I, we were just having a little celebration, just the two of us. Weren't we, Schatzie?" The dog wagged its body in response. Felix made an apologetic gesture, as if to begin to remove the hat.

"No," said Anna. "I don't want to disturb . . ." But she allowed Felix to take her coat. She entered. The faint smell of sulfur rose from her body, now in contact with the warmth of Felix's rooms. With a faint swoon of warmth and delight, he caught the dusty, deliciously nose-wrinkling odor that rose from her skirts. But the Rat seemed unaware of all this, her spine bent, hands primly folded, her eyes on the floor. She willed her twitching thighs to be still.

"Come in, my dear Countess." Felix said a bit belatedly over the music. He spread his hands. "The music, you see. It is the waltzes I miss. They help me concentrate. Sometimes I play them. When we are alone, just the two of us."

Anna sighed.

"Do you dance, my dear Countess?"

"I used to. No longer."

"Ah," said Felix, wrinkling his brow. Tactfully, he went across the room and lifted the needle from the phonograph. The pro-testing silence screeched just once, loudly, and then *Don Quixote* fell on the floor between them, shattering into broken shards. Felix smiled as if he had willed it. The subservient silence awaited their words. "This is better, *nein?*" he said. "Now we can have our little talk."

"Tell me," he said when he had settled Anna, now with a cup of tea. "What is it that I can do for you?" Felix sensed the Rat's distress.

Gratefully, she raised her head, her eyes brimming, the whiskers at the corner of her mouth trembling. Her little nose twitched, and she sighed as she looked at him. She said imploringly, "My dear Doktor, it is only to you that I have come. You were so kind to me last week. And I felt . . . I felt . . ." Something was guiding her speech. She looked at him with her most melting smile. She wanted to tell him that time was running out. "I could not stop thinking about you," she said instead. And with that, in a most helpless wave of her little paws, she gestured toward her lap, now overspread with skirt and petticoat. "You have seen?" she asked.

"Yes." Felix nodded. "I know now."

"And can you . . ." The Rat did not finish the sentence, but, holding her breath, she looked meltingly into Felix's eyes.

Felix's eyes took in her entire body.

"Perhaps you would like to see more, my friend. Would you like to see everything?" she asked.

Felix could hardly breathe. He leaned forward and took one little hand in his. "Yes," he replied gently. "Yes, I would." Then, mustering confidence, he jumped to his feet, the birthday hat still on his head. Schatzie, as if in alarm, also stood up heavily. "First of all," said the doctor, assuming heartiness, "perhaps you would like to visit my laboratory."

The Rat, still in the throes of mustering her courage, did not seem to hear. Felix held out his hand to her. "Come, my Countess," he said. Trembling, Anna allowed herself to be drawn to her feet.

Within her bowed breast, conflicting emotions struggled. "Felix," she thought. "So it has been Felix all along." The laboratory: so it was true. Everything she had heard. "For you, my old friend," she thought. Then, as she willed her thought waves to be transmitted, she quickly translated her thoughts into Esperanto and sent them through the clear, bright, winging air to Herbert: "It is true. It is Felix." Did Herbert hear? He didn't need to. "Pay attention," Anna told herself sharply. But to Felix, she allowed only the misted, vague emotion of her lovely eyes and little twitching nose. Her iron will she would conceal; she focused on getting her way.

"Then," she forced herself to say gaily, "perhaps you will show me your 'everything' first."

"Schatzie, come!" cried Felix. "We show our friend the laboratory, *nein*?" Schatzie didn't want to follow, however. The minute the Rat and Felix left the room, she climbed laboriously back onto Felix's couch behind the screen and, sighing softly, curling her tail end toward her mouth, lay down, looked after them indulgently— play, my children, play—and closed her eyes. "Schatzie!"

"Oh, leave me alone," thought Schatzie. "Isn't it enough that I wear this ridiculous hat?" The elastic was bothering her, and she scratched herself. The hat lay at an angle, and Schatzie's breath came in even snores as she sank more deeply into the faded brown velour of the cushions.

"This is my laboratory," Felix said as he guided Anna into the small closet-like space. He had his hand on her shoulder, and he could almost reach the place where her spine had finally curved, bowing forever her little neck. A sudden urge to touch her hump came over him. But he suppressed it.

"Look," he said as he opened the curtain that covered the labeled shelves. "Here is the secret of life, my dear Countess. This is where life begins. You," he said, addressing her, articulating each word slowly and carefully, as if this presentation had been planned, the one he had been preparing for all these years, "you are looking at the very creation of life. Matter into matter." He stood back, his arm on her shoulder, surveying his life's work. "And God said, 'Let there be light.' "

Together, they regarded the jars. A strange phosphorescent greenish glow rose from the shelves, and there was a gentle vibrating humming about them. Inside each jar, pale green liquid swirled, dreamily, in a counterclockwise direction. Anna stared, mesmerized.

"It is a time of rest," explained Felix. "All life must take its rest." The waters swirled, and an even pitch became discernible to the Rat, one single vibrating note, the note of A, held and reiterated from each jar. A, the tone of the universe. A, the tone that instruments tuned to. A, the alpha, the alpha-bet—the universal A.

"Listen!"

From the closed refrigerator, also, came the sound of A, loud and clear, piercing, as the severed quartet fingers cried out from their concealment. "Aleph. We Are Alive!" All of New York was sounding to the tone of A: the skyscrapers, the trumpets, the solemn shafts of sunlight piercing, as in the inside of a cathedral, the dark streets.

Anna shivered. The kitchen pulsed with eerie light and sound. The sweetish odor of the fluid enveloped her. It was sickish, like ether, or violets, dying ones, mixed with formaldehyde and other meaty odors. Liverwurst.

Inside the jars she could discern small hairy fragments of things, floating, diaphanous, in cloudy fluid.

"Look carefully, my Countess." Felix's voice was warning her. It pierced the odor. "Look. Here you will see my miracles."

Anna leaned forward, her dark eyes straining to read the fragments within. But she could not.

"Look," urged Felix in a whisper. And he began to point out the specimens within. "Schatzie," he whispered reverently, indicating the jar. "It's a piece of her tail." Slowly, he enumerated his favorite specimens and his plans for them. "Schnitzler. The genius Hombrisch. The famous beauty Frau Knoect. And others. Why should genius and beauty be allowed to leave the world?" He began to explain his theories to the Rat. "I decided to consecrate my life to the continuance of what is great and beautiful," he explained. "My whole life. But I think I have found the secret now." Modestly, he pointed out to Anna the jar that held a fragment of his own scrotum. "Man at his best. The culmination of desire. The preservation of the species.

"It is we who have been forced to leave, who are the best that Europe has to offer," he continued. "We cannot be allowed to die." He explained how he had studied, waited, and collected. How he had brought nothing with him when he left but his precious specimens and jars. And notes, too, of course. His friendship with Helmut. The chain of suppliers who could be trusted to send him fresh specimens, smuggled every few months. The correspondence. The careful observations and the recording of them. "Just the fact that these cells have survived, are still living, might already be enough. But look, they are growing." Felix explained how he had found their proper nourishment. "The staple German diet, modified." How his specimens were thriving. "Someday humanity will thank me," he said. He paused. "But that will take a while."

His mood shifted quickly. "Mankind is stupid, don't you agree, dear lady?" He threw back his head and uttered a few quick sardonic barks, which somewhat approximated laughter as onstage. "Hah. Hah. Mankind is so stupid. Stupid!" he hissed. His fingers tightened on her shoulder and he suddenly crooked his head, peering into her face. "My dear lady, we must save mankind from itself."

Anna felt faint. She was trying to comprehend, trying to gather this information as quickly as possible, thinking, "I must tell Herbert." "But this is remarkable," she said.

"Yes, isn't it," replied Felix, satisfied, spreading his hands. He started to take down his notebooks, the painstaking observations, timed and dated, and opened them to show her. "My records. It is so important to keep careful records." Anna looked, uncomprehending. "You see, it is perhaps a secret now. But one day, people will want to know. It is important to make no mistakes."

Felix bent toward Anna. She was looking carefully at everything in a kind of trance, hardly breathing, only her nose and the whiskers twitching. In a few minutes, he would have her entirely convinced. In a lavish, generous gesture, he flung open the refrigerator door, and the hum of A increased perceptibly. "Here, my dear Countess. This will explain it all to you. My pride and joy! My most recent acquisitions, and look how well they are doing."

There was a jagged screech as the severed fingers of the Quartet protested against this invasion of their privacy. But it was momentary, that sound, and they immediately returned to their peaceful circling. "The Tolstoi Quartet," Felix announced. "But we are going to make of them a new Quartet. A better Quartet. A more tasteful, less offensive Quartet." He bent down to the jar. "Aren't we, my boys?" he said. "Eh?"

There was again a momentary spasm of protest, as if a moment of Alban Berg had crossed the peaceful rumination in A. But then the fingers were passive again.

"Bad boys!" Felix said, leaning toward them. "*Schrecklich!* Are you being bad boys for our lady here? You should be ashamed of yourselves! Please, may I remind you of your manners!" The severed joints continued to float languidly. "Bad boys!" he hissed again. Felix shut the refrigerator door. "It will take them a while to get used to it. But they will." He was confident.

He ushered Anna back into the main room. He felt expansive, happy. "This is the first time I have told anyone about this, dear lady. But I wanted you to know, to see what your old rascal Felix has been up to all these years."

Anna leaned on his arm, dizzy. "Felix?" she asked anxiously. "Does anyone else know about this?"

"My friend Helmut in Germany. And yes, I have other friends. In high places," he said significantly. "They have, perhaps, an idea." Modestly, he added, "Perhaps one day you will even read my name in the papers. They might even establish a special Schweitzer Prize for me. But"—he waved a finger—"it is too soon, my dear lady. For we must have definitive results. But I have hopes."

Sitting down beside the Rat on the couch, he moved the sleeping Schatzie aside. "Perhaps you have some questions, my dear Countess?"

Without waiting for her response, he sprang up again and rushed into the kitchen for the decanter of wine, cut crystal, and two small glasses. "The true elixir of life," he joked, raising his glass to hers and cocking one bushy eyebrow ironically.

Anna drained hers in one gulp. She gathered her forces and looked Felix directly in the eye with her limpid gaze. "So I was right to come here," she said with determination. "You know why it is, my dear friend, that I have come to you? Only to you?"

Felix seized her hand, pressing his lips to her dry little back of the hand and then the palm.

"Yes," said Anna. "You are the only person who can help me. I have thought about this for a long time. But now the time has come. My time," she added significantly.

"No," Felix protested.

"I am an old woman now," said the Rat, "and there is no more need of me. But first, my dear Doktor, I have a favor to ask."

"Anything." Felix felt faint.

Anna looked at him meltingly, her gaze piercing his bosom, right into his very soul. "You know, my dear Doktor," she began, "I have never felt what other women feel. . . ." She let her voice trail off.

"You mean . . ." He looked at her and thought he understood everything. His chest swelled with feeling. She had come to the right person.

Her answering gaze indicated her misshapen body. "Yes. I want you to take me. I want you to make me feel what I have never felt, what is a woman's highest privilege. That transport, that abandon of self, that total surrender to another human being." As she spoke, she could see the effect she was having on him. Pity and greed crossed his face simultaneously.

"Yes," she added. "Take me!"

With a murmur—was it sadness, regret, comfort, or perhaps love?—Felix reached up and for the first time touched the Rat's humped spine. It felt like bone, the vertebrae curved and mangled. He stroked her back gently, and the Rat allowed herself a small sigh.

"Use me," the Rat whispered to him. "Use me in every sense of the word. I want to shiver like other women. And in return for those divine services, I shall offer you my entire body, and all the marks upon my body, those very marks. I know you want this. I'll do it any way you want it. Do with me what you will! But take me, my friend, take me quickly. I long to be in your arms. Forever." She gazed upon him, a beautiful supplicant.

Felix began to throb. "Little Hänschen" reared up in pride. This went beyond all his dreams. "Thank you, my Führer," he thought. Never had he been asked to perform such an act of mercy. "An honor, dearest Countess, an honor. May I address you by name?" He hardly dared such familiarity.

Anna's body began to vibrate and glow, and from her cells also came the tone of A, a faint hum growing louder. Felix, encircling Anna's shoulders, felt his body vibrate in answer. A, like the violin sections of an orchestra tuning up. He picked up the tone and echoed it. "Alive!" He could have stayed like that forever.

Faintly, Anna recalled something. "Wait. I must tell you this before we go too far," she whispered, and she put her hand on Felix's. "They know. My friend, I have come to tell you we must be quick. They know."

"What?" Felix lifted his head sharply.

"Yes." And quickly, in a whisper, Anna told him what she had heard from Herbert.

"Herbert? David?" In an instant, Felix understood. "Of course, that is why I have had no response from Helmut these many months. My letters have been intercepted." Quickly, he tried to recall what it was he had written. Had he been elliptical enough? "Wait!"

He refilled the crystal decanter—why hoard this precious wine?—and came back with it. "Now, my dear lady, tell me again."

The Rat did not know too much, but while she murmured again the little she had overheard, Felix was mentally packing. He had been ready for this always, of course. The sulfur odor from the Rat's body, warmed by the steady passage of intoxicating wine, rose and filled the room. Felix's nostrils quivered with delight. There would be time for everything, he knew. He put his glass aside, took hers from her hand, and set it down. Now! It was time to act immediately. They looked at each other. "Everyone needs a master," Felix said, "even Rasputin. Even"—he straightened Anna's skirt—"even you, my dear lady." His chest swelled with pride. "Isn't that so, my dear Schatzie, hmm?"

The dog, hearing her name, raised her head and her tail thumped twice before she fell back asleep.

"So it is Rasputin who has branded you so," Felix murmured softly to the Rat. "Do you still love him? Is that it?"

In answer, Anna took the doctor's large head in her two small hands. "That was the past," she whispered. "Today I have come here to give myself to you. In the interests of science, of course," she added. "And in the interests of love. Take me. One last time."

"Is it true?"

"Yes. But we must be quick." The stench of sulfur rose around them both. She gathered her wits about her, though the light was fading from her eyes.

Felix kept his hands on her thighs, and the embers of the enormous heat of Rasputin's fingerprints glowed under his.

"You see," said the Rat, "I have found out—don't ask me my sources—that our war is almost over. Soon I shall be just another old lady, boring everyone with my stories, dependent on everyone, a bother. I want to be free to meet my Maker unspoiled, to forget all the troubles, just to be peaceful." She paused, then continued. "Here I am, dependent on Herbert's family, and for what? I see how hard Ilse works, I see the children growing up, and I ask myself, 'Anna, why do you go on living?'"

The doctor stared intently into her face.

"And I answer myself," she said. "'There is no reason to go on.'"

"What is it you would like from me?" Felix was nervous. "You know I am at your service always."

"I want"—the Rat leaned forward and took both his hands in hers—"I want to give Rasputin to you for your experiments. I want you to take him from my body."

Felix held his breath.

"And I want you to take me, too. For I know one is impossible without the other."

Felix started to protest.

Anna stopped him. "Do not say you can never accept. Do not say you can never find the way. For I have seen your work now. And I know you can."

Felix's mind was racing. It was true, he knew; he could and would accept. He could do it. His final proof. The final experiment he needed to prove the validity of all his experiments.

"You see," said Anna, as if reading his thoughts. "I came here today to give myself, my entire self, to you." She looked into his eyes significantly. "My entire self," she repeated.

Felix whimpered.

"Do not be afraid, my friend," she said. "Do you not see that this is what we both want?"

Felix nodded, pressing his lips once again to her lap. Anna took his head in her hands and raised it so that Felix's gaze met hers. "It shall be so. But, my dear Doktor," she said slowly, clearly, "I ask only one thing in return."

"Anything," Felix replied.

"In return," said Anna clearly, "I ask only for the Tolstoi Quartet musicians' fingers."

"The fingers?" They looked at each other, astonished.

"Yes," Anna repeated. "The fingers of the Tolstoi Quartet."

Felix did not hesitate. For these were troublemakers, and the fact of being offered a whole living person—no, two persons, already regenerated, in exchange for mere body parts—well, there was simply no choice.

"Done, my dear lady." He raised his wineglass. "You see how Felix answers you. Just name your price. You shall have it. I shall do just as you wish."

Anna fixed her eyes on his and, while he watched, began to undo the brooch at her throat. "Come to me, my *Liebchen*," she whispered. "Come to me now. While there is still time."

In one quick gesture, Felix flung himself onto the floor beside the couch and Anna's feet. In a kneeling position, he clasped her body and pressed his large oily head into her lap. He reached up and caressed her, the whole length of her little bent body.

Rasputin gathered the forces of his old rage, and Anna's body grew hot where once he had touched her. The odor rose in the room. Anna quivered.

Felix kissed Anna's body through her skirt and petticoat. And as he did so, intoxication overcame him. "My darling," he murmured. "My darling little Countess. My Anna." Familiarity permitted.

With a voluptuous sigh, forced out of her unwillingly, the Rat gave in to pleasure. She had not been called "my darling" for such a long time. She closed her eyes, and her left whisker thrummed. Felix stroked her body gently. In a swoon of pleasure, they vibrated together.

Gently, Felix slid his hands over Anna's hump again. He trembled, and his entire body, not only the sexual location of feelings, became aware of itself and the sensation of love. He stroked her. The handprints, stimulated, also began to caress the Rat, sliding themselves into her secret places. "Oh," the Rat moaned, for they burned her. They probed, fingers of fire.

"Does it hurt? Tell me where it hurts."

The handprints, which could not bear to be touched, which had never, not since those fateful evenings, felt the presence of a man near them, began to sizzle and hiss in warning.

In a resolute gesture, Felix raised Anna's skirt and petticoat and forced himself to look. "Rasputin." Anna opened her body to Felix's hands.

Each place the Monk's hands had touched the Rat, her body flared red, like a hot coal, then ash white, and then, around the edges, a blackened mark appeared. There was the smell of cinders. The long, bony fingers still clasped her thighs, twisting like ivy or mistletoe. They had grown into her, yet one could see their own imprints dancing crazily as they wound. At Felix's approach, they burned themselves in deeper, holding on for dear life.

Felix made himself look with clinical interest. "I must write Helmut of this," he thought. Then, in an instinctive healing gesture, he leaned forward and put his lips on the hand marks. There was a sizzle of heat as the wet surface of his lips was seared by the molten passion of the prints. But where he kissed, the dance of fire subsided. He kissed her everywhere. And when he was done, the handprints lay still on her body, subdued, and the flesh began to resume its color again. But Anna herself was unconscious.

"Now, my boys," Felix said to them, "you see who is the master here."

Anna lay back across the sofa, her life force almost spent.

"Wait!"

Felix rushed into the kitchen and flung open the refrigerator door. The fingers, thinking they were going to be fed, woke from their slothy green dream, circling peacefully, and sensing his presence, they began to drum impatiently on the glass. "We are here we are here it is Mozart!"

Felix could not stand them. "Stop this at once." The little fingers stopped. "Boys, I have news for you." cried Felix. "You are soon to be released." The fingers did not understand, sensing only the vibrations of his voice upon the sides of their prison.

"You are going to be permitted to help a beautiful woman. One of the last," he added. "Prepare yourselves."

The fingers waited.

"But before this happens," commanded Felix, "I want you to play for me one last waltz."

The finger joints turned to one another uncertainly.

"You hear me, boys? Today I shall be giving you your liberty. But the price is one last waltz. None of that dissonant stuff, either," he warned them. "You know what I mean." The fingers were silent in their green fluid. "Play for me now all the Strauss waltzes, and by tonight you will be free to rejoin the hands of the Tolstoi Quartet." He leaned close to the jar. "And if you disobey your Uncle Felix, you will never see liberty again."

The fingers turned to one another uncertainly and began to take up a jerky swimming motion.

"Yes, that's the idea," said Felix. His mood changed to slightly manic. "Play, my boys, play!"

The joints of the fingers swung into the most famous waltz— *dah dah dah de dummm*—and began turning in the jar in time to the music.

"Yes, that's it. That's it exactly!" cried Felix over his shoulder. He forgot to shut the refrigerator door as he ran into the next room, back to the Rat. She was waiting for him, her eyes trance-like, turned up, her entire body exposed to him and for him alone, to do whatever he wanted with it, her breath almost gone from her body.

"May I have this dance?"

Chapter 24

WHAT PASSED THERE

S chatzie," Felix murmured as he circled past the watching dog. "Do not think I have forgotten you. It is only that human must seek human, do you not think? It is the law of the species, is this not so?"

Felix scrutinized the Countess carefully. Perhaps he had put too much anesthetic in her wine. He didn't think so, but he was worried. He lifted her eyelids; the pupils stared back at him, enlarged. But perhaps it was better that he had given her a large dose. He had practiced before on people who were almost dead. Enough of that, not to think. That was another life, before his desires were fulfilled.

If the Rat understood, she gave little sign; she just tightened her arms around Felix and held him close, ever so close. She smelled the odor of his cigar, the scruffy man smell of him, and her being was suffused with his odor. Her body assumed its own outlines now.

"Felix, shouldn't we . . . ," the Rat slurred.

"We have all the time in the world." His fingers caressed her. His organ swelled. The waltzes played on through the darkening afternoon.

The Rat sank into dreamlike lassitude. "Soon it will be time, my dear Doktor," she managed to say. She tried to wake up.

Felix kissed her words back. "I am master here. You need not worry," he crooned. *Ta tah tah dee dum!* Everything circled to the universal note of A. Twilight darkened the windows; the city throbbed beneath them. As they danced, they watched the shadows lengthen, darken. Even Schatzie was a shadow dog, watching them as they circled solemnly, holding each other and, in a free hand, a long-stemmed glass. "Music, music." Felix sighed. "Yes." The Rat was silent.

"How much time did they say I had?" asked Felix finally. Part of him did not even care. "Human warmth, my Helmut, human warmth . . . friendship, kinship, the closeness of a woman, the hump, the little Countess, imagine. . . ."

The Rat did not seem to hear Felix, so absorbed was she in her own dream of closeness. Finally she murmured, "Not much time, I am afraid."

Recalled to themselves, they smoothed their vulnerable, imperfect bodies. "Not much time."

"You tell me, dearest Countess, when you are ready." Felix kissed her long, drifting fingers.

"Yes . . . ," she signaled, her eyes closed. He kissed her eyelids. "Yes." Her hand drifted over his narrow chest.

"I assume they will be coming for me soon. They know where I am, is it not true?"

"Yes." Anna was in a swoon of decision, preparing to enter some other world.

"I am already packed. I have already foreseen this," Felix said. "I have always known that someday, somehow, mankind would find a way of stopping me. My bags have been ready for a long time."

Felix thought of his arrangements, the ticket long since bought, the letter sent to Helmut, giving emergency instructions. His laboratory could be dismantled in minutes. His large trunk, the one with the careful shelves prepared, each with its leather strap to hold in precious specimens, was ready to be sent to the address of a willing woman friend, a contact of Helmut's in Venezuela. Felix looked forward to his new life there. He had heard many good things. It was rumored that the Führer himself planned to live in South America one day, had even had a grand villa built for him there. There was a room prepared for Felix. "In my Father's house are many mansions," he thought. He imagined the place prepared for him, the choice bedroom, the laboratory promised in the basement of this villa, with real shelves, not just a kitchen cupboard.

"I have all faith in you," the Führer had said.

Music played from the open refrigerator. The afternoon passed from dusk to night. The contents of the apartment seemed to swirl in the milky, darkening light. It was as if they were enclosed in a jar, a jar containing elements of life: oxygen, a watery, permeated air that nourished them as they swirled slowly, counterclockwise, thrumming to the universal tone of A—A-live—as did the groups of cells where life or semilife was being formed. A city held them, and beyond that city a continent, a planet. They danced, supporting each other, like little stick figures in a larger enclosure. Their eyes were focused on their own private reveries.

"Is there anything you'd like, dear lady?" asked Felix. "I mean, before?"

"Nothing," Anna replied. "I am at peace now."

"Good. It is good to be at peace."

For the first time, the Rat felt her body united within a larger universe of music. The grasp on her body and soul that she had endured, first because of her deformity, and then because of her experiences with the Mad Monk, now fell away from her consciousness. No longer was she the prisoner of a consciousness of her body; she finally became her body, inhabiting herself as if for the first time, from the inside outward. She forgot herself, her bent, tortured fishhook spine, and, in that forgetting, became beautiful. Dreamily, she opened her heavy-lidded eyes and regarded Felix. Turning her palms upward, Felix felt all his tenderness flowing toward the Rat.

"So this is love, this sensation. . . ." Felix surprised himself. Then he corrected himself, for he truly loved Schatzie also. And the Führer. What love of woman could replace love of ideals? Though Felix knew he was soon to be the agent of destruction, or at least partial destruction, he also knew that he would be the agent of liberation for the Rat, too.

Perhaps he would be able to bring her back again, unmarked, a new Countess Anna, to live a new, proud life in a proud body. But it was not the regeneration of the Rat that interested him so much, despite his feelings. No, it was Rasputin. The regeneration of a political mastermind. Felix wondered what Rasputin would be up to in the current world in which he would soon find himself.

Well, never mind, that was not his affair. "I am a scientist," he reminded himself sternly. "I am a scientist first and foremost."

As the stars and planets circled New York City, the sky began to glow. The sounds of the city were hushed; only a jazz samba beating itself upon the waves of the night rose up to their ears and caressed their damp hair.

"Listen." Anna raised her face to the night air, closing her eyes, as if memorizing the sensation.

The sky was beginning to lighten, almost imperceptibly. "We still have a few hours," Felix murmured, pressing his face to her hair.

"My dear," the Rat said gently.

"Yes, perhaps you are right." Quickly, he ran into the kitchen and said something to the Tolstoi fingers. "The last waltz," whispered Felix tenderly as he took her in his arms. "My beloved Countess, may I have this waltz?"

Once more he held the wineglass to her lips, that wine into which, unseen and quickly, he had slipped something else. "Mercy," he thought. "And compassion. My Hippocratic oath." He watched as her eyelids became heavier and heavier. Before she could sag totally in his arms, he led her back into the kitchen and helped her onto the shelf. Dreamily, Anna lay down, curled into a small shell of herself, becoming the size of a shrimp.

"Gently." Felix held her hand as she eased herself into the large jar that awaited her. She found a comfortable position and adjusted herself.

"Easy, my beauty," he crooned.

The Rat curved and curled herself into the large-bellied earthenware jar. It was the one Felix had used in former times for making pickles and sauerkraut: his biggest jar. The Rat had no difficulty finding her curvature in the jar. She closed her eyes. Felix watched until she was fully asleep. The Rat did not move, but imperceptibly, as by a force larger than herself, the rhythm of the spheres, she began to circle slowly inside the jar. Slowly. Felix watched her, breathing his love into the rotating enclosure her curved body made.

As Anna sank further and further into her trance, the jar began to glow, and a strong greenish light flared up from it. There was a heavy odor of sulfur, mixed with the sweetness of violets and all the other flowers the Rat had ever worn on her body. The scent of grass, the scent of clean clothes and sunlight, all this rose from her body also. But over all was a yellow-green wrinkling odor.

The odor rose and gathered itself forcefully. Before Felix's watching eyes, the handprints revealed themselves and shimmered as if phosphorescent.

The prints danced upon the Rat's body. Felix watched as they grew stronger and brighter in outline, sizzling in their dervish dance. The Rat sank more and more peacefully into her drugged sleep. But the hands cried out in their shining presence. Their hot smell filled the room.

Hastily, Felix now began to empty the shelves in the kitchen, filling his large trunk. He ran back and forth as daybreak threatened. He would leave no trace of himself. Felix thought of Herbert, of David, of the whole group who wanted to stop his experiments. His escape had been planned. He had always been prepared for its eventuality. "Come, Schatzie," Felix commanded. But Schatzie did not move. She snoozed as if drugged. Felix did not worry too much about her. He found his ticket and papers. He was almost whistling as he packed quickly. The photo of the Führer was the only one he took. The photographs of children, the little ones who had been his patients, they could stay on the walls. A museum. He had no time now.

Accidentally, Felix's sleeve brushed against the counter, where a row of jars stood waiting to be packed. There was a crash as one slipped off onto the floor. "Ach, *Dummkopf*!" Felix muttered to himself. There was no time, no need to clean up the mess of broken glass and liquid on the kitchen floor. He was running out of space. He would not be back.

"We must be quick, eh, Schatzie?" Felix asked. The dog did not respond. Felix opened the refrigerator and emptied the jars into the trunk. Each jar had its place and was cushioned. Carefully, reverently, he placed the jar containing the Countess and the handprints in its special place in the trunk. Felix wrote a quick note to Helmut. Then he wrote another to Herbert and David, and placed it openly on his desk, where it would easily be seen. He left a special jar behind as well. He had already drugged Schatzie, who was sleeping soundly.

At six in the morning, the movers arrived, ready to take Felix to the dock, to the ship that would take him to his new destination.

Felix tapped the trunk. "Careful with that." Inside, the future slept in its jars, circling head to tail, as if in mothers' wombs. The Rat dreamed on, shrinking more and more into herself, circling head to feet, as if her body had been made for this moment. A greenish light came from the trunk, even as the men carried it carefully. The handprints sizzled and leaped with excitement, merging their hot will to live with all the other animate parts of beings that Felix had collected. A smell of phosphorus rose from the trunk as two strong men staggered under its weight.

"Jeez, man, what you got in there?"

"My personal effects, gentlemen. My worldly effects." Felix planned to tip them well. He smiled as he walked, and with satisfaction, he inserted his monocle into his eye socket. He did not wake the sleeping Schatzie, but rolled her in a blanket and tucked her under his arm.

Before closing the door of the apartment behind him, Felix took one last look upward at the angelic faces of the many children he had served. They looked down at him out of the frames, into their future lives, their loves, their own children. "For Uncle Felix with love." "This, too, has been part of my real life," he thought. "This, too."

He felt pride, even now, at this moment, holding his dog in a rug under his arm, and a small shabby suitcase in his other hand. As Felix stood at the top of the stairs and supervised the downward descent of the trunk, he thought again of the children and said good-bye to them in his heart. Too bad he did not have enough place for their sweet faces in their glass frames, but his trunk was already full, given over to the sacrament of glass jars holding new life.

"I will make many more children," he thought. And he squared his shoulders with pride. A super-race of superchildren. "And most of them from me," he thought. "So now, my new children," he addressed the specimens within the trunk, "we go forward. Forward, into a new world."

The vermilion cry of four stringed instruments screeching in unison illuminated his departure. "Don't leave us. Don't leave us here alone!"

"Sorry, my boys. I am truly sorry. But it's *auf Wiedersehen* for now. Till we meet again."

Felix closed the apartment door behind him, walking behind his trunk. There was the sound of a plucked string from the apartment he had left.

Was all the wine of the night before making him giddy? Or was it the sudden rush of early-morning air striking his face and body? Why was this precipitate departure filling him with such joy? It was freedom, freedom to end a life that had already become too entrapping. It was the freedom of picking up, packing up, and leaving. Soon there would be the usual troubles: papers, officials, the effort of finding a place to put down his trunk and suitcase. What if the Führer's house and place for Felix were not already prepared? In a part of himself, he knew that might be possible. Only . . . only . . . "No, my Führer will not let me down," he thought. Felix forced his thinking into more positive channels again. For he was leaving his worldly practice to devote himself full-time to the regeneration of life. Already, as he said good-bye to his New York surroundings, he was preparing himself for the work to come.

"My children, we have work to do!" he called gaily down to the two moving men who now, near the final turn of the landing, set the trunk down on one end and took a breath. "It is a new day!" cackled Felix.

"Oh yeah?" The men regarded the little doctor sourly. Felix's monocle glittered in the early-morning daylight, and his bushy hair stood on end, making an aureole around his head like the illustrations in the German children's book *Struwwelpeter.* "What is he so happy about?" They looked at each other.

"A fine morning, gentlemen," said Felix, stumbling down the stairs after them. Felix struggled under the weight he was carrying. In his small suitcase, he had managed to reserve a special place for his photograph of the Führer, and his own personal specimen, the bit from his own sex. Otherwise, the bag was filled with his journal observations and notes, a few personal grooming items such as his mustache comb, and that was all. Under the other arm, he held his heavily sleeping dachshund. "Wait for me," he panted.

"Forward!" The merchant ship *Calypso* was ready down at the docks, with instructions to carry its secret, most important passenger to Venezuela. A laboratory and a job were already waiting for him. On board, Joe Riley, the young captain, waited. In the port of La Guaira, the beautiful one-legged whore, Carmelita, was also waiting hungrily for Joe. The parrot on his shoulder, Sugar, took an instant dislike to Felix, and as he walked onto the deck, Sugar, squawking, hurtled out and grabbed him by the nose.

But Felix was now safely on the boat and out of the harbor, turning from time to time to gaze back at the receding skyline of New York with mingled pleasure and regret. Then he allowed himself to look fully forward, to the horizon, toward which the boat was steaming. Felix finally put Schatzie, still in her rug, on the deck near his feet and lit a cigar. He leaned on the rail. For a brief time, at least, he could relax.

Three hours later, when David and his men from the federal government, carrying their solemn warrant of arrest for espionage, came to Felix's apartment, they did not even have to break open the door. David sounded the bell a couple of times. Then he tried the handle. The door swung open, welcoming them inside. Above, the somber faces of little children watched them enter, impassive. "To Uncle Felix with gratitude." The apartment was hushed.

"Anybody here?" But there was no one, no answer. "This the place?"

"Yes," said David.

But just as David had suspected—in fact, as he had halfway hoped—Felix was no longer there. David felt a mixture of exasperation and relief. He rubbed his grainy eyes. Cold morning light leaked all over the place, revealing the shabby carpet and curtains. Felix's office was tidy, the instruments carefully laid out beside the sterilizer, and the examining table with a fresh sheet on it. All was impeccable.

David went to Felix's desk and halfheartedly opened and shut the drawers. He was hoping to find nothing. And his hopes were rewarded. "This is it, gentlemen," he said. He wanted to go home, home to Ilse and the children, back to that little room where he could at least lay his head down for a moment and take a few hours' repose. But he could not ask for that. His personal life he kept secret from the men with whom he worked. Of course there was a dossier on him; he knew that. But as long as things were not spoken aloud, David could keep his family alive. Somewhere, he was important, needed, and the core of a family. Somewhere in the world—in fact, right here in New York, across town, if anyone cared to know it. "Oh, hurry up!" he thought, as the agents opened and shut each drawer again.

David walked into what had served as Felix's kitchen and blinked. A large jar stood on the counter. From it rose a briny smell, and a glow. Within it, now totally silent, curved and imploring, lay the meek little fingers of the Tolstoi Quartet. David looked, first at the jar and then away for a moment, clearing his vision to look again more closely. The fingers lay without sound. On the counter, there was also a large crinkled envelope. David took it. "Whistle the first few lines of the Mozart—you will know which one—and these boys will find their way to their rightful owners. Sorry for all the trouble. Heil Hitler." Felix had scribbled this in Esperanto.

From the mess of brine and glass shards on the floor at his feet, in a great heave and shudder, a small dachshund staggered up, groveling and licking at David's shoes. "Schatzie!" said David, thinking he recognized the dog. The dog he called Schatzie snuffled and snorted, wiggling the entire back half of her body in ecstatic greeting. The dog shook off the glass shards from her short hair. And it was then that David saw that this dog, now wagging her behind most enthusiastically as she begged to be loved, to be picked up, gathered in, and taken home to a family, had a slight but visible deviation that made it impossible to call her Schatzie. The dog, a Schatzie replica in almost all respects, differed in a most important one. This dog, now thumping unmistakably in greeting, had two tails. Two tails! Yes, two perfect tails.

David recoiled from the dog. Then, in one gesture, saying, "All right, all right," he patted the dog and bent down and picked it up. "All right." The fingers began to drum a strange rhythm on the glass.

David felt in his bones the beginnings of relaxation. All he wanted was summer, which he knew was coming, and then, for his family, a quiet place with a garden. In his mind, he saw himself teaching little Philip to play chess. Music filled the dream space where he watched this scene, his father aging, watching this with him. Then David watched himself also aging, sitting in the garden with his wife and children, then Maria growing up, then Philip.

He put his arm around his wife, who sat with a basket of apples, which she was peeling, while the wind blew its autumn leaves about the garden. There was music coming from the house behind them. Ilse looked at her husband lovingly. He tightened his arm around her; no need to say a word. Maria and Philip married; their children played in the garden. David and Ilse were old now, peaceful. The War had ended long ago. And at their feet in that autumn garden, an old dog watched them and laid its head on its paws. The old dog, the family dog. *Thump, thump,* a soft brushing sound that accompanied them always, hardly noticed, so constant was it through their lives. The sound of two tails, two happy tails wagging in unison. "Yes, Mitzie. Dear Mitzie," they crooned to the dog.

Thump, thump. Swishing through life.

Chapter 25

THE LIVERWURST SOLUTION

Before leaving, David picked up the smoky lab jar that held the fingers and queasily closed it. The liquid was oily and the fingers started to circle. He put the jar in his briefcase and walked to midtown. That afternoon, he waited at the Automat. "Enjoy the dance," David said to the jar. "It might be your last." The fingers gyrated madly in their amniotic brew.

David waited a long time in front of a curdled cup of coffee. He knew that the members of the Tolstoi Quartet, informed by his father, would come to him. Finally, by late afternoon, curious and pulled by news they could only half understand, the musicians arrived. "We expected your father, Herr Hofrat." They looked at David suspiciously.

Their eyes were furtive yet hopeful. Shabby and unwashed, clutching their instruments, the Quartet seated themselves at the scratched Formica table. The chairs protested as the men pulled them in. "So, my boy, have you brought news for us?"

David unscrewed the lid of the large jar and placed it on the table. Furious green fumes rose up. The men peered at David and then at the jar and its contents. They looked at one another, while David nodded encouragement. One by one, they slid their damaged hands into the open jar. The life-giving fluid was noxious, pea green and bilious. It rose up to meet each violation of its surface, and lapped, carnivorous, to catch each hand.

Voraciously, each severed finger leaped onto its place on the hand of its rightful owner as if to strangle it. They attached themselves and started sucking greedily.

The shock was so secret and so immediate that no one could speak. It had happened so suddenly. Without a further word, the men pushed back their chairs and left the Automat.

David sat there wondering what to do with the jar and where to pour the remaining liquid. He dumped his leftover cup of coffee into the jar, and quickly, before anyone could notice, he, too, ran out of the Automat. The jar waited on the stained table. That evening, it would be added to the huge ever-steaming pot of unusually strengthening pea soup. There would be a number of street fights in the city the next day among the temporarily insane warriors who had ordered soup for lunch.

The Quartet walked through the city grimly without speaking. Their left hands were tightly curled around their newfound brothers. A green cloud surrounded them. "Welcome back," crooned the restored hands from every cell as they caressed their prodigals. Holding their precious left hands carefully, the musicians entered the subway and took the long trip back to their underground living quarters. Their shabby basement room was home to them now. And all of New York City was their city now. They walked the last blocks. The great-spired city, its dusk like conflagration, reverberated with magnificence. The organ notes of sunset were calling to one another, orange-purples and a corolla of reds. Sound ricocheted from the gleaming towers. A hundred thousand little lights went on. "We've been here all along," they blinked. "Did you just notice us?"

"And where have you been, my darlings?" asked the fingers of the restored missing ones. "We have been waiting so long for you."

"Wait and find out," thought the pinkies impatiently to themselves. They couldn't bear to be touched, for they were different now. But the hands could not keep from caressing the soft pads, the fingertips no longer calloused, of the newfound fifth fingers.

"We have been so lost without you. Now we are complete." They stroked each other in the safe snail of the closed hands. The pinkies shook off the grasp of thumbs and loving palms. Being fingered by others irritated them.

Once back in their room, the Quartet could not wait to try their beautiful new hands. The instruments bucked in their cases, ready to be let out. "Easy, boys," the musicians soothed as they carefully released their instruments and began the ritual of wiping them down. They were gentle and loving, and the left hands lay compliant.

"Bach," the first violinist declared. "It must be Bach. For thou shalt have no other God before Bach. The hushed harmonies of God." He stopped, and the musicians hesitated. "No," he said, correcting himself, "Mozart. Mozart is more joyful."

"Yes!" cried the fingers in finger language, unwinding themselves from one another and stretching. The lost brothers twitched in the presence of their newly attached siblings and tried to free themselves from this quintuplet group behavior.

As the first strains of the Mozart Quartet No. 1 in G Major began, it was evident that something was wrong. Discordancy and squeaking erupted along the fingerboards. Since the musicians were rusty, they tried to ignore the involuntary misbehavior of their left hands. They pressed closer to their instruments, urging the music forward with their bowing arms. But the hands cramped and the fingers squabbled against one another.

For the newcomers, these regenerated fingers, were not "normal." They had become superfingers. They were no longer team players. After being nourished for so many months by Felix's brew of liverwurst and other life-enhancing substances, they had evolved into a master race of little fingers. They stretched in strange ways, made sexually suggestive motions, and clambered all over the strings of their instruments in lewd postures. They threatened to break the others' knuckles. Angrily, they shoved and scratched. "Move out of the way!" They reached out and hammered the notes of all the parts.

But the other fingers and thumbs would have none of this. Calloused, with strongly developed muscles, they also fought back. "Keep off, this is my note," they insisted, shoving just as hard. Nevertheless, the old fingers were being pushed out of their way by the superpinkies, and they could no longer hit the true notes. Those new digits were dominant, prehensile. They could do anything, reach any note at any moment, and hit the top harmonics, too. They were aggressive and warlike. "We're the boss now!"

While the fingers quarreled about who would be boss, the musicians stopped playing. "What is it?" asked the second violinist. "What are they doing?" He looked at his twisted fingers, excitedly scratching one another. "Listen."

"Can it be? I think they were playing Wagner." The cellist sighed. "It sounds so dark and so horrible. This is not Mozart!" This was the dawn of a new race, a master race with master fingers. It was the sound of triumph and victory.

Outshouting the sweet notes of Mozart, the little fingers tapped the *Meistersinger* overture, which Hitler had decreed for every rally.

The Tolstoi musicians listened to the music and watched their alien fifth fingers knocking out every note. The new fingers were celebrating the immolation of the old order.

The Quartet realized that the new fingers had to be retrained.

The musicians decided to use a system of punishment and reward. Recognizing that only Germanic authority would work at first, they reluctantly began spanking their lost fingers. The new pinkies were strong-willed, but the Quartet simply would not tolerate Wagner. Each time they pushed another finger out of the way, each time they secretly plucked down a Wagnerian note, the musicians whacked the offending fingers with their bows. "This hurts me more than it hurts you!" they grunted. Then the cellist cried, "It hertz!" The four men doubled over in laughter.

Deprived of the elixir that had sustained them, and without Felix's formula, the fingers slowly shrank. They were no longer special. They missed their liverwurst mixture, pig fat and innards, which the Quartet, on principle, refused to serve. To stave off all noxious Germanic influences, the Quartet switched to Italian salami instead. The little fingers became weaker and more compliant. The men worked hard to accustom them again to the familiar classical tuning, to move them down on the strings, to get over the habit of pressing the strings slightly higher and sharper, when the rest of the fingers were peacefully obeying their traditional tuning.

For tuning had changed. In the middle of the nineteenth century, some composers and players had started adding additional stretch to their instrumental tuning, But in 1939, Goebbels, then Minister of Propaganda, made it official. He decided to change the tuning of all musical instruments. The note A was cranked from 432 hertz to 440. The old classical tuning of A, as it stood, was too calming, too inward. Goebbels wanted something that would incite the crowds. Though not discernible to the human ear, this change moved the whole tuning up, one whole tone sharper and more insistent. The director of music, Furtwängler, supported this edict. It was known that Verdi, Italian and individualist, had refused to alter all his tuning, while Richard Wagner, his nineteenth-century contemporary, had complied. The operas of Wagner, Teutonic, nationalistic, now with an entire industry devoted to them at Bayreuth, inspired the passions of the Führer. That was enough reason for Goebbels's decision. He did a few experiments in support of the edict. And the music of Wagner was on the last program given by the Berlin Philharmonic Orchestra before it was forced to close its doors at the end of the War.

The government-ordered tuning was effective at inciting mob violence. People went berserk more easily, and no one knew why. Soon all of Germanic-conquered Europe was screwed to a higher pitch. Beneath the perception of hearing, the tuning raised the level of crowd anxiety and patriotism. It was a do-something tuning. Inspired by this new level of sound, crowds went wild. People could be easily persuaded now. Political speeches rose to a shriller tone, and the music did, too. An immense collective destruction rose uneasily at the sound of military bands, the warlike sounds of triumph and anxiety. Later, European orchestras would tune their instruments even higher, some to 444 and beyond.

The members of the Tolstoi Quartet had never been made aware of Goebbels's edict regarding the new tuning, and even so, they would have ignored it. But the new fingers were restive. The Nazi 440 they were accustomed to made the old tuning sound a little flat to them. Each time the little fingers inched their way a bit above the normal note according to the old tuning, the Tolstoi musicians whacked them again with their heavy horsehair and Pernambuco bows.

After a while, the pinkies were forced to play melodically with the others. Hitched like oxen forever joined to the rest of the hand, the new fingers became sullen and sluggish. They drooped, were less eager to dominate all the notes and the other fingers. They feigned sleep and finally refused to move at all, falling asleep during passages where they were called up to excel, lulled into laziness by the more interior sound of the old tuning. They buckled and lay down on the job.

"Work for a living!" the men cried, flogging their fingers unmercifully. Sore at night, resentful and full of self-pity, the pinkies finally learned. And so they went back to work.

When the pinkies started to behave again, the men allowed them a tiny smear of liverwurst on their knuckles. But it would take a lot of smears of liverwurst to retrain those hands to play as one. And a long time to get the little fingers out of their reflexive Wagnerian obsession and back into harness with good old Mozart.

Chapter 26

OBEY

"A deline." Herbert took the thin hands of his ailing wife in his. "Wake up. I have news." Beside her bed, David watched, as if from a distance, his mother and father.

Adeline stirred, as if to avoid the two men. Perhaps she had been dreaming. "Open your eyes, my dearest," Herbert coaxed.

The frail woman moved her head again, as if in protest against this harsh presence, this intrusive light that tingled at her eyelids. She moved her thin hands.

"Look," Herbert said, awed. "She is practicing."

"Mother . . . ," David began timidly. But he was frightened of her, this old woman with the savage ability to wound.

"My little girl." Herbert seized her hands in his and kissed them. Adeline withdrew her hands and regarded him suspiciously. If she squinted, she could make him out to be a total stranger, an intrusive one. Not the one she had loved best. No, not that one.

"You did this!" she hissed to him, malevolent as a goose, indicating with her fierce gaze the entire women's ward. "Look at me. I am nothing!"

In despair, she sank again into her sallow reverie. But her fingers plucked on, practicing the piano on the top of the folded sheet.

"Stop that, my darling." Herbert again took her two hands in his. "I have something to tell you."

She did not respond. "Something remarkable. Something marvelous," Herbert coaxed. "A surprise for you."

David turned away, impatient. He hated his father's cloying way of humoring his mother, who, for as long as he could remember, had always been impossible. What hypocrisy, their formal relation. "I grew up without love," he thought for a moment, and tears sprang to his reddened, exhausted eyes. He was condemned to care for these two mad old people forever.

"So when am I going to get my turn to live?" he demanded of the silent, invisible Michael. "It's your fault, leaving me with them like this. 'When?' I ask." The spirit of Michael said nothing, curled slyly around the steam pipes.

Herbert was still leaning over Adeline's bedside, whispering soft, crooning words of love and encouragement, and Adeline shook them away. "No," she said to Herbert impatiently. "Leave me alone to sleep."

David sighed, forced once again to witness his elderly parents in their approach-avoidance dance. "Papa, get to the point," he interjected impatiently.

The two old people hardly noticed him, so intent were they on playing their script. "Look," said Herbert finally, cupping Adeline's chin in his hand. "David's here."

"David?" Adeline's wondering gaze fell on him. Did she see him at all?

The ghost of Michael smiled in its sly way and slithered closer.

"I'm so tired of your suffering," David said to his dead brother. "That eternal suffering. Always. Where is the place for me in this family? You've taken all the air. Oh," thought David, exasperated, "just as you always have. It was always you. Michael the gifted, the special, the sensitive! How I have hated you."

"Brother, I forgive you, for you know not what. . . ." Michael wreathed himself closer to his family in a sanctimonious, ingratiating way.

David tried to get a hold of himself. "I forgive you, too," he thought, feeling guilty at once for the fact of his ruddy survival.

He thought of his younger brother. "How could you be so different from me? Mama's favorite. You should have been the same. But Mama divided us." The steam pipes hissed in the bare room. In the nearby beds, troubled old women tossed and muttered.

Now the spirit of Michael wreathed itself about the body of David. "That is true, my brother. We were different. Now you are alive, and you must live for me just the same."

Together, the brothers, one dead, one alive, regarded their aged parents, the tableau they made on the bed. "Take care of them for me," said Michael.

David brushed away the smoke that was his brother and tears sprang to his eyes. "My brother," he whispered, overcome by tenderness. "It was always you I loved best." He thought of the golden-haired boy who had been Michael.

Michael ruffled David's thinning hair. A gust of heat—or was it a current of air?—from the pipes caressed David's neck.

Adeline opened her eyes and stared at her grown son beside her. This time, her eyes were lucid, focused. "David. What are you doing here at this time of day?" she asked accusingly. "Why aren't you at work?" Adeline turned to Herbert. "Why isn't he at work?" Then turning back to David, she asked harshly, "And how are Ilse and the children?"

"Fine, Mama. Just fine. Maria's at the top of her class, and Philip will be starting kindergarten soon."

Adeline fell back on the pillow again and allowed her eyes to fog. "That wife of yours, is she still working as hard? She ought to be home with your children. The woman has no sense." Her hands resumed their plucking.

"I'll tell her," David muttered.

Herbert shot him a glance. Then, as if barely tolerating this interruption by his elder son, Herbert leaned forward and began again. "Listen to me."

Adeline said nothing, but it was clear in her grouchy demeanor that she was temporarily in truce mode.

"Are you ready, my darling? Because I have brought some special visitors to see you today."

"No visitors!" Adeline hissed, turning her aristocratic head away from her husband. But it was too late. "Why do you always bother me?"

"Too late," cried Herbert, the magic maker. He sprang to his feet and twirled twice on his toes, then extended a raggedy arm toward the doorway. "Come in, my good fellows."

The members of the Tolstoi Quartet, who had been waiting outside in the hospital corridor as if in the wings of a great hall, entered the room. They walked briskly, their newly shined shoes making a brisk staccato on the tile floor. They were dressed today as for a performance, wearing their suits with tails, their best ones, and the shirts starched to the chin. They carried their instruments unsheathed in gloved hands.

Adeline's mouth fell open. "Prop me up," she commanded her husband, and suddenly she was imperious and ramrod straight against the pillows.

"The Haydn," the first violinist said as he tucked his violin firmly under his chin. He nodded to the others, who immediately assumed their positions, the cellist sitting on the bed next to Herbert as if he had every right.

The first violinist plucked a string delicately with one gloved finger, and the others tuned quickly. "Now," said the leader. There was no hesitation. They began.

Like butter, like warm golden light, like prayers, like small white shining doves, the notes flew upward to the vaulted ceiling of the grimy psychiatric asylum.

It was heavenly music—that is to say, music that was always meant to be, music that existed even before the first notes sounded. The notes carved a place for themselves in the universe, just by their sounding, which had always been there. It had been the listening world that had been hollow, waiting to receive them.

"We are here; we are together once again." The musician's gloved fingers found their way over the strings with ease, as if there had never been a period of silence.

Adeline clutched her frayed pink bed jacket to her throat. For once, she forgot to complain. Herbert held her other hand in his. The two old people watched and listened to the Quartet with baby-shining eyes. David, watching them, saw how it was between them, how it had been. These two people who had happened to be his parents, who had happened to have their world destroyed.

"I am listening," whispered Michael from under the bed. Did David imagine that whisper? No matter. Haydn sang of different times, of happiness, a reality without words, a moment of sunshine and flowers. Music issuing into a garden where a child sat frowning at a chessboard.

"Forget!" sang the music. The first violinist caught David's eye while he played and, from his stance on tiptoe, winked at him, smiling. The instruments swayed like Thoroughbred horses, and the musicians rode them, rode the music.

All over the ward, old ladies were sitting up in their beds, forgetting to whimper or moan. Birds dipped and swooped through the room, silver light, like drops of water falling, shining, from a waterfall of sound. The instruments gleamed, their varnish catching the dazed morning light and sending it back upward in sheets of unison, of sound.

Adeline allowed herself to look directly at her husband, her eyes luminous. Herbert's eyes replied, "Do you see how I have always loved you?"

"Oh yes," Adeline's gaze replied. "And I you. My darling, it was always you I loved best. Always." Her eyes were steady.

"You are my dearest. My only one."

David caught all this, though not a word had been said, though above it all the music soared, singing its own crescendo of joy. The woody notes rippled.

How had David managed not to see the love that had always been there between his father and his mother? The world that had been jagged healed itself in that moment. He longed to throw himself on the hospital bed beside them both.

As if reading his mind, Adeline said, "Come here, my David." She motioned to him, patting the bed next to where the cellist was happily playing. "Come here, our darling."

Now David held himself, softened, his head in his arms, next to his mother and father.

Adeline stroked his head. Haydn played a counterpoint to his emotions.

"Our boy," said Herbert also, patting his grown son's thinning hair.

David wept, finding his way back.

The last notes of the Haydn finished with an upswept flourish. The sound, shivering, hung in the air after the musicians had lifted their bows, their arms lofting the final notes upward. There was a silence, the memory of sound.

The old ladies of the ward burst into feeble applause, the ragged sleeves of their nightdresses fluttering. "Bravo!"

But the family did not move: David, Herbert, and Adeline, bent in tableau. David lay with his head buried in his mother's lap while she absently stroked him with restless fingers. Beside her on the bed, Herbert, too, sat with his surviving son. It could have been a stable: the old ladies, watching figures in a child's Christmas crèche, the musicians in obeisance like wise men. "Only . . . only, the religion is wrong," thought David, "and the setting as well. From whence came the metaphor? Abraham and Isaac? Cain and Abel?" "Bless me, Father . . . ," he murmured into the bedclothes. "Forgive me, my brother."

The musicians removed their gloved hands from their instruments' strings and bowed. Like plunging horses, the instruments also bowed their necks, whinnying slightly. The men began to speak in perfect thirds. The faint after-harmony floated, winged black notes, upward into the room. "We can play again!"

"All thanks to Herr Hofrat." The first violinist did not say more, as if knowing this was a private topic.

"And thanks to the young Hofrat, too," the second violinist added, holding up a gloved hand and wagging it.

"A miracle," echoed the other two men.

"No." Herbert hunched his shoulders humbly.

"Yes." Adeline caressed his cheek. "It is a miracle."

"So now"—the first violinist beamed, rising on his toes again—"we prepare for Carnegie Hall." He turned to Adeline. "And you, dear lady, will, I hope, accompany us?"

Adeline turned to Herbert, cupping his chin in her hands and forcing him to look directly into her eyes. "Herbert, are you mad? What are you thinking of? How could you imagine I would be capable?"

Turning to the Tolstoi Quartet, she added, "My husband must have been insane ever to promise you such a thing." She softened a bit. "I am an old woman now. It is a long time since we played together in Vienna, and now I beg you to excuse me." The queen, refusing to carry money.

"My darling," Herbert remonstrated.

"No, Herbert," said Adeline firmly. "Be quiet. Stop exaggerating." Turning again to the Quartet, she was coy. "You see, I prefer at this time in my life to play only for my husband. I am not interested in the public; not at all." She gestured disdainfully at the ward, at the old women now nattering themselves to sleep again. "That world is not for me. I want only the private world of my family now. Don't argue with me," she snapped at Herbert. "My mind is made up. I shall go home to live with my husband and son and grandchildren," she announced. "It is time to pick up our lives again. And I shall play the piano again. But no, gentlemen, not for the public. Never. I despise the masses too much."

Adeline's eyes changed. "My Herbert, my David," she whispered.

"Say 'My Michael!'" the steam pipes pleaded.

"Michael." Adeline's heart groaned. "My Michael. Come." She opened her arms. "It is you, dearest child, I have always loved best."

"I am here," said the steam.

"It is you whom we always loved best," David and Herbert echoed silently. "Stay with us. Always."

"I will," the ghost of Michael promised.

The doors of the train closed, the train pulled out of the station, and their pale, frightened boy tried desperately to tear open the doors again.

"Look!" The first violinist was holding up his gloved hand, interrupting their joint reverie. "Our hands are as good as new."

"Better," added the second violinist.

"Only, the strangest thing . . . ," the first man continued. The rest of the Quartet, instruments included, watched him expectantly. "You see," he said, "our fingers are fine now. But our repertoire has changed."

"We were rehearsing the other day and—"

"Amazing," said the cellist, sounding the bass notes.

"We found that—"

"Everything came perfectly."

"But we can no longer play modern music," the first violinist said.

The four men nodded in agreement. "Yes, it is true."

"From now on, we play only the classics. Haydn. Schubert. Bach. Beethoven. Mozart, of course. Dear Mozart. And in exactly six months, we shall play in Carnegie Hall. It's all arranged. So you see, Herr Hofrat," he concluded with a flourish of exactitude, "the Tolstoi Quartet is, as usual, right on schedule."

"Are you certain you will not join us onstage, dear lady?" the first violinist asked once more, for form's sake.

"No," replied Adeline regally. "I shall be in the first row to hear you. And afterward, I shall give a supper for the Tolstoi Quartet. A magnificent supper." Her eyes brightened. "Everyone will come. Champagne. Caviar!" Her eyes glittered and she spoke more quickly, feverish, as she began to mutter her guest list.

David and Herbert looked at each other, then looked away. "Calm yourself, my darling," Herbert said mildly, patting her hands.

"Everyone always loved my parties," she said. "And you will, of course, play for us after the concert."

The members of the Tolstoi Quartet were beginning to feel uneasy.

"Yes, of course they will," Herbert said.

"Herbert," commanded Adeline, her voice rising. "You stupid little man. What are you doing, just sitting here? What are you waiting for? Go off and find the nurses and get me out of here."

Herbert hesitated.

"Do what I say this time, for once," she said impatiently. "Ohh!" She looked at David. "David, go home and tell your wife that your mother is coming back to live. Go on!" She pushed him gently. "I am fine now. I am well. I want to see my grandchildren."

As David hesitated, she reached out and took him in her arms. "My darling boy. You will see, we will be happy together. Ilse needs the help; the children need someone to oversee their education."

David doubted that, but now was not the moment to say anything. He would just have to break it to Ilse somehow. He looked at his father, but his father's face and hooded eyes warned him. Obey.

Adeline turned to Herbert, who sat helpless, looking at the equally helpless Tolstoi Quartet. "Men," said Adeline, "have they no sense?"

She looked at the men around her. "There is so much to do," she said. "Pick up our lives. Prepare for your magnificent debut in New York. The guest list. We do not have much time. We are not getting any younger. Herbert." She shook her dazed husband. "Do you hear me? I want to live our days together, not rot here in this hellhole." She gestured to the ward.

Michael tightened his grip about her neck.

"I know," she muttered impatiently. "But the past is past." She willed herself into clarity. "It is time to go home," she commanded.

Home! A complicated concept.

Chapter 27

DIVERTIMENTO

Home. A difficult concept in a new world. How to find oneself at home again? America banged with the sound of its newness. Far away, the blanketed cities of Europe huddled, the rust of blood on their stones. All that dark tragic history, that sense of cynicism and fatalism, led to a point of view that would be known, in the more dignified sense, as "European philosophy." All founded on certainty, fear, and the inability to prevent death. Europe reeked of death. As it did of philosophy about death.

Here hopes rained like gold, promises burned the land to a crisp, and there was no history to be seen in the hastily thrown-up houses of the United States of America. "Thank God, no history," thought the refugees. By which they meant, no history from which to hide.

The major parts of their lives were lived in the key of Memory, the darkest chord of all. They were to resonate to that combination of notes for the rest of their lives, even their children, and those children's children, would always feel in themselves that urgent straining, moaning sound. Lives lived in the key of B minor.

So to find again the concept of home. Would they ever? And did it matter, finally, in the end? Home would be burdened, secretive and surreptitious, dark and quarrelsome, with moments of coziness and even, if one dared, a little tenderness. And in the end, they would have lived together, grieved, loved one another to the best of their abilities, and survived the Old World and the New.

Herbert's ears, large and translucent, thrummed to the A sound. In the New York Public Library, hunched though he might seem, his heart fluttered with excitement, even when he seemed most humble. He floated on the stairway, or slightly above the floor of the reading room, close to the angels of libraries, the angels that bent over the newspapers draped on the racks and whispered "Shush, shush" soothingly. Herbert was near them, supported by golden light. Herbert vibrated to the A of *Animus*, of *Angel*.

Was he, as rumored, the Grand Vizier of the International Society of Freemasons? A former minister? The keeper of the ward room? Was he the former head groom of the stables of the Austro-Hungarian Empire? Was he the undersecretary of trade? Or the valet of that undersecretary? He floated joyfully on the universal tone of the A, the tone of the new world. A for *Aid*. A for *Adjust*. For *Antagonist*. A, also, alas, for *Appease,* his basic nature. A for *Arms*.

"I am Alive." Herbert's blood sang, "I am useful. Use me, my dear people. Ask me. As long as I Am, I shall Assist. This is my reason for being." He bent his head in gratitude. How else to repay the debt of being Alive?

How could it be that he lived and his younger son did not? Herbert would have exchanged places—he saw always the eyes of his grieving wife—but fate had not decreed this. His purpose was to stay Alive, to bring his family and others to the new land, to quiver to the universal A, to refuse to submit to B minor. "Lord, you ask too much of me!" Herbert's shabby shoulders hunched under their burdens.

"Only what you can support," was the answer that came, sealed by that heavy ring, the moist lips upon it, his papery, dry hands seized between the clutching hands of others. The wet, too-prolonged kiss, the reverent but insistent pleading. Did no one but he sense the deep irony of it all?

"Lord, I am just a little man."

"My servant."

Herbert knew he was addressing a void. An atheist from early childhood, a rationalist, a believer in Esperanto and the goodness of man, a believer in rational solutions to the world's conflicts, he was ironic enough to know that beliefs ultimately meant nothing. He was not afraid to express, even to himself, that there was no God. Even if, sometimes, he prayed to this No-God, involuntarily, trying to impress his own will on circumstances. Herbert believed in power. It was only power that could command, from time to time, a power made of money and threats and goodwill and the gift of his personality.

Still, in spite of it all, Herbert held on to his belief in mankind and its need for communication. Chess, Esperanto, rational appeals to human solutions, the international rights of man— these were the only hopes. Oh, yes, and children. His grandchildren. His own personal hopes. Soon he would begin reading Goethe with Maria. She was almost old enough. Only in his grandchildren could he hope to pass on the traditions of learning. If there was to be any pride that Herbert would allow himself, it was only when he thought of his grandchildren.

Herbert could not envision a time when he would not frequent the Automat, making deals for human lives. He could not imagine a day not spent at the New York Public Library, where, out of the gloom of the great hushed hall, small figures broke from the general dimness to fling themselves at his feet, presenting their appeals. He felt each life, each loss, as if it had been his own. But in another way, like a giant rock in the water, he felt nothing. He was implacable-seeming, even while he was being imperceptibly worn down.

"Bless you, Herr Hofrat." He allowed his ring to be kissed. His eyes closed for a moment in remembered pain. But there was no time for his own feelings, really. "Bless you."

"I am of service," he replied humbly. "I am at your service. What can I do for you?" He waited, he listened, his large ears backlit, his head like an aureole.

Tonight, shoulders bent, as always, under the shabby overcoat, Herbert waited beside the outstretched arm of the usher, before the ranks of seats in the front row of Carnegie Hall. He stood aside to allow Adeline to enter.

Adeline was wearing her best finery today: the silk dress, low cut over the shrunken bosom, the fine pearly stockings, the shoes, the kid gloves, alabaster to the elbow, with little pearl buttons all the way up. She wore her good fur jacket with the silk lining, into which was woven, over and over, the coat of arms of the Emperor Franz Joseph, delicately embossed. Most important, she wore slung about her neck a stole made of little dead foxes, two of them, their sharp teeth still yapping in protest, their small dark eyes open, veiled and glassy, as in the moment of death. Their entwined tails dangled over her left shoulder. And Adeline wore her hat, black and smart.

The rest of the family followed. Maria was enthralled by the foxes, their sharp glassy eyes and black-button noses. She, too, wore her best dress. She and Philip, solemn in their importance, had promised to sit quietly throughout the entire concert.

As Herbert stood aside to allow his wife to enter the front row, a ripple of whispers swept the hall. "Herr Hofrat," the voices rustled, like many little leaves, leaves of the weeping willow, shaken out of weeping into a moment of recognition. "With his family."

The rustling of the audience gathered force, swept from the first rows to the last and up into the first and second balconies. "Herr Hofrat!" Leaning forward, the audience was composed almost entirely of refugees, all of whom had turned out to hear their own, their finest musicians in this city of strangers.

Herbert, embarrassed, sank into his seat. But Adeline stood up immediately, poking him with her elbow. Applause ricocheted off the chandeliers, the royal red velvet curtains, the gilded moldings. Herbert became smaller. Graciously, Adeline turned and faced the audience. She inclined her head regally while she adjusted the little foxes, their bared, snarling teeth, around her neck with one delicate gloved hand. She bowed, her nostrils flaring with the exhilaration of being once again center stage. There had been times when she had been applauded like this in the past. She smiled, self-satisfied.

But the audience would not be quiet, would not sit down. On their feet, they continued to applaud. Their cries rose to the ceiling. "Herr Hofrat!"

Herbert hunched modestly in his seat. But finally, when it was clear that the audience would not stop until he did something, he raised one hand and gave a little wave. "Thank you, my friends. Now, please, sit down."

The great animal of the audience swelled. There was the noise of many people creaking, the rustling of old coats, the smell of wet wool, the readjusting of bodies into seats, and a few coughs.

Herbert hated displays of any kind. "I am so tired," he thought.

A hush in the hall, and a single spotlight on the rich velvet curtains. The chandeliers were dimmed, their luster fading slowly. Maria leaned forward in her seat. Her chest would almost burst with the beauty of anticipation, royal red excitement of the just-before.

The Tolstoi Quartet entered onto the stage in Germanic precision, stopping in front of Herbert, aligned, to bow once, briskly, before taking their seats. Instruments gleamed in their gloved hands. The first violinist nodded. And then the music began.

Mozart, of course. The music poured, con brio, out of the musicians' instruments. They swayed, obedient to their masters, bridled, then lifted and galloped. The chariot of the music took hold of Carnegie Hall, and as in the chariot of Phoebus Apollo, the audience was borne upward, up toward the sun itself. Life, the giver of life: Mozart, a golden god, like rays of the sun, showered notes upon the listeners.

The music lifted the listeners to the rafters of the great hall and then opened the roof so that they were dispersed into the starry sky. And through this music, they were vouchsafed another glimpse of the Europe they had left.

Not the Europe of sighs, of darkness. Not the Europe of prejudice disguised as new intellectual thought. Not the Europe of bigotry and jealousy. For hadn't insatiable jealousy been the innate cause of this diaspora? The Jews knew it, much as they tried to hide their scorn for the stupidity of "the blond, blue-eyed ones." The jealousy. How they feared it. It started among children way before the school yard. But in Europe, nothing stopped it. The Continent ran on jealousy. Territorial expansion, covetousness. A small, mean series of countries where everyone knew everybody else's business.

As the music lifted in Carnegie Hall, another Europe, the "real Europe," or perhaps the "best of Europe," was to be heard, reminding the audience of its presence. The unreal, romantic Europe of storybooks. The Europe of beauty, of delicate music and flowers and wine and flirtatious glances. Beautiful meals served beautifully. A Europe of gracious people who wished only to enjoy themselves and think about the meaning of life at the same time. A Europe that valued education. And culture. And beauty, carefully cultivated. The cafés open along the boulevard Unter den Linden. The Tiergarten, with its many flowers just waiting to bloom in neat gardens along the paths. The churches. The *Platzes* and squares. The crystal, the china, the pastry gleaming with sugar and butter in the elegant rooms of the Hotel Sacher. Love affairs. Perfume. Music. Baroque architecture.

The naked Klimt girls, with their jeweled long hair and jeweled eyes, swirling above eye level. The grapes and cupids and goddesses on the stone windowsills of buildings. The ornamentation of life. Everywhere, what was man-made was made to delight the senses. Nothing was simply what it seemed.

Listening to the concert, the refugees strolled once more along the Ring. They sat in the park and let the sun warm their tired bodies. They drank *Kaffee mit Schlag*. They talked, talked endlessly. About everything and nothing. Once more, they felt the hopefulness of their philosophies. Philosophy that would soon blow to nothing in the light of history. But for now, a belief in education and in culture. Rational man. Some kind of hope.

As if that could somehow veil the underlying barbarism that they had up until now believed was to be found only in America and in some regions of Siberia. Places where the natives were not civilized enough to appreciate Mozart.

When the concert was over, the Mozart, the Haydn, and the Beethoven, the audience would not be quieted. Encore after encore. Finally, the first violinist held up a white-gloved hand.

And the Tolstoi Quartet sat down again and played one Strauss waltz after another until the sun came up on a new day in New York.

Only then did the audience agree to go home, picking up their old coats from their chairs, folding the programs and carefully putting them away and taking themselves and their sleeping children out into the streets of New York. Day was beginning in this icy new world, sharp and beautiful and bright. The first rays of the frosty morning sun touched the first skyscrapers. The Quartet packed up their instruments. They were getting ready for their tour now. Mozart and the old masters were in their guardianship.

Herbert ushered his family out into the breaking day. Maria sighed, lavish with the music she still heard. The family clasped the music to them as Adeline did her little foxes. They wrapped their coats, their music around them. The wind beat against David as he tightened his coat around his neck and, with his free hand, held Ilse against him. Neither of them spoke. Ilse carried Philip, and Maria clung to the hem of her coat. Herbert and Adeline walked together thoughtfully.

Maria heard the silver strains of the music as she walked, half-asleep. In counterpoint against it, jazzy, optimistic, came another sound. Morning in New York: another song.

"Come, children," Ilse said briskly. "Look, we've been up all night." The children tried to clear their eyes.

"Remember this." Herbert sighed. "You will not hear a concert like this again."

At home, a supper—now a breakfast—had been laid out in the little room. All was waiting for the family, the Quartet, and the audience known to Herbert and Adeline. They would host their friends, drink and talk into the full bloom of day.

Walking homeward, Ilse and David thought exhaustedly of

their couch, and their desire to be quiet together, to sleep. "Father has so many friends," David said, sighing, resigned, when the celebration had only been in the planning stages.

"We do this for your parents," Ilse reminded him. "It is our farewell to the city of New York." She looked at David tenderly. "Soon we shall have our own room together. Be patient, my darling."

"Herr Hofrat!" The Tolstoi Quartet, flushed and shining and out of breath, caught up with the little family just as they entered the foyer of the apartment building.

Far away, in a turquoise and fuchsia land of palm trees and jungles and dust, the homunculus that had once been Anna, the little Rat, stirred uneasily, enclosed in a jar. And the fingerprints of Rasputin blazed, dancing once more to music sensed rather than heard. The marks on her body flickered out forever.

Felix, ensconced in an underground laboratory, happily engaged in holding her jar up to light, found himself humming. He whistled, recognizing it was Mozart he was whistling. "Beautiful, eh, Schatzie?" he said as the dog wagged her behind, happy that her master was in such a good mood. Felix squinted once again at the jar. "It was a good trade, was it not, my darling?"

Chapter 28

O MY AMERICA!

"Maria, hurry up. We haven't got all day." So saying, Ilse left her daughter at the door to the now-denuded room. She had so much to do. She stood for a moment, uncertainly, then changed her mind again. Philip was with her parents-in-law at the zoo, so at least they were happily occupied. Perhaps if she hurried, she might have some time to organize the little house a bit before they all came back from their day.

"I'll be back for you in a little while. Just wait here. Be a good girl."

It was moving day.

Room. Doom. Gloom. These new American words clanged together in Maria's head as she stepped, for the last time, across the crumbling threshold into what had been the entire world just a few hours before.

Now the room held only vacancy. Its secrets blew across the floor, and the graying curtains fluttered listlessly. The clothesline, which had supported the blanket dividing Maria's little section from that of her grandfather, still delineated a space, but the space was open. The room was dirty, she saw. The cold-water faucet in the sink dripped, a worn brown track wending its way toward the drain. Gone was the small hot plate upon which Anna had prepared the morning tea. The sooty windowsill, which had held the family's milk and cheese, was an empty slab of stone. Out in the hall, the toilet gurgled horribly.

Maria shivered, alone in the desolate room. Her body felt hollow, shabby. She had grown, even though she had not wanted to. Her dress was again too short; her knees stuck out from the frayed hem. Washed forever, thin with the washing of it, the dress, made by Ilse, candy-striped and gay as an American girl was supposed to be, hung in listless folds about her body. Her long hair was limp, too, exhausted from brushing against her body. She rubbed her eyes. Her chest ached.

"I am leaving home," Maria told herself. Leaving home. Nothing, not her mother's bright false optimism, not the teasing love of her father, could cheer her up. She and Philip were nothing, she saw: two children, torn from their home. For what? A little brick doghouse far away?

"Why, Mummy?" Maria had asked. But her mother had not answered. The child was not important, Maria knew. It was only the grown-ups, the grown-ups with their squabbles and problems and sometimes their marvelous stories.

"I hate you," Maria muttered to her absent mother. It was only the old ones she liked. Some of them. Sometimes.

Obscurely, she blamed her mother for Aunt Anna's disappearance. If only her mother had taken the trouble to be nicer to the Rat. Anna, with her wonderful stories and romantic, suffering life, had been replaced by her grandmother Adeline, who was capricious and temperamental and forever having hysterical fits to which the whole family had to pay court.

Maria recognized in Adeline a definite threat. Before Adeline's arrival in their little room, Maria had been Herbert's pet. Her grandfather had fussed over her, lavished his love and attention. Maria smiled smugly. Even little Philip, a stupid baby boy, could not compete with the affection she, the elder grandchild, received. Philip? She traced a circle with her toe in the fine dust on the floor. Oh, he was cute, all right. But why did everyone expect her to love him? Well, she didn't, wouldn't! He was okay in a pinch, when there was nothing else to do, no one else to pay attention to her.

Maria smoothed her dress, then quickly, surreptitiously, felt her chest. Her little nipples stood up, hard as pencil points. She fluttered her hands over them. "You are beautiful," she whispered to herself. "You are my little beauty."

Who was saying these words? The wallpaper closed in on her—the buglike flowers she had always hated.

Maria stood in the small, stuffy, enclosed space and put her hands on her stomach. "You are my little beauty." Her stomach gurgled.

She put her hands down lower, there.

"No," Maria said firmly to the whispering. "I am not. I am dead. Can't you see?"

"You are not dead."

A wave of desperation rose up in the girl. She was dead. Nothing. Dead, a piece of garbage. All the hatred she contained for others—her mother, her brother—must mean that if she were not already dead, then she deserved to die. To be dead.

Maria felt faint.

"It's all right, my little darling. You'll be all right."

"But I hate everyone. I hate them so!"

"Yes."

Maria allowed the room to engulf her. It gave forth its wrinkly, cobwebbed, dusty smell. She felt completely alone in the world. There would never be anyone who would really understand her.

Overcome by a feeling of sadness and loneliness so suffocating that she thought she would never get over the pain of the weight of it on her body, she sank into the far corner and covered her face. Her dress lay in the dust, the brave stripes fading even faster.

Maria wanted to be forgotten, left behind in the room while the family moved away. She was ruined for life, and no one in the family could even see that. All they saw was the hollow shell of a little girl, a "good" little girl. But that "good" little girl was a mockery, a farce. A pretend person, not real. A bad girl, in fact, a shell of a person, someone who would never grow up, never love or be loved.

Her mother and grandmother could not imagine her feelings. Somehow, Maria knew, Uncle Felix had taken the soul out of her, removed the essence of Maria, and substituted a fake puppet, a sawdust doll who went through the motions of being good. "I'm dead," she told herself.

The curtains rustled, waving their thin fingers across the sunlit sky outside. "Listen."

As Maria crouched alone in the corner of the room, the whispering grew louder.

A thin ghostly hand brushed her hair back from her forehead, smoothing as it went.

Maria did not dare remove her fists from her eyes. She sat, still hunched over, but now she was listening, her whole body, ears and every cell, straining to hear what was being said to her. "You are not dead. You are alive."

The ghost of Michael regarded her with compassion. Or so she imagined. "Michael?" Maria could not breathe. She had only heard of him, always in the family.

Michael curled his ghost presence around her, stroking her with softness, the softness of a cat's tail, softer than Mitzie, who had a rough Germanic coat. "My child," he said, stroking her.

Maria did not move.

"Listen carefully to what I am saying to you," he said. "You are alive. It is I who am dead. Do you understand?"

Maria's breathing stilled to comprehend what was being said to her. Was it the curtains whispering? Was it the breeze? The sunlight? The dust, easing against itself across the pitted floor? Far away, the toilet gurgled, and cold water still dripped from the single faucet of the sink, etching its rusty snail-like train on the horrid white porcelain. All blurred to distant sound. What mattered was that tender voice, that soft caress, brushing the hair from her face and stroking her.

"Yes," the voice continued. "Take my strength, my life. It is for you." The ghost of Michael wrapped itself around Maria protectively. "Think of me always, if you like. You are the child of us all. Our hope. You must live for all of us.

"You are not dead." He rocked Maria as she crouched, trying to listen and not listen at the same time.

How long he held her, Maria did not know. The shadows of late afternoon darkened the corners of the room, and still she sat, unmoving. Something was loosening itself. She felt her chest open, swell with sadness for Michael, and then for herself. A warm melting began.

The warmth rose through her body into the center of her abdomen, into all the hurt places, and then, finally, into her chest. There was a sharp, tight pain, so piercing that she became it for a moment.

"Yes, cry. It is better." The skinny hands of Michael held her forehead. "If you can cry like this, then you are not dead."

Maria sobbed for her ruined childhood, her hollow body. She cried for all the times she had contained herself—been quiet when she wanted to scream—for all the times she had been a "good" girl. She cried for the lack of love and understanding she felt. For her parents, who were so caught up in their own problems of survival that they had no time for her, no time even to see what was happening to her.

She cried because she had no right to cry in a family with a history such as hers. She cried for her loneliness, for her inability to deal with the husk she had become. She cried for the love she so desperately craved. She cried for what she perhaps would never find.

And most of all, she cried for her own selfishness, her clandestine longings. "I have no right to live." Her despicable selfishness in the face of everything else. Even now.

"And then he did to me—unspeakable things." Maria could hear the Rat's voice, incantatory, as she recounted her tale. Over and over, stopping always at those words: "unspeakable things."

"It does not matter," said the voice of Michael. "Forget it. You must go on, my girl, for all of us."

"And you, Michael?" Maria's asked sadly. "Do you suffer a lot?"

"No." His eyes looked deeply into hers and now he smiled. "I do not suffer. I am happy to be around the family. I'm always here, you know."

"I don't believe in ghosts," Maria told him firmly.

"No one does. Call me a memory, then," he said. "A memory you can hold on to."

He smiled. Her crying had subsided now. "One day," he promised, "you will be a woman, as beautiful as your mother and grandmother. And you will love and be loved. Really."

"Really?"

"Yes. Do not let anyone break your spirit. I don't want to hear any more of this dead business. Survive, my girl, survive. It is the only way."

"Will anyone ever love me?" Her pleading entreaty.

"Of course." The voice of absolute conviction.

Michael, entering the boxcar once more, the boxcar that was to take him toward extinction again, turned and looked back at Maria. The conductor blew his whistle; the train pulled out of the station, gathering speed. But this time, Michael did not fling himself against the closing doors, pressing his desperate face to the outside for the last time. He stood at the opening, a casual, smiling, jaunty figure, a lithe young man, smiling and waving at Maria as he left. "Don't forget," he called. He blew her a kiss. "Happiness will come."

The tightness unlocked in Maria's body. Her stomach, with its terrible cramping, relaxed. Her chest and throat were open. She breathed. Molecules of sunlight entered her heart.

"Not dead," she told herself. And now the warm slow tears of release and relief. She felt her body, stroked it. "I am not dead."

What did the move out of New York accomplish? Everything and nothing. Madness to go on doing what one has always done while history manages without us. Some people, betrayed, are taken and lost. A few people evolve; some merely survive. Perhaps these are synonymous. There are no solutions, "final" or temporary. History is merely hindsight, the impotent illusion of control. Why some people were killed. Why others were crowned. Stupidity rewritten. More unnecessary suffering will come. More history to write.

Winds blew about Europe, and the human race, scurrying and dislocated, mammalian creatures, shuffled to find food and shelter, to bury themselves in dark earth far from conflict. What was survival now? Some luck, some treachery, some confidence in self and long-acquired values. Whatever it took to manage. Selling out. Endurance. A willingness to learn new languages. Luck. Flexibility. A little courage. Some help. A lot of luck.

Like a rock laced by water, Herbert stood in the midst of his historical moment. Each wave overtaking him made a slightly different pattern on his surface, then fell back into the general oceanic pool. Each person, each life bore with it a slightly different need and despair, yet they were of one body, one saline gathering, the surface shimmering and shivering.

Rounded, granite, Herbert endured the water pouring over him and then rejoining its source. The wave broke from its smooth surface to trace its longing upon his veined perception. Then, soothed and dispersed, it fell back again. Herbert was, for a moment, visible. But then the next life came, claimed him for a moment, wrote its history upon his body, and left.

His daughter-in-law was much more practical than that. His son David was already growing older, weakened by the past. Adeline screamed her wants, growing less powerful each day, baffled by loss. Ilse, like a small flower growing between stones, pushed new life forward.

It was Ilse's will that forced her family to move. Ilse had no patience with the past. She refused mere survival; down-to-earth, she wanted something more. She arranged it so obviously and quietly, they had no choice. Before they knew it, they were living another life. Outside of the city, in a small boxlike house with their own beds, each of them. Ilse needed some space for herself; she could hardly stand the family around her. "Come on," she said to herself impatiently. Gently, she pushed them all around. "I know this is best." There were many things that Ilse did not say aloud. She just managed to make them happen, quietly. It was easier that way. She insisted on moving: she was pregnant again.

"Put your hand right here," Ilse told her daughter a few weeks after they had moved. "Can you feel the baby? Can you feel it kicking?"

Maria put her hand on her mother's body. Nothing, and then a faint flutter trembled underneath her hand. "I feel it!" she said in wonder.

Philip, watching the two of them, ran across the small lawn to put his head, too, against his mother's stomach. As he did so, he managed to butt Maria's hand away. "Do you feel it?" Ilse asked her little boy tenderly.

"This is no time for another child," David had groaned, raising his body from his wife's after she had told him the news. "We are already overworked. I cannot manage even as it is." He was exhausted, impatient. First the move, then this. He was still commuting, coming back once a month or so, irritated to find himself so quickly displaced and taken over by Ilse's plans.

"Of course this is the time. This is exactly the time." Ilse stroked her husband. "My darling, we will be so happy in this new country. You will see."

"Where will we put it?" He meant the child. David was exasperated. Already his parents, with their loud squabbles and reconciliations, were dominating the small house. Was he never to have any peace?

"In our bedroom, of course."

David groaned and fell back onto the pillow next to his wife.

Outside, on the lawn, Herbert and Adeline were reading the papers and arguing. The new Schatzie, called Mitzie now, lay beside them, thumping her two tails. "You are right. You are always right, my darling," Herbert was saying mildly.

"Don't be so irritating!" Adeline snapped.

Mitzie slobbered and rolled over.

"That dog! How could Ilse be so stupid as to take on a dog?" said Adeline. "With everything else she has to do."

Herbert seemed not to be paying attention.

"I am sure those children are neglected," continued Adeline

fretfully. "What with their mother insisting on going to work every day. Totally neglected."

Herbert did not bother to point out that it was Ilse's job that was feeding them all, nor did he bother to mention that it was David, his precious son, who had brought the dog home in the first place. He put down his newspaper, leaned forward, and covered his wife's hand with his. "My dearest girl, do not trouble yourself. You are right," he soothed. "You are always right, my darling."

Adeline stared into space, plucking at the ruffles around her neck with a thin hand. "I miss my piano."

Herbert sighed. "Of course you do. We must be patient." Already in his mind he was boarding the elevated train into Manhattan, where, later this afternoon, he had a series of appointments at the library.

"A baby." Maria raised her hand from her mother's lap and looked lovingly into Ilse's face.

"I hope it's a girl," she said. "I can't stand boys."

Ilse laughed, brushing the hair back from her daughter's face. "I know, little one."

And at that moment, the War ended so quietly that the family hardly noticed. For a long time after, their lives did not change. Which is to say that their lives had already been changed, irrevocably.

The photographs and articles began to filter out of Europe, filling the newspapers and magazines of the American households. Suddenly, they were confronted with the starving faces of the now dead. Americans were shocked. But the refugees were not.

"I don't want the children to see these," Ilse said as she continually gathered up the old newspapers and discarded them. Although Adeline screamed at her, Ilse threw the papers away just the same.

"Nasty girl!" cried Adeline, her dark eyes quite mad.

"Shh," said Ilse. She was determined that her children would not grow up with these nightmares.

In the face of the incoming materials, David spent more and more time in his basement office in Washington, clipping and sorting and examining documents and photographs. There was so much to understand.

Herbert, in the New York Public Library, pored madly over the newspapers hanging from their racks, searching the world press.

The thin bodies pressed against barbed wire, yearning for liberation. Many died before they could live again, but their faces and bodies stood before the world, a reproach.

No one told the Gypsies the War was over. They stayed in the death camps, longing for liberty, within the open gates. No nation wanted to take them, although they now could go free. After the treaties, the Gypsies, uninformed, still stayed imprisoned, their wills broken, waiting for what, they did not know. They died in droves, mouths pressed close to the open air.

"My brother." David rubbed his tired eyes and put down the magnifying glass. Then he picked up the glass again and turned to another stack of materials.

"Bless you, Herr Hofrat. Thank you." Though petitioners fell to the floor in front of Herbert, seizing his hand and pressing their lips to his ring, there was no one who could help Herbert himself. No one. "Michael, where are you?" Herbert searched and searched.

But Michael was gone. They were never to find him among the other faces.

And now there was so much to do. So many petitioners, so many people needed to be resettled. The work of getting on with life, now that the War was over. Hooray. Information must be falsified. Perhaps now there would be no more wars.

Several months later, David decided to commit himself to this new life, this new country, and his place in it. A new house. A third baby. It was time, he told himself as he took the train back from Washington to spend the weekend with his family. Time to become "American."

When he arrived, it was morning, a cool, fresh morning after a night rain. No one saw him arrive. He walked anonymously down the sidewalk to where the house stood, identical to all the other houses on the street. But it was his.

The smell of newly cut grass rose to David's nostrils as he stood outside the house that Saturday. It was a clean smell, clear and acrid and lemony at the same time, rising from the street directly toward his appreciative nose. He could see his neighbors already outside. There were no fences here, no barriers. David looked at all the other tiny houses, the driveways, the plots of furry lawn being mowed. American front yards, neat and open and squared off for everyone to see. Nothing to hide. If he wanted, David could look right into the other windows on the street, identical to his own.

His parents were already carefully smoothing open the latest *New York Times,* drinking coffee in their dressing gowns. They would have ironed the pages open first to make the newspaper more readable, arguing all the time. He could hear his mother's voice rising, querulous.

The front door opened, and his children ran down the steps, laughing. They didn't even see him, a drab man standing at the end of the walk. Between them, they were hauling Mitzie, now dressed in a baby's little nightgown, with a lace-edged baby bonnet tied around her head, from which her floppy ears protruded. Mitzie's two tails wagged from the skirt of the baby's nightgown, at the same time as her mournful, wrinkled face scrunched up, seeming to say, "Yes, I am ridiculous. But love me anyway."

"Mmmm. My baby!" Maria cried ecstatically, leaning down to plant a big kiss on Mitzie's nose.

"My baby!" echoed Philip, imitating his big sister. Mitzie did not protest. Her tails just thumped a little faster.

"I will have to teach them both to play chess," David thought.

Somewhere, far away, another garden, walled, hummed in his memory, and music poured into the space under the linden trees. An enclosed garden, full of music and happiness. Two brothers. The memory held no sting. His language stayed in his mouth like butter and honey.

The green smell of his neighbors' newly cut grass filled his lungs, and the soft sun touched his body as David stood and looked down the length of the street. He watched as his wife came to the door, her belly heavy. She smiled out at the children playing but did not see him yet.

David fixed this all in his mind. Then he started slowly toward the house, pushing back his sleeves. He had many projects this weekend. The first thing would be to get out the lawn mower, the gadget the Americans used that looked like a child's push toy, and trim his own little patch of grass.

ACKNOWLEDGMENTS

To my amazing editor, Victoria Wilson. Her painstaking work has shown me what great editing entails. Thank you for giving me the opportunity to work with you and with this iconic publisher. To my agents, Carolyn French and especially Don Fehr. Thank you, more than I can say, for believing in this book through all the rewrites. Thank you also to Audrey Silverman.

To the Fulbright Commission for Franco-American Relations. To Jeannette Ambrose, Pronob and Sara Mitter, Dominique Masson, and others who found me places in which to write this book. To Odile Hellier especially.

To friends Kate Frank, Elena Dodd, Marilyn Taylor, and Jennifer Mascola. To Jeannette Littman, Virginia Larner, Claire Bruyère, Robert and Gail Melson, Keith Winstein, Eva Hoffman, Elizabeth Knoll, and others. To my cousins, Marilyn Rinzler and Elizabeth Morse, who share so much with me. To the gifted Victoria Root: a special thank-you.

To beloved France, which has continued to examine its dark World War II history, notably during the capture of Klaus Barbie and the Maurice Papon trials. To the work of historian Robert Paxton, and to Mavis Gallant, Martine Beck, Sylvie Weil, and Hazel Rowley. To Jean-Pierre Ledoux, who took me to see important sites. To Inge Hoffmann and her seminar, who explore ways of understanding the past.

To my parents, who read the first draft, were surprised, and—would you believe it?—laughed in all the right places. To my mother, Doris

Drucker, who explored and shared her past with me. And, of course, always to my father, Peter Drucker, who gave me the little confidence I have. To Nova Spivack, helpful reader, and Joseph Murray, my steadfast companion. To Marin Spivack for his thoughtful support.

To memory: its denials and recognitions. To my characters, especially those over a "certain age." To the refuge of New York. To the Grimm/grim world of childhood.

To the American Academy of Rome. To Vienna, and its attempts to present itself as a frothy pastry shop. To teachers, who gave me a voice. To the solace of reading. To the music that I love and have played, which animates this book.

To "my America, my new-found land!"

Thank you,
Kathleen Spivack

A NOTE ON THE TYPE

This book was set in Adobe Garamond. Designed for the Adobe Corporation by Robert Slimbach, the fonts are based on types first cut by Claude Garamond (c. 1480–1561). Garamond was a pupil of Geoffroy Tory and is believed to have followed the Venetian models. He gave to his letters a certain elegance and feeling of movement that won their creator an immediate reputation.

Typeset by Scribe, Philadelphia, Pennsylvania

Printed and bound by Berryville Graphics, Berryville, Virginia

Designed by Iris Weinstein